WELL HUNG OVER IN VEGAS

KIMBERLY FOX

Well Hung Over in Vegas

By Kimberly Fox

Sign up to Kimberly Fox's exclusive newsletter to hear about new releases and to get exclusive content, including an extended epilogue from this book!

Sign up at:
www.AuthorKimberlyFox.com/newsletter.html

Do you like Paranormal Romance?
Kimberly Fox has an extensive paranormal romance catalog that she writes under Kim Fox.
Check out her PNR books at
www.AuthorKimFox.com

www.AuthorKimberlyFox.com

Proofreading by: Beverly Bernard

To all you lovely freaks who make Vegas such a wild &
unforgettable place
Save me a drink I'm coming to see you soon!
(As soon as I can get these damn clinging toddlers off of my leg...)

1

Dahlia

Is that a man's watch?

I stare at it in disbelief, but there it is, tick ticking away like a bomb that's about to go off. There's a man's watch lying on my night table.

Wait a minute. This is not my hotel room.

The wallpaper is different, and the lamp is not the
—*Why is my underwear on the lamp?*

My heart is racing as I peek under the covers. *Holy shit, I'm naked.*

I'm naked in a stranger's hotel room. A male stranger from the looks of his watch. A *rich* male stranger according to the diamond encrusted Rolex logo on it.

Why am I naked in a stranger's hotel room? I try to think back to last night, but my head is a blur of spilled shots, wobbly heels, and—*oh shit. We had sex.*

It's all so blurry with my head pounding like a jack-hammer at a Metallica concert. I can't think.

Yes, I can. *Think, Dahlia, think.*

But all I remember is a flash of me arching my back and screaming out as a rich male stranger fucked me like an animal.

I close my eyes, trying to build up the courage to turn my pounding head to see who is there. Courage isn't coming. It's time for a pep talk.

Okay, Dahlia. It's time to face whatever fucked up reality you got yourself into. Just do it. You're a winner. You clawed your way up to the COO position at Hospitech with only a high school degree. In only ten months, you cut the company's costs by twenty percent and increased their profits by a record thirty-two percent. You can do this. Turn your head.

I swallow hard, my mouth tasting like a dry sewer, and carefully turn my head to peek over my shoulder.

Oh, shit!

I whip my head back around and pull the covers up to my chin, feeling extremely naked.

Well, there's definitely a male.

I couldn't see his face with it sunken into the pillow, but I did see his body—muscular chest, chiseled abs, arms out of a comic book that are covered in tats.

He's naked too. At least we have something in common.

I peek back over to get another look. My heart is now pounding harder than my head is.

His muscular thigh is sticking out of the crisp white sheets, and I carefully tilt my head up to see if he's showing anything else.

The corner of the sheet is resting over his package, his hard pelvis with the mouth-watering V visible in all of its glory. I let out an audible gulp when I see the tip of his trimmed pubic hair sticking out.

Shit!

Too loud.

I drop my head back down and hold the blankets up to my chin, closing my eyes impossibly tight as he lets out a deep groan and starts moving around.

What's the game plan here, Dahlia?

I always have a game plan. I always have a backup for my game plan and a backup for my backup.

But this is unexpected. He's thrown me off my game. I don't even know what sport we're playing.

He gets up with a heavy breath and shuffles to the bathroom like a hungover zombie. Mr. Rich Naked Stranger doesn't even bother to close the door as he fills the toilet bowl with last night's beverages.

I explode out of the bed like my pubic hair is on fire. I have less than ten seconds to get dressed before he comes out and sees my kibbles and bits.

Pants first. No time for underwear. I yank them up my legs as I keep an eye on the door and an ear on the stream of liquid that's hitting the water in the toilet bowl like a fire hose.

Where the fuck is my bra? Arghhhh!

I leap across the room when I see it hanging off the desk. I yank it on with my pulse racing, already looking around for my shirt as I snap the clasp closed.

My head is pounding, my stomach churning, and I'm nearly hyperventilating as my bulging eyes dart around the room looking for my shirt.

I'm on my hands and knees looking under the bed when the toilet flushes and Mr. Rich Naked Stranger walks out.

"Looking for something?" he asks in a deep groggy voice.

Yes. My dignity. My self-respect. Have you seen either of them, or are they gone for good?

"Just my—" The words vanish from my throat when I turn around and see Mr. Rich Naked Stranger in all of his naked glory.

My eyes are level with his cock that's hanging down low between his muscular thighs. I can't seem to take my eyes off of it. That was in me last night. I know because my hoo-ha is still achingly sore.

With a shake of my head, I pry my eyes off of his dick and drag them up his hard body, my pulse racing dangerously fast with every inch that I climb.

His abs are a work of art. They look like they should be on a statue of a Greek God in some dusty old museum instead of in front of my blushing face.

"What are you looking for?" he asks, running a hand through his messy brown hair.

My eyes follow his hand up, and I swallow hard when our eyes meet. He's gorgeous—stunning, actually.

Jade green eyes that bore into me, ripping away any chance of me answering him intelligently. I just stare up at him with my mouth hanging open. "Uhhhh."

How can someone look this hot right after crawling out of bed? His hair is messy and disheveled in a perfect way. His face looks like it could grace the cover of magazines with his strong masculine chin that's dotted with the perfect length of stubble, his sexy lips that are curling up into a smirk, and his tanned, golden skin tone that makes his eyes pop impossibly bright.

I shake my head, catching myself. *How long was I staring?*

"My shirt," I blurt out, ducking my head under the bed. *Yes! Thank God!*

I grab my shirt that's under the bed for some reason and pull it out. "I was just looking for my shirt."

Now, I'll be looking for the door.

"Are you leaving?" he asks as he walks over to the bed. He drops down onto his back and folds his hands over his flexed abs as he watches me. The sheets are right beside him but he doesn't bother to cover his naked package.

Well, I don't have to look. Maybe one more peek.

"We can go again if you have some time," he says, staring at my breasts.

I quickly put on my shirt with shaking hands and glance at the closed door.

"I can't," I say, trying to sound casual and relaxed, although my voice is unusually high-pitched and tight. "I have an important business meeting." And it's true. I do.

In two hours, I'm meeting with Mack McMillan, the seventy-five-year-old billionaire who just bought the company I work for.

Why I was out drinking last night to the point where I woke up here and not studying about the acquisition is anyone's guess. I'll figure that out later.

But first things first. I have to graciously get the fuck out of here with what little shred of dignity I have left.

"That's too bad," he says, his cock still in plain view. "I got a stupid thing this morning anyway. Maybe I'll catch you around."

He steps off of the bed and walks over to me, way too naked for eight a.m.

"Can you please put some underwear on?" I ask, turning away with burning cheeks.

I can hear his frustrating smirk. "No problem," he says, walking over to the leather couch. "Although, it didn't seem to bother you last night when you had those tight little lips wrapped around it."

"Well, that was last night," I snap back, trying really hard not to take one last look as he steps into his bright red boxer briefs.

Who the hell wears bright red underwear? It's so impractical.

"Okay," I say with a firm nod. "I'm leaving."

"All right," he says, standing up straight and giving me a sarcastic salute.

I'm so bad in situations like this. Mainly because I'm *never* in situations like this.

How do I end this?

A wave? No, too awkward.

A kiss on the cheek? No, too friendly.

A gentle punch on the shoulder? No, too thirteen-year-old male.

I go for the old classic handshake and step forward with my hand out.

He grins as he takes my hand in his, swallowing it whole as he cups it with his other hand. "It was a *pleasure* to meet you," he says, leaning in as he locks those dreamy green eyes on mine.

A flood of warmth flows through me, raising every hair on my arm and causing my skin to tingle. Now I can see why I woke up here.

Now I get it.

That sexy heart-stopping look would be enough to get any girl out of her party dress, even a straight-laced, goodie-goodie like me.

This guy is pure sexual energy wrapped up in a beautiful bad boy package. He's got it all; the flawless muscles, the sexy tattoos, the handsome face that always seems to have a cocky smile on it that you just want to smack off but end up kissing instead.

He'd be nothing but trouble.

And a woman in my position can't afford to have trouble.

A clean break is what is needed here. "All right," I say, sliding my sweaty hand back. "Keep it groovy."

I close my eyes before I see him laugh at me. *Keep it groovy? Are you fucking serious, Dahlia? Did your grandmother teach you slang?*

I just turn to the door and hurry out without looking back. The opportunity for a graceful exit already passed, and I failed miserably.

Now, I just want to get into the hall where I'll be safe. "Okay," I say, my eyes on the floor as I open the door and rush out. "Bye."

He steps forward, smiling. "Keep it groov—"

I close the door in his face before he can finish and then sprint to the elevators down the hall faster than Usain Bolt on speed.

"Come on," I mutter, my finger hitting the lit-up button like a woodpecker. "Let's go."

I glance back at his closed door, praying he doesn't open it. I made a fool of myself enough for one morning, and I just want to get back to my room.

It's then that I realize that I don't know where I am. The hotel looks familiar but a hotel is a hotel. They all look familiar.

The Parisian. It's written on a sign over the elevator.

Good news and bad news.

Good news is, I'm in my hotel and don't have to take a taxi back to my room without any underwear on. *Shit! I forgot my underwear on the lamp!*

Bad news is, I might see Mr. Rich Naked Stranger again

in the halls. Double shit if I'm with my boss while it happens.

The elevator dings and the stainless-steel doors slide open. My heart is pounding as I jump in and immediately press the door close button a few dozen times.

I take a deep breath of relief as the elevator starts moving down to my floor.

Fucking Las Vegas.

My coworker Emily warned me that Vegas can turn even the straightest of librarians into a party-crazed slut.

I didn't believe her.

I've always been the straightest of the straight.

Boy, was I wrong.

I hate being wrong.

The doors bing open, and I step out onto my floor, leaving a piece of my dignity behind that I'll never get back.

I still don't know what happened last night, but I'm ready to put it behind me. I have an extremely important business meeting to get to, and I'll just try to get over this hangover and focus on that.

As long as I don't see *him* again, I'll be fine.

2

Dahlia

"WHAT HAPPENED TO YOU LAST NIGHT?" Emily asks as I sit down at the conference table. Our boss is in the corner playing air guitar with his earbuds in. He always listens to Kenny Loggins before a big meeting. He says it pumps him up.

Mr. Wallace is ignoring us for the moment, and I'm glad he is because I could use as much time as possible to get over this raging hangover of doom.

The adrenaline of waking up next to Captain America's body double ran out a long time ago, and all I'm left with is a queasy stomach and a head that won't stop pounding.

I'm not in the mood to talk, but Emily is not letting it go. "I turned to get my phone to take a picture when I saw you standing in a fountain, but when I turned back you were gone and I didn't see you again. What happened to you?"

"I don't know," I say, dropping my head onto the desk with a thud.

"You look like shit."

I close my eyes, enjoying not having the bright lights in the room burning my retinas. "Thank you."

"Look at those black rings under your eyes," she says. "You look like a raccoon who stayed up all night getting high on bath salts."

"Okay, Emily," I groan, wondering why I ever drank anything, ever.

"Remember the Crypt Keeper?" she asks, ignoring me. "From Tales from the Crypt? You look like him if he got a makeover but then fell into a barrel of acid."

"Okay!" I say, raising my pounding head. "I get it. I look horrible."

"No," she says, tilting her head as she examines my face. "Horrifying is the word I would go with. Maybe even soul-crushingly awful. You're making me want to start a charity for you."

"I hate you," I groan, dropping my head back onto the table. This is going to be my first meeting with the new owner of the company, and I feel like I woke up in a bus station.

"You look like Gary Busey had a baby with a turtle," Emily says.

She pulls her phone out and starts taking pictures. "This is going on the company website," she says, snapping away. "It's going to be your new profile picture."

I reach up and give her the finger. *There. Put that on the company's homepage.*

"Look at your shirt," she says, stifling a laugh. "You have sweat stains under your armpits. You look like you just got finished tarring a roof in the middle of July."

"All right," I snap. "I know I look horrifying, but I can't help it. I don't know what happened. I had one drink with you guys, and then all hell broke loose."

"All hell broke loose on your hair," she says, cringing as she looks up past my forehead. "Your hair looks like you have a possum living inside of it."

She pulls her muffin towards her as she scrunches her nose up. "Does the possum bite?"

"I hate you," I say, dropping my head back onto the table.

I can hear in my boss's headphones that Footloose is almost over. Two more *everybody cut*s and I'll have to start acting professional.

With a last energetic strum of his air guitar, Mr. Wallace takes off his earbuds and sits down.

He cringes when he sees my face. So, it's not just Emily's normal sarcasm. I *do* look like shit.

Great.

"I was worried we were going to have to bail you out of jail," he says, sitting across from me. He folds his hands together on the table as he stares me down. "Office cocktail parties are supposed to be professional. It's not a time for you to get white girl wasted and relive the glory days of Spring Break."

"Sir," I say, dipping my chin. "I can explain."

He crosses his arms over his expensive suit and leans back in his chair. "Please do."

"Uhhh." I have nothing. To be honest, I have no idea how I went from classy cocktail to sloppy sloshed. It doesn't make any sense.

"Some people just can't handle Vegas," Emily says, shaking her head as she watches me with a look of pity on her face.

I glare back at her. If looks could kill, she'd be blowing the devil in hell.

The intercom beeps on the phone, and Mr. Wallace gives me one last frown before answering it. "Yes."

"Mr. McMillan is here."

Mr. Wallace exhales long and hard. "We're ready for him."

The three of us stand up as we wait for the new boss to enter. I clasp my hands in front of me to hide the sweat stains that Emily so graciously pointed out.

Mr. Wallace is nodding his head, his lips moving as he sings under his breath. "*Kick off the Sunday shoes,*" he whispers, getting himself ready.

Oh, no.

What the hell is he doing here?

He walks in looking as fresh as the bright sun in the Caribbean sky while I feel as fresh as a urinal cake after a Super Bowl party.

It's *him*. The naked guy from this morning.

He looked good naked, but he looks absolutely delicious in a dark gray suit with a classic white shirt and black tie. The material is tailored to his muscular frame, and I gulp at the size of his broad shoulders and round biceps. His hair is no longer a sexy mess but looks just as good combed and gelled to the side like he had a team of stylists rush into his room the second after I left.

A sudden coldness grips my core as he ducks under the low doorway and shakes my boss's hand.

"Wow," Emily gasps beside me.

Wow is fucking right.

There's an army of hummingbirds in my stomach fighting for space. I want to crawl under the table and hide. I want to turn invisible or melt through the wall. I want to do anything but stand here in shock with my mouth hanging open, but unfortunately, it's all I seem to be capable of at the moment.

Maybe if I stand really still no one will see my cheeks turning as red as my new boss's boxer briefs.

"Hi, Mr. Wallace," Emily says, hopping forward with a big smile on her face. Her chest is thrust out for his visual enjoyment. "I'm Emily."

"Hi, Emily," he says, bowing his head slightly as he smiles back at her. "Please, call me Tyler."

"Okay," she says, clasping her hands behind her and looking as giddy as a school girl who just got asked out by her crush.

Tyler turns to me and jerks his head back in surprise when he recognizes me. I'm not sure how he does recognize me since I looked like an angel last night, and right now I look like a troll who lives under a highway overpass.

His beautiful jade green eyes are locked on me as his sexy lips curl up into a grin—those same lips that last night were on my... nevermind.

Mr. Wallace butts in when we just stare at each other in shock. "This is our COO, Dahlia Winters," he says, introducing me.

Tyler reaches his hand out, and I hold my breath as I slide my hand into his. It's no big deal. It's just a handshake. A handshake from a hand that was caressing my naked breasts and sliding in and over my hoo-ha just a few hours ago. No big deal.

I want to die.

He grins as he takes my hand in his, cupping it with his other hand like he did an hour or two ago in his hotel room. "Hello, Dahlia," he says, his deep voice coming out like the purr of a lion. "I'm sure it's going to be a *pleasure* working with you."

I give him a firm handshake back and nod my head, pretending like we just met. "It's nice to meet you as well," I say, trying to keep my voice steady. "I am looking forward to having a respectful, professional relationship with you."

Emily pries her eyes off of Tyler for a second and turns to me with a confused look on her face.

"Definitely," he says with a grin. "I can't wait to see what happens."

"Should we get started?" Mr. Wallace asks, motioning to the conference table in front of us.

The four of us sit down, the boys on one side and the girls on the other like we're back in elementary school.

"Would you like a coffee?" Mr. Wallace asks him, already sucking up to his new boss. "We also have donuts or fresh fruit."

"No, thanks," Tyler says. He looks at me and licks his lips. "One of your employees generously gave me their peach and it was *delicious*."

My eyes drop to the table, and I stare at the grains in the wood, trying to pretend like this is not happening.

Mr. Wallace nods. "I'm sure you'll find that the employees in our beloved company are very generous. They'll provide you with *anything* that you need."

"Anything?" Tyler asks, still looking at me.

I stare at the table, trying to stop the rush of blood to my cheeks. It's not working.

"Anything," Mr. Wallace says, thankfully answering for me. "Will Mr. McMillan senior be joining us?"

"No," Tyler answers curtly. "I'm taking over the company."

"Great," Mr. Wallace says, laying on the smiles and nods

extra thick. Emily looks just as thrilled, and I guess I'm the odd one out. I just can't shake the knots that are swirling around in my stomach.

He's my new boss.

I slept with my new boss.

Shit.

I've worked so hard for the past six years at this company. I clawed my way up from the reception desk to the Chief Operating Officer by working weekends, forgoing my social life, and doing basically the complete opposite of what my hippie parents did throughout their lives, and I feel sick that I might have thrown it all away over one drunken mistake.

"I'll be handling the acquisition," Tyler says. He pauses for a second and then continues. "And all of the necessary *restructuring*."

The three of us gulp at the same time.

Tyler's company, McMillan Worldwide Inc., is a company eater, a huge monster of a corporation that thrives on swallowing smaller companies and then tearing them to pieces. They are known for buying up manufacturing companies and then restructuring them by closing all of their plants and factories, only to reopen them overseas where the labor is cheaper and the profits are bigger.

The company I work for, Hospitech, is their most recent victim. We do important work manufacturing specialized hospital equipment that saves thousands of lives every year.

And I'll be damned if I'm going to let the corporate monster take us down without a fight.

I stare Tyler dead in the eyes—his beautiful, mesmerizing, jade green eyes. "And by restructuring, you mean closing our factory down and shipping it overseas?"

He leans back as he holds my eyes from across the table.

He's trying to get a read on me, probably wondering why the girl who had her legs behind her head for him last night is now starting to attack.

"The Hospitech factory has been in the town of Summerland for eighteen years," I explain. "It's the main source of work for the residents. If you close the factory, there will be no more jobs for the people of the town. The local businesses will fail, the whole economy of the small town will collapse."

My body starts tensing up as I picture having to hand out fifteen hundred and ninety-two pink slips to the loyal factory workers. The town would be devastated. It would never recover.

I start to sweat as I picture every little shop in town closing one by one: Camilla's bakery that makes the best gingerbread cookies on the planet, George's auto shop, which has the only mechanic who is incapable of lying, and the little mom-and-pop hardware store owned by Brenda and Pete. Pete is so nice that he even insisted on installing the Christmas lights that I bought from his store.

"He never said anything about closing down the factory," Mr. Wallace says, defending the new boss already. "Let's give him the benefit of the doubt."

I sit back in my chair, grinding my teeth as I look over at Mr. Wallace. He's nodding at Tyler with a big fake smile on his face. This guy is always looking out for himself and *only* himself. He knows what's going to happen here, but he's not going to do a thing to stop it. All he wants is a job in the new restructured company, and as long as that happens, he doesn't care if the factory gets shut down and all fifteen hundred and ninety-two workers get a thank you, a sympathetic smile, and a pat on the ass as they're ushered out the door for good.

If he won't fight for our employees, then I will. I'm not letting them go down without a fight.

"Are you going to close the factory?" I ask, staring Tyler down and challenging him to lie.

"We haven't decided on that yet."

"But it's a possibility," I fire back.

"We haven't decided on that yet," he just repeats.

"Who is *we*?" I ask. "I thought you were taking over the company. Don't you make those decisions?"

Emily is looking at me like I'm crazy, but I can't stop. Maybe it's the hangover, maybe it's the embarrassment of having slept with my new boss, maybe it's the rumored layoffs, maybe it's the fact that I can't stop thinking about his bright red underwear and the way that it fit so snuggly around his muscular thighs and nice big cock, or maybe it's all those things, but my claws are out and I'm attacking my new boss.

Career self-destruct in three, two, one...

Tyler smiles, and I hate that it sends a flood of warmth surging through me. "You have every right to be concerned about your job and the jobs of your coworkers," he says, clasping his hands on the desk in front of him. The sleeves of his tailored suit slide up his forearms giving me a glimpse of his tattooed skin underneath. I can see the bottom of a green stem that leads up to a tattooed rose.

I know that it's a tattooed rose because a quick memory of last night flashes into my mind, making me cringe— Tyler's muscular body hovering over mine as he slides deep inside of me. I moan as I turn my head on the pillow, gasping as I look at the beautiful rose tattooed on his forearm.

"I do make the decisions," he says, staring me down. "But I do consult my father before any major decisions are made. My father started McMillan Worldwide Inc. when he bought a failing ashtray manufacturing plant back in nineteen seventy-one. I'm not sure if you've been paying attention, but he built it into a billion-dollar company. I'd be stupid not to listen to his advice."

"Even if his advice means destroying a whole town?" I ask, feeling my face get warm. "Entire families without jobs, no food to put on the table, no money to buy diapers or pay the bills?"

Emily leans over. "Tone it down, Dahlia," she whispers.

Tyler sighs and turns to Mr. Wallace. "I thought this was just supposed to be a meet and greet."

"It was," Mr. Wallace says, bowing and shaking his head like a servant trying to appease an angry king. "I apologize profusely." He turns to me with a look that warns me I'm going to pay for it all later.

Tyler turns back to me and grins. "No harm done," he says, smirking at me. "I like your spirit. McMillan Worldwide Inc. needs more people like you, people who will fight for what they believe in and fight for their employees."

Yeah, right. He's saying this now to save face, but I'll probably be the first to go.

"It's been nice meeting you all," he says, pushing his chair away from the conference desk and standing up. Mr. Wallace jumps up so fast that his chair topples over behind him.

"I'd like to invite you all to stay for a few days," Tyler says, "while we figure things out. I'll be working here as well."

"I'd love to stay here and work with you," Emily says, pressing her tits out for him. She's my best friend in the office and one of my only friends outside of work, but for some reason, I hate her and I want to claw her eyes out.

"That's good to hear." Tyler turns to me and grins. "And don't worry, Mrs. Dahlia. I'll be keeping it *groovy*."

Every cell in my body is screaming at me to look down at the table, but I hold his gaze, glaring back at him.

I want to get back to the East Coast factory where I work and live so that I can forget about this little blip in my flawless career, but I'm not about to leave this careless driver at the wheel of my company without my supervision. So, I guess I'll be working here in the West Coast sales office for a few days. I just hope my first week in Vegas goes better than my first night.

I'm still not sure what the hell happened.

"I'll be seeing you all around." Tyler nods and then leaves the conference room.

"What the hell was that?" Emily asks me as soon as the door is shut.

Mr. Wallace looks furious. "That was highly inappropriate. That is our new boss! How do you think that made our company look?"

"It's not our company anymore," I say, taking a deep breath to try and calm the blood boiling up inside of me. I'm wound a little too tight at the moment.

"You're not even going to have a job if you continue on like this," he snaps.

I'm not in the mood to listen to one of his lectures.

"Oh, go listen to some Kenny Loggins," I say, marching to the door.

He slaps the table, clearly offended as I storm out of the room. "Kenny Loggins is a musical genius!" he shouts. "A *genius!*"

Tyler is in the middle of the office surrounded by smiling faces. They're all looking up at him like he's a famous rockstar and not the douchebag that I know he is.

Oh, well. At least he'll be out of your life soon because there's no way he'll let you keep your job after that little outburst.

I fight back exhausted, hungover tears as I lower my head and slink back into my temporary office.

All thirty-eight employees laugh at Tyler's joke that probably isn't funny as I close the door behind me.

Less than twenty-four hours in Sin City, and I've already slept with my boss and torpedoed my career.

Emily's warning on the plane keeps ringing in my pounding head: Some people just can't handle Vegas.

I should have listened.

Because I am definitely one of those people.

3

_____

Dahlia

"YOU FUCKED HIM?!?" Emily screams, *wayyyyy* too loud.

"Will you shut up?" I scream in a whisper back to her. I jump up from behind my desk and rush to the window of my closed office, looking out in a panic to see if anyone heard.

Martha turns to me with a disapproving look on her miserable face, but no one else seems to have heard.

"I can't believe you fucked him," Emily says, staring at me in shock. "You lucky bitch! I totally wanted to fuck him."

"You still can." I say it with a shrug like I don't care at all, but I definitely do. My fingers twisting into claws ready to scratch her eyes out are proof of that.

"What was it like?" she asks, staring at me as she gives me her complete attention. She's sitting on my desk, turning as she watches me walk back to my chair and plop down.

"I don't remember anything," I say, rubbing my throbbing temples. "I woke up with no memory of the night before, but we were both naked and we definitely had sex." My sore hoo-ha is proof of that.

"Maybe he roofied you," Emily says, staring at me with wide eyes. "You're so lucky."

"I don't think so," I say, closing my eyes. *Why are the lights so bright in here? I didn't realize the West Coast office is located on the surface of the sun.*

"I only had one drink," I explain, trying to machete my way through my hazy memory to figure out what happened. "And I got it straight from the bartender. *He* never touched it."

She's still staring at me with jealous eyes. "He's so hot."

"He's okay," I lie. He's definitely more than okay. He's absolutely gorgeous. If he was a Greek God, he would be the God of sexy smiles, obsessive crushes, and goosebumped skin.

"We have to figure out what happened," Emily says, looking very serious. "Think back to the moment that led up to you sleeping with him."

"What's the point?" I ask with a sigh. It's not like I'm going to be able to keep my job after this morning's disastrous meeting.

Emily is looking at things a little differently. "What's the point?" she asks, staring at me in disbelief. "This is beyond you, Dahlia. This is bigger than just you."

"I know," I nod, seeing her point. "I want to save the factory too."

"Not that," she says, crinkling her nose up. "You slept with the hot son of a billionaire. Teach me your ways. Please!"

I wish I could help her out, but I have no idea what happened. It's all a murky fog of regrets.

"Let's go through your purse for clues," she says.

She hops off my desk and grabs my purse before I can say no. "We'll take a look-see," she says, turning it upside down on my desk. Tons of pennies come raining down on my desk and I cringe as the rest of the contents come pouring out after them.

"What is this?" she asks with a wide grin.

"What is *that*?" I ask, staring at the big box of Magnum condoms in shock. I was in such a hurry this morning and was so focused on trying not to puke that I just grabbed my purse without looking inside. If I had, I definitely wouldn't have missed that.

"Magnums," Emily says with a smirk. "I knew it."

Well, that explains the sore hoo-ha.

"Looks like you had fun last night," she says, peeking inside. "Only three left in a box of twelve."

I grab a loose condom off the corner of the desk and toss it at her. "*Four* left."

Emily is grinning like a perverted Nancy Drew. "Either you had seven other cocks inside of you, or Mr. Billionaire is a sexual stud that fucked you eight times. Either way, the plot thickens."

Something that I've never seen before catches my eye in the pile of makeup, keys, and other crap. I grab a flowered necklace from the pile and turn it around in my fingers.

"Is that a lei?" Emily asks. "Add one more lay to the eight cocks. Did you fly to Hawaii or something?"

I shake my head as I stare at it.

She grabs it from me, tosses it on the pile of junk, and grabs a pamphlet. "What's this?" she asks, unfolding it like an accordion. "Sunshine Happy Church? Did you join a cult?"

My stomach drops as I see my name scribbled on the sign-up form. *Oh, my God. I joined a cult!*

She tosses the pamphlet back on my desk and picks up a handful of pennies. "Why do you have about ten dollars' worth of wet pennies in your purse? You're like a homeless lady."

"I have no idea." I guess that explains why my purse was so heavy today.

"Well, that's it," I say, stuffing everything back into my purse. "No more clues or explanations. Just a bunch of junk."

I toss the condoms into the trash and then pick them up and stuff them back into my purse after thinking twice about it. I don't want the cleaning lady to think I'm a huge whore who got rammed by at least eight monster cocks.

I grab the last thing off the desk, my checkbook, and gasp when I see what's under it.

"No!" I shout, throwing the checkbook back on it. *It's not there if I can't see it.*

"Is that what I think it is?" Emily asks, smiling like a professional gossiper who just found out the juiciest secret in the history of secrets.

"No," I say, shaking my head in disbelief. It can't be. Life can't be that cruel.

But somehow, I know that it's true. I get a quick flash of last night. I'm wearing white. There's plastic pineapples everywhere. A Bible with the back cover ripped off.

Oh, God.

"I have to do it," Emily says, grinning as she slowly reaches for my checkbook. She picks it up and then slams it back down over the diamond wedding ring, staring at me with wide eyes.

"I must have found it," I say, swallowing hard as my

heart races. My breaths start coming out quick and ragged. But I remember the feeling of it on my finger. It was a little too big. It was so shiny.

My mouth is so dry as I shake my head, desperate for an explanation. "Someone must have dropped it. I must have picked it up to give it back to them."

Emily is trying to stifle her giggles as she watches me. I'm not convincing her.

I'm not convincing myself.

She goes to lift up the checkbook again.

"Don't," I say. I can't handle the truth of what's under there.

Why was I wearing white?

She doesn't listen and slowly lifts it up. Just as I feared, there's a diamond wedding ring sitting on my desk.

"Holy shit," Emily gasps as she stares at it.

Holy shit is right.

"Did Tyler McMillan buy you this?" she asks, lifting it up.

I feel like Gollum as I have a fierce urge to rip *my precious* out of her hands. I sit on my fingers instead.

"Don't be ridiculous," I say, shaking my head. "I must have found it."

Emily rifles through my checkbook and grins when she sees the last check. "You have a check written out to The Pineapple Chapel for eighty bucks. Sounds classy."

I rip it out of her hands and my mouth drops open when I see my drunken handwriting scribbled on the check.

"Look," I say, showing it to her. "The check isn't even ripped off. It's all good. Everything will be okay." *Please, everything be okay.*

Emily just shrugs, not looking too convinced. "Maybe he paid. He is a billionaire after all." She raises her eyebrows.

"So are you if you are indeed married. Can I borrow some money?"

I grab the ring and checkbook out of her hands and stuff them back in my purse. "Out," I snap. I'm way too hungover and tired to deal with this right now.

"Are you two going to have kids?" she asks as I point at the door.

"Get out."

"Maybe you're pregnant right now," she says with a chuckle as she gets off my desk.

"Now!"

"Don't worry," she says, laughing as she walks to the door. "I won't hold this rude outburst against you. It's probably just the pregnancy hormones kicking in."

"I'm not pregnant!" I shout as she gets to the door.

"It's okay," she says with a grin on her frustrating face. "You're a married woman now. We don't know to whom, but we'll find out."

She ducks out of my office and quickly closes the door as I throw my purse at her. It slams into the door and falls to the floor. I hold my breath as the ring rolls out onto the cheap carpeting, mocking me.

I can't be married.

I don't want to be married.

I can't have a successful career if my brain is preoccupied with thoughts of love all the time. If my parents taught me anything, it's that.

"Shit," I whisper under my breath as I stare at the ring. I don't remember what happened, but I remember that I wore that ring before.

And I'm pretty sure I know who slid it on my finger.

～

IT'S ten minutes until five o'clock, and I'm still pacing my office, trying to build up the courage to go talk to my new boss.

My new boss who may also be my new husband.

I glance back at my window on the fifth floor. Maybe I can jump out and escape. Maybe I'll get lucky and land on my head.

Someone walks by my office, and I nearly jump out of my skin. I take a deep breath as I see Martha shuffle by the window.

This has been the single worst day of my life and that's saying a lot. I grew up with two hippie parents who let their kid do all of the adult stuff, so I've had my share of bad days.

All afternoon, my mind kept racing to every worst-case scenario possible.

Maybe when I try to tell Tyler that I think we got married, he'll fire me, close the factory, and sue me for everything I have.

Maybe I married a homeless man.

Maybe I married a goat.

People start getting up and putting their coats on as the clock ticks closer to five. Computers get turned off, and happy hour plans are being made as I peer through the blinds at Tyler's office. His door is still closed.

Just go. Just do it.

It's easy to say, but it's another thing entirely to get my feet moving.

Emily walks by my office with her coat on and starts giggling when she sees me. She stops and stands straight, holding her purse like a bouquet and starts stepping down the hallway like she's a bride walking down the aisle.

I hate her. So much.

My stomach starts rolling again as she disappears and I

turn back to the closed office door. *This is all just a big misunderstanding. It's nothing.*

I open the door of my office, pretending like I'm not about to throw up, and step out into the hallway.

I'll just tell him the truth, we'll get it fixed, and then we'll both break out laughing.

My hand slides over my stomach as my veggie wrap from lunch threatens to make a grand reappearance in front of everyone.

This may even be a good thing. We'll probably share a laugh and become closer. Maybe we'll even be friends.

I dry heave when I arrive at the door, and it's settled: I'm swan-diving out of my five-story window instead.

His door swings open when I'm spinning on my heels about to make my high-heeled getaway.

"Dahlia," he says from behind me. Every muscle in my body clenches in panic.

I slowly turn around with dry unblinking eyes. Even his impossibly good looks can't make this situation any better. Somehow, it just makes it worse.

"I have to talk to you," I say. My voice is so hoarse. My mouth is so dry. It feels like I slept in the desert.

"Should we go in my office?" he asks, rubbing his chin as he stares down at me. "Or would we be more comfortable in my hotel room?"

I march into his office without acknowledging his sexual invitation with a comment. He chuckles as he follows me in and closes the door, watching me as I sit down in the chair in front of his desk.

"What can I do for you, Miss Dahlia?" he asks as he sits behind the desk. He stares at me with interest, probably not knowing what the hell to expect.

Whatever he's expecting, it doesn't have shit on what I'm

about to bring up. I toss the ring on the large oak desk between us and wait for his reaction.

"Are you asking me to marry you?" he says, looking down at it with a furrowed brow. "It looks a little bit small for me."

"I found this in my purse."

"And I found a Tic Tac in my pocket, but I didn't throw it on your desk."

I cross my arms over my chest as we stare each other down. "What happened last night?"

He leans back in his chair and raises his chin, all while keeping his bright green eyes on mine. "I don't remember."

"That makes two of us."

We stare at each other with tight eyes and clenched jaws, not saying anything for at least thirty seconds.

I raise my eyebrow as I break the silence. "Did you put something in my drink?"

"Did you put something in *my* drink?"

I huff out a laugh. "Why would I put something in *your* drink?"

"I don't know," he says, watching me as he rubs his chin. "Because I'm rich and you want my money? Because you're trying to get pregnant? Because I'm hot and you want my big dick? I don't know the reasons why crazy broads drug men."

My mouth drops open. The balls on this guy.

"Are you saying I'm a crazy broad?"

He shrugs. "Are you saying I'm a rapist?"

We stare at each other for another few tense seconds.

His eyes drop to the ring on the desk. "What's with the ring?"

"You tell me," I say. "I found it in my purse with a check written out to The Pineapple Chapel."

His face drops.

I lean forward. "What?"

He opens his shocked mouth but nothing comes out.

"What is it?"

He shakes his head as he closes his eyes. "I thought that was a novelty gift or something."

"What?"

"I found a marriage certificate in my hotel room from The Pineapple Chapel. It had my name on it with another ridiculous name."

Oh, shit.

"It wasn't Dahlia," he says. "It was-"

"Rainbow Solstice the First." We both say it at the same time.

It's my real name. The one that only my hippie parents use.

"That's me," I say, turning red as he looks at me with confusion. Even after twenty-eight years, I'm still ashamed of that stupid name. "If you tell anyone, I'll kill you."

"About your name, that we slept together, or that we're married?"

I clear my throat. "All of the above."

He leans forward, staring at me like he's trying to see into my skull. "We got married? What the hell?"

"Do you remember *anything* about last night?"

He shakes his head. "I remember meeting you at the bar."

"Me too."

"Then we had that drink."

"*Your* idea," I say.

He just ignores me. "Then you stormed away, and I wasn't feeling very well so I started walking back to my hotel room. That's all I can remember."

"That's all?" I ask, sitting on the edge of my seat.

He looks around like he's sifting through his perverted mind and then shrugs. "That's all."

I exhale in relief. *He doesn't remember the sex. Thank God.*

"Do you remember the night?" he asks, tilting his head slightly as he looks at me. "Or the sex?"

I shake my head like there's a spider trying to crawl into my ear. "No. Definitely not."

"But we still had sex," he says. His green eyes start to wander over my body like he's trying to figure out what his damaged memory is making him miss out on.

"It didn't really happen if neither of us can remember it." *Did it?* I'm sure there's an old dead philosopher somewhere out there who would back me up on that.

His eyes drop down to my chest and he smiles. "Should we start the honeymoon now?"

"No!" I snap back at him. "I want an annulment."

His face lights up in a smile. "Sure, we can do it in the butt. I'm down for whatever."

"Not anal, you moron. *Annulled.*"

He bites his bottom lip as he looks out the window to the beautiful view of the Vegas Strip in the distance. "Although, this could be good," he says. "My parents will give me the company now."

"What?" I ask, leaning forward. "You're not actually running the company? Then what was all of that big talk in the meeting about?"

Tyler rolls his eyes. "They won't sign the company over to me until I'm married."

"So, you're not in charge?" Maybe I can save the factory after all if I can make a good impression on his father, the real billionaire owner Mack McMillan.

He shrugs. "I am now. I'm married."

"I'm not staying married so that you can con your

parents into giving you their lifetime's work. I want an annulment."

"Okay," he says with a roll of his eyes. "I'll set it up."

I also want to talk to him about his father's plans for the Summerland factory, but now is not the time. I just asked for a divorce, it may be a bit much to ask for a favor right now.

We agree to let this little incident slide and never talk about it again.

"Thank you," I say as he walks me to the door. "I really like working for this company, and I don't want a night of... well, whatever the hell that was, to ruin it."

"It won't, Miss Rainbow Bright," he says with a grin as he opens the door for me.

The look I give him makes him take a step backward. "My parents were hippies."

He's trying to stifle his smile.

"Big hippies."

"I can't wait to meet them someday," he says as I walk out. "They are my in-laws."

"Not funny," I say to him over my shoulder. "Get the annulment. Right now."

"Yes, boss," he says, throwing me a salute.

I walk back to my office feeling better than ever. Tyler doesn't remember the sex, he's not my real boss, we're putting an end to the mistake of a marriage, and the day is finally over. Now I get to go back to my hotel room and crawl into bed like I've been fantasizing about all day.

My other boss, Mr. Wallace, pokes his head through the doorway. "Can I speak with you, Dahlia?"

"Sure," I say, waving him in. Even he can't ruin my mood. "I'm sorry about last night and this morning," I say, shaking my head as I place my palm on my chest. "I don't know what happened. I haven't been feeling like myself since I got here. And I'm sorry about insulting Kenny Loggins. He is truly a musical genius."

He lets out a breath and smiles. "No worries," he says, nodding like all is forgiven. It was the Kenny Loggins comment that did it.

"You're the only one I can trust," he says, walking into the office. "I have a meeting with Mr. McMillan senior tomorrow at lunch, but I have to head back home to Summerland early."

"Is everything okay?" The Mr. Wallace I know wouldn't miss a meeting with billionaire Mack McMillan for anything short of an emergency.

"Yup, yup," he says, nodding as his eyes cloud over. "My son and his friends were caught tattooing their teacher's forehead, but I'm sure it's not as serious as it sounds. He's at that rambunctious age right now."

"Right," I say, nodding along even though I wouldn't put 'rambunctious' and 'tattooing a poor woman's face' in the same category.

"I need *you* to meet with Mr. McMillan senior," he says.

My heart starts drumming a happy beat in my chest. "Really?" I ask, trying to stop myself from hugging him.

It's an opportunity to erase this disastrous day and start fresh with the real boss. I know I can impress him and get him to like me. From there, I can convince him to save the factory *and* the town of Summerland.

"He still calls the shots, no matter what his son says. This is a very important meeting for the factory workers, for us, and for the town. I'm counting on you to nail this meeting."

I nod so fast that I get dizzy. "I can do it, boss. You can count on me."

"I know," he says, placing a hand on my shoulder. "I'm constantly impressed by your business sense and work ethic," he says. "Except for today."

I thank him for the opportunity, and he leaves to go take care of his soon-to-be-jailed son.

Wow. A real opportunity to impress the boss. The *real* boss.

It's going to go great!

As long as he doesn't find out that we're currently related...

4

Dahlia

I'VE NEVER BEEN in awe of a door before.

But I've never been at the front door of a billionaire's mansion either. The intricately carved door is the most beautiful piece of wood I've ever seen, well, with the exclusion of Tyler's wood. That was pretty damn beautiful too.

I take a deep breath and ring the doorbell.

You got this, Dahlia.

I'm nervous, but I'm ready. I'm meeting with the seventy-five-year-old billionaire Mack McMillan, the new owner of my company, my new boss, *and* my new father-in-law. But he doesn't have to know that last part.

This is strictly a business meeting, a one-on-one meet and greet where I can impress him with my industry knowledge and try to save the factory and all of my coworkers' jobs with it.

I studied the stats and figures all night until I fell asleep on the floor, curled up with a calculator for a pillow and spreadsheets as blankets. I know my stuff. I've memorized all the facts about his company, can talk about every factory and office, and I've even come up with ways to save money in several departments.

He's going to be so impressed with me that he's going to want me to move into his personal office.

From what I heard, Mack McMillan is a hell of a business man, and I'll finally be able to see how I stack up against the best of the best.

As long as his son's name doesn't come up, I'll be fine.

I hear footsteps shuffling on the other side of the door, and I glance back at my rental car that's being driven away to the parking lot by security. It's too late to escape.

I smooth out my jacket as Mack himself opens the door. A wave of wealth, affluence, and power hits me as the door swings open.

His intense green eyes lock onto mine, and I gulp. He's shorter than I expected—his tall son must have gotten his height from his mother—but he still reeks of confidence and authority. He's good looking with a kind face that reminds me of an older version of Tyler.

I clear my throat as he stares at me, waiting for me to say the first word. Classic power move to throw me off my game. I'm impressed.

"Hello, Mr. McMillan," I say, trying unsuccessfully to keep my voice from shaking. "I'm Dahlia, the COO of Hospitech. It's a pleasure to meet you."

I thrust my hand out while keeping my shoulders straight back, waiting for a handshake that never comes. His lips curl up into a smile as he looks down at my hand.

"Ha!" he says, breaking into a wide smile. "That's a good one. Tyler said you were a funny one."

Tyler?

"Sir, I-"

He interrupts me when he rushes past my extended hand and wraps his arms around me, giving me a tight bear hug. "I'm so happy to meet you," he says, giving me an extra squeeze.

My chest tightens as my mind races, searching for answers that aren't coming.

"Is that her?" a female voice squeals from inside.

A gorgeous older lady with curly blonde hair, big breasts, and an outfit that would make a Kardashian stop and turn her head, rushes over, squealing with her hands raised over her head.

"My daughter-in-law!" she screams, crashing into my other side and completing the Dahlia sandwich.

My thoughts are frozen. My brain is broken. I could have sworn that I heard her say daughter-in-law, but that couldn't possibly be right because I haven't died and descended to the depths of hell.

Or have I?

While Tyler's two parents cling onto me like needy spider monkeys, *he* walks into the hallway, cringing as he watches.

My jaw is clenched so tight that my teeth are dangerously close to shattering as I glare at him. My nostrils are flaring like a dragon's. If I could breathe fire, his face would be a pile of ashes.

A pile of sexy ashes.

"Sorry," he mouths as he walks over with his hands in his pockets and a nervous look on his face.

I'm going to kill him.

"Mom, Dad," he says, "meet Dahlia. My new wife." His voice cracks with the last word.

I just glare at him. He's going to get more than just his voice cracked by the time this is over.

My two new unwanted in-laws finally release me, and I'm forced to drop my scowl and smile.

"It's so nice to meet you," Mack says, grinning as he stares at me in awe.

Tyler's mother clasps her hands together and squeals again, making me swallow hard. "I can't believe you two got married!"

"I can't believe it either," I say, giving Tyler a dirty look. "I nearly faint every time I think about it."

"That's what true love feels like," his mom says as she grabs my hand and pulls me inside.

His father takes my laptop bag that's full of ways to optimize, streamline, and monetize dozens of his company's departments and tosses it on the bench like it's a useless sack of potatoes. "Did you just come from work?" he asks, looking at my professional yet classy pantsuit that right now feels wildly inappropriate. "We have a strict no business talk in this house."

"Great," I mutter, thrilled that I spent all night preparing for this meeting.

"Come in, come in," his mother says, waving me into the enormous kitchen. It looks like Extreme Home Makeover threw up all over this place. "I want to know everything about you. Tyler hardly told us any details."

"Well," I say, narrowing my eyes on him. "We're still learning all about each other." All I know about him is that he likes to wear bright red underwear, and his cock is longer than any of the bananas lying on the counter.

"We sure are," he says, walking over. He approaches me like a scared tourist about to take a picture with a tiger. If he gets any closer, my claws are going to come out.

"Tyler," I say, giving him a sweet smile despite the fire brimming from my eyes. "Can I talk to you for a second? Alone."

"Sure," he says, swallowing hard. He turns to his mom and dad and excuses us.

"What the hell is going on?" I ask when we're back outside out of earshot. "You told them we're married? Are you fucking crazy?"

"Well, technically we are married," he says, rubbing the back of his neck.

He takes a step back when I take a step forward. "A marriage is more than just a piece of paper with a bunch of tacky pineapples on it."

"Not according to the state of Nevada it's not."

"Well, according to me it is," I snap back. "What happened to the annulment?"

He takes another step back. Probably a wise move. He should be running away from me in a full sprint with the way that my heart is pumping so hard.

I'll be lucky if I don't get fired at the end of this because of him. He's ruined any shot that I had at impressing his father, Mack. Six years of working hard at Hospitech down the drain.

Because of *him*.

"What. Happened. To. The. Annulment?" I speak slowly trying to shove every word into his thick skull.

He gulps. "I thought that maybe we could hold off on the annulment for a while."

I rub my forehead, trying to ward off the headache that's rushing forward. "You didn't think to consult me on this? Or before you told your parents?"

"I knew that you would have said no."

I'm livid. I want to rip his beautiful head off of his body

and laugh as I watch his sparkling green eyes turn to a dull gray.

"*Then why the fuck wouldn't you get an annulment?*"

I'm screaming so loud that the security guard who took my car starts walking over, looking unsure.

"Are you okay, Mr. McMillan?" he asks. His hand is hovering over his pepper spray.

"Great, Wilbur," he says, giving him a thumbs up. "The new wife has a bit of a temper."

I grind my teeth as I glare at him. "You haven't seen my temper," I say in a voice that's ice cold. "This is me *very* controlled."

He gulps and takes another step back. One more and he's going to fall off the front stoop into the bushes.

"Just hear me out," he says, showing me his palms. "I think you're going to like what I have to say."

"If it's not 'you're on Candid Camera' then you're going to be very disappointed."

He's talking so fast now. He knows that I'm two seconds away from storming back into the house and telling his parents the truth. "You want to keep the factory open, right?"

I don't answer, but I'm listening.

"And I want my parents to sign the company over to me," he says, his voice racing. "We can work together."

"I think we did enough *together* already."

"If you stay cool and tell my parents that we're married," he says, scraping a hand through his hair, "then I'll get the company, and I'll make sure that your factory stays open."

I stare at him for a full ten seconds before moving. "How can I be sure that you won't screw me over and close it the second you get the company?"

"If you can't trust your husband, who can you trust?" he

asks with a smirk on his face. "Kidding, kidding," he says when he sees my face. "I promise."

I don't want to trust him. I don't want anything to do with him, but I've been over the numbers and I know that whoever is running McMillan Worldwide Inc. will see the same thing that I've seen. The factory in Summerland is too expensive. They could save at least twenty-five percent in production costs if they close it up and move to Mexico. That would be disastrous for the town. Everyone would lose their jobs, their homes, everything. If there's something I can do to prevent that, then I have to do it.

"How long is this going to go on for?" I ask. I can't believe I'm actually considering this.

"Just a few months. You can go back home next week, and I'll stay here. Once the company is transferred to me, I'll tell them that we had a falling out, we'll get that annulment you want so badly, and we'll go our separate ways."

"And the factory stays open?"

He nods. "I pinky swear."

I want to pull my hair out and strangle him with it.

He looks at me with hopeful eyes. "What do you say?"

The front door creeps open before I can answer. His mother pops her excited head out and smiles. "Quit hogging her," she says to Tyler. "I want to get to know my new daughter-in-law! Champagne is served. It's time to celebrate!"

She holds the door open and looks at me with raised eyebrows. "Coming?"

"Yeah," Tyler whispers. "Coming?"

I turn to his mother and smile as wide as she is. "I sure am, *Mom!*"

She squeals in delight and races back into the mansion, leaving the door open.

My smile vanishes as I turn back to my new husband. "What's your mother's name?"

"Thank you," he says, exhaling in relief. "You won't regret this."

I march past him into the house. "I already do."

He follows me in and tells me that his mother's name is Kirsten. I'm shaking my head the whole way into the kitchen until I see his parents standing around the marble island with four full champagne flutes in their hands.

Mack hands me one, and Kirsten hands Tyler one. "I never thought this day would come," Mack says, tearing up as he raises his glass. "I never thought my son would settle down. I was worried he would stay a playboy forever. I can't wait to meet the girl who finally tamed him. You must be a miracle worker."

"I am," I say, shooting Tyler a look. "It's a miracle that I'm still standing here."

"Thank you for sticking around," he says, smiling as he raises his glass in the air. "To many more years of health, wealth, and happiness."

Mack wraps a heavy arm around my shoulder and raises his glass, smiling from ear to ear. "Cheers."

I force out a smile as I clink glasses with my new unwanted family.

"Tell us how you met," Kirsten says, ushering us to the table. Tyler pulls out my chair for me and then sits on my right as his parents sit in front of us.

"It's a great story," I say, nodding. "Tyler tells it so well."

His parents turn to him with big smiles as they wait for it. I may be playing the sweet new wife, but I'm definitely going to make him pay for putting me in this awkward situation. "Tell them about the part with the elephant," I say, making it harder for him. "And the aliens and how you tripped on the apple pie and fell into the barrel full of warm beer and how Shaquille O'Neal helped you up."

"Wow!" his mother says with wide, excited eyes. "This seems like quite the story!"

"It is," I say, trying to stifle my giggles. "Wait until Tyler tells it. It's even better than it sounds."

"Don't build it up too much," Tyler says, placing a hand on my thigh. He gives my leg a hard warning squeeze, but it just makes me laugh even harder. "The story is not *that* good."

"Aliens, Shaq, *and* an elephant?" his father says, staring at him with complete attention. "It doesn't get better than that!"

"Don't forget about the apple pie and barrel full of warm beer," I say, batting my eyelashes at him.

Tyler sits up straight and clears his throat. "So, I was at the premiere of Shaquille O'Neal's new movie called... Alien Basketball Players."

I burst out laughing. Could he have picked a more ridiculous name for a movie?

"She's laughing already," he says, placing his hand on mine. "It's not even your favorite part yet, honey."

"I can't wait," I say, watching him with rapt attention.

"So, after the movie, which was horrible by the way. Don't bother seeing it."

"I don't think they could even if they wanted to," I say, between chuckles.

He flashes me a wide-eyed look. "Anyway," he continues. "After the movie, they had an elephant there as part of the festivities. Shaq was riding around on him and throwing pies into the crowd."

"Oh, I don't like when they bring elephants into the city like that," Kirsten mutters, shaking her head in disapproval.

His father leans forward. "They were throwing *pies*, into the *crowd*?" he says with a furrowed brow.

"Of course," Tyler says, and I laugh at the casualness of his reply. "It's what all of the young kids do these days."

"Oh," his father says, dropping his eyes in thought.

"So," Tyler says, turning to me with soft eyes. "I saw this beautiful girl standing in the crowd, and time just stopped. It was incredible. I never believed in love at first sight, but when I saw Dahlia standing there with the sun on her gorgeous face, I knew there was no turning back. I knew that she was going to be it for me. The one I always want to be with."

His parents let out an 'awww' as I shift in my seat and undo a button on my jacket. *Is it hot in here?*

"But then," Tyler continues, "I saw an apple pie flying at her, and I just reacted. I dove in the air and knocked it out of the way just as it was about to hit her."

He takes my hand and turns to me with a smile that makes my breath quicken. "We've been in love ever since."

"That's so sweet," Kirsten says, tilting her head as she looks at us with doe eyes.

"What about the barrel of warm beer?" Mack asks.

"Yeah, Tyler," I say, shaking my head to get the hearts out of my eyes. "Tell them about the barrel of warm beer."

"We were leaving to get a cup of coffee," he says, trying not to laugh, "and I slipped on one of the pies and fell into Shaq's barrel of warm beer. He helped me out."

His mom looks confused. "Why was there a barrel of warm beer out?"

Tyler shrugs. "Shaq is a giant, Mom. He drinks beer out of a barrel."

"Oh," she says, tilting her head as she tries to process it.

"So how have you two been?" Tyler asks them, desperately trying to change the subject.

"Oh, no," Kirsten says as I take a big gulp of champagne. "We're talking about you two. We're finally meeting Dahlia after you've been dating for *two years!*"

I spit a mouthful of champagne all over my new father-in-law's face.

Tyler jumps up to get a napkin while Mack stares at me with wide eyes as the champagne that was in my mouth a few seconds ago, drips down his shocked face.

"Goodness, dear," Kirsten says, leaning forward with a look of concern on her face. "Are you okay?"

I nod as I wipe my chin with the back of my hand. "I'm sorry, sir. It was the bubbles."

"No problem," Mack says as Tyler returns with some paper towels. "It's been a while since I've had a glass of champagne thrown in my face by a pretty girl. No harm done."

He wipes his face as Tyler sits down beside me. I turn to him with a tight smile. "I'm sorry. Did she say two *years?*"

"I did," Kirsten says, nodding happily. "Is that not right?"

Tyler shakes his head and answers before I can. "It went by so fast. It feels more like two months."

"Two *days* is more like it," I mutter.

He smiles nervously at me, begging me with his eyes to be cool.

"I can't wait for tomorrow night!" his mother says, squealing again. "I can't wait for you to meet everyone!"

"Mom," Tyler says, gulping as he turns to her. "Maybe we could put the party on hold for a while."

"Tomorrow night?" I repeat as a large empty pit forms in the depths of my stomach. "Party?"

"It's just a small dinner party," Tyler says, nervously rubbing his hands down his pant legs.

"No, it's not," his mother says, waving a dismissive hand at him. "I invited the whole family and all of our friends. I just can't wait for them to meet you!"

I glance back at the door, wondering how fast I can sprint out of here, grab my car, and drive to Mexico.

"You have to be here at seven o'clock sharp," she says.

I turn to Tyler with a grin. If he's going to pull a fast one on me, then I'm going to pull a fast one on him. "Will that leave us enough time to go shopping for the wedding present you promised me?"

"Wedding present?" his mother asks with a big smile on her face. "That's so romantic."

I turn to her and smile like a good daughter-in-law would. "Your son is *very* romantic." She looks thrilled. "He promised to buy me a new car for a wedding gift. I said no, but he insisted. He said I could get any car that I wanted."

"A new car," Mack says, nodding as he watches me.

Tyler shifts uncomfortably in his seat. I love making him squirm.

"I'll have Harvey meet you at the Ferrari dealership tomorrow," Mack says nodding. "He'll take care of you and help you get something nice."

Tyler lets out a panicked cough. "Ferrari dealership? Dahlia is not a very flashy girl, Dad. I think she would rather have a Honda or a Toyota."

"Nope," I say, shaking my head. "A Ferrari sounds nice. I can get used to flashy."

"Then you came to the right place," Mack says, pulling out his phone. He googles something and then hands me his phone. The cars on the page look like a rapper's wet dream. "I would suggest this one here," he says, pointing to a bright red Ferrari that looks like it's from the year 2036. "It's a bit pricey at $360,000, but you don't get married every day. If you're not going to splurge on your pretty new wife, who are you going to splurge on?"

"Yeah, Tyler," I say, turning to him with a grin. "Who are you going to splurge on?"

He wipes the sweat off his temple and laughs nervously.

"All right, Pumpkin. Whatever you like."

I try to hide my evil smile. Ten minutes into this marriage, and I already have my new husband wrapped around my finger.

He doesn't know what he got himself into.

5

Tyler

"WE LOVE HER!" my mother squeals when Dahlia finally leaves.

My heart is still thumping away. I was terrified that she was going to rat me out, but she didn't. And all it cost me was a brand-new Ferrari.

But honestly, I don't care what it costs. As long as she's willing to keep up the charade for a while longer, I'll pay whatever she wants.

"Good choice, son," my father says, patting me on the shoulder. "I'm proud of you. It's a good decision to settle down. You'll see in the long run that family life beats the bachelor life. Diapers, Friday nights in, and minivans may not be as luxurious and exciting as models, parties, and fine Italian cars, but it brings the type of happiness that money just can't buy."

He can keep his type of happiness all to himself. I only want the type of happiness that hot models can provide.

"Thanks, Dad," I say. "I hope you're right."

"Come," he says, waving me to the backyard. We walk outside as my mom grabs the phone to call her friends and brag all about her new daughter-in-law. My chest tightens when I see how happy she is. I might have gone too far this time.

She's going to be crushed when she finds out that Dahlia and I are nothing but strangers who shared an intimate moment that neither of us can remember.

But they're not leaving me with much of a choice. They refuse to sign the company over to me until I 'mature' and drop the party lifestyle. My father has told me many times that he didn't work nights and weekends for the past five decades, building up a fortune to hand over to me and see it get wasted on private jets, expensive cars, fine champagne, and pretty girls who only like me for my money. I take offense to that. The girls like me for my big cock too.

"Sit," he says as he pulls out a chair by the pool. "I think it's time to talk about the future of the company and your role in it."

My heart starts racing as I sit down beside him. This is what I've always wanted.

"I like the new changes you've made in your personal life," he says, nodding as he looks at me. "It gives me hope."

A thickness settles in my throat as I listen to him. My father's always been the type to put work before fun. Even after he made his first ten million, he was still driving a rusty old car that you could hear from down the block. That's why I was so surprised to hear him so excited about getting Dahlia a new Ferrari. It's so not like him. He must really like her.

"It makes me think that you might be ready to take on a bigger role in the company," he says, looking relieved that he can finally take his retirement.

"I am," I say, nodding excitedly. I may like to party hard on the weekends, but that doesn't mean I don't bust my ass every day in the office, working as hard as I can to grow the company. But try telling my stubborn old man that. It's hard to teach an old dinosaur new tricks.

It's always been my dream to run the company. I've wanted my father to hand me the torch so I can run with it and show him what I'm really made of. I want to show him what I can do.

I can definitely run faster than my cousin, Nick. I've always feared that he would hand the torch to him and not to me.

"Good," he says, nodding as he sizes me up. "That's what I like to hear. I was surprised to hear that you were married, but now that I think about it, it's pretty fitting. You've always flown by the seat of your pants and been a little too carefree for your own good. I was worried that your live-in-the-moment attitude and lack of concern for any consequences would get you into trouble someday, but it seems to have worked out for the best. Dahlia seems like a good catch for you. She's got a good head on her shoulders. I think she'll keep you in line."

"Life has definitely become more interesting since she showed up."

"The good ones always have that effect on men," he says, smiling as he looks back at the house where Mom is still blabbing away on the phone.

"I'm done with the partying," I lie. "I've sewn my oats. I'm ready to settle down, and I want to run the company." I lean forward, locking eyes with him. "I can do it, Dad."

He takes a deep breath as he leans back and looks away. "I know you can," he says, looking uncomfortable as he stares at the pool. "You definitely have the business sense and skills to run it, but I have thousands of employees to think of. I have to pick the person who will be the perfect fit to lead the company into the next few decades. You shouldn't get any special treatment because you're my son. McMillan Worldwide Inc. is bigger than us. Thousands of families depend on the paychecks we give them. If the person I choose is not up to the enormous task of running it, those families may see their only source of income disappear. I can't have that. I have to consider everyone and pick the absolute best."

"Nick," I mutter. I know he's on my father's mind right now. He always had a close connection with his brother's son. Sometimes I was jealous of him growing up, thinking my father wished he was his son instead of me.

My father nods. "I'm not going to lie to you, Tyler. You're a man now. Nick is a consideration. He's smart, clever, resourceful, and a hard worker."

He's also a lying, stealing creep. My father doesn't know him like I do. All my father ever saw was Nick's good grades and polite attitude. He never saw the darkness that Nick has buried deep inside. My uncle, Nick's father and my dad's brother, died years ago, so Nick and his brother Jason grew up without a dad. I think my father has always ignored Nick's negative side out of pity.

He always chooses to ignore the missing money from the departments Nick runs, attributing it to accounting errors instead of what it clearly is: theft.

"But don't worry about that right now," my father says, standing up. "This is a good step in the right direction. We have a marriage to celebrate."

I swallow hard as he stands up with a smile on his face, feeling like a liar and a creep myself.

IT'S midnight when my phone lights up. It's my beautiful new wife, probably telling me to have a good night with some sweet dreams.

Nope.

Dahlia: What the hell did you get me into?

I text back.

Tyler: What are you wearing?

Dahlia: Sweat pants and a Garfield hoodie. I'm married now. I've stopped trying.

Tyler: Send me a pic... minus the Garfield sweater.

Thirty seconds later she sends me a photo of her hand giving me the finger.

Tyler: Not quite what I had in mind.

Dahlia: What are you doing to me? I'm freaking out over here!

Dahlia: How many people do I have to meet tomorrow for this thing???

Tyler: Only about a hundred. Don't worry. The new car will help calm your nerves.

Dahlia: A hundred people?!? Did I say I wanted a new car? I changed my mind and want a new yacht.

Dahlia: Bring ALL of your credit cards.

Tyler: It won't be that bad.

Dahlia: Your mom looked so happy today. I feel bad.

I sigh when I read the text. The last heart I want to break in this world is my mother's. She never thought I would settle down with a girl, so she had it in her head that she probably wasn't getting any grandkids. This changed it all.

But it's something I have to do. I can't let the company fall into Nick's hands. He's going to undo everything my father worked for. I can't let that happen, even if my father can.

Tyler: It's all going to work out. Everything always does.

Dahlia: I believed that until I woke up married next to a stranger.

Tyler: A naked stranger.

Dahlia: Oh, believe me. I haven't forgotten that part. It's etched into my brain forever.

Tyler: I impressed you that much?

Dahlia: Traumatized is more like it.

Tyler: You don't remember anything???

Dahlia: Nothing. You?

Tyler: Nada.

Dahlia: So strange...

I lower my phone and take a sip of scotch, thinking of the girl on the other end of the line. The girl who is my new wife.

I don't know much about her besides the fact that she's smoking hot with a bit of an uptight bitchy attitude, but in all fairness, she has every reason to be a bitch with me right now. I could have gotten the annulment, but I didn't.

If that doesn't bring the bitch out in a girl then I don't know what will.

My phone lights up when I'm thinking of her smile and the cute freckles that dot the tops of her cheeks.

Dahlia: I'm going to sleep now. I want to be fresh and alert for when I buy a car that's way too expensive.

Tyler: Goodnight. Any chance of a last minute nude pic? We are married...

Dahlia: Any chance of a last minute annulment? I do hate you...

Tyler: You don't even know me.

Dahlia: Yet we're married. I guess we'll never know what happened that night.

Tyler: I guess not.

What a waste. I had sex with that stunning girl and I don't remember a thing.

What the hell did happen that night?

6

_____

Dahlia

THREE NIGHTS AGO...

"WILL YOU RELAX?" Emily says, shaking her head at me. "We're in Vegas."

"For work," I answer back. "Not for going on a bender."

She laughs. "Have you ever even been on a bender? And I'm not talking about a fender bender with that old clunky car you used to drive."

"I have."

She snorts out a laugh. "When?"

"I have done plenty of naughty things," I say, feeling my cheeks heat up. "But now is not the time for drinking in bars. We should be studying for tomorrow's meeting."

We have a big meeting with Mack McMillan, the billionaire business giant who bought out our company. I really want to make a good impression on the commander-in-chief, so that's why I'd rather be studying in my hotel room instead of drinking in a bar. Emily doesn't share my view.

"Oh, relax," she says, waving a hand at me. "It's going to be fine."

Mr. Wallace walks over with a beer in his hand. "Beer always tastes so much better when my kid is miles away from me," he says, smiling to himself as he sits at the table. "And it always tastes better in Vegas."

"Dahlia has never been," Emily says, giggling at me. "Which is probably a good thing. I don't think she could handle Vegas."

I roll my eyes at her. I'll see what *she* can handle in tomorrow's meeting. I'll be answering questions like rapid fire and impressing the heck out of our new boss while she's hungover under the table. She'll see.

"What are you even drinking?" she asks me. "Please tell me there's alcohol in there."

"There's alcohol in there," I lie.

She grabs the glass out of my hand and tastes my drink. "This is a Shirley Temple," she says, staring at me in disbelief. "Will you go to the bar and get yourself a proper drink for once? You're in Vegas, not Disney World."

I take a deep breath and look at my watch. *How much longer do I have to stay here before I can go back to my hotel room and prepare for tomorrow's meeting?*

Emily looks to our boss when I don't move. "Order her to go get an alcoholic drink," she pleads. "This is such a buzzkill."

"I'm not here to be your drinking buddy," I say, getting annoyed. *I'm here to impress Mr. McMillan.*

Mr. Wallace is sick of our bickering. He's been traveling with us and dealing with it all day. "Just go be a normal person for once and get a drink," he says, taking a big sip of his beer.

I push away from the table with a roll of my eyes. "Fine." I could use a break from them anyway, and a white wine spritzer to sip on sounds pretty nice right now.

"And no white wine spritzers," Emily calls out to my back. "This is Vegas, not Sunday brunch. Get a real drink."

Ugh. Am I that predictable?

I feel eyes on me as I walk to the bar, feeling a bit out of my element. I've never been a fan of the bar scene. I don't understand how girls can meet guys here. It's just full of creeps and perverts trying to take advantage of drunk girls.

Oh, great. One of those creeps sitting on the corner of the bar has his eyes on me. I turn to flash him a bitchy look but my stunned face freezes in a twisted grimace when I see what he looks like.

If the rest of the men in the bar are like warm flat beers, he's like a fine expensive wine: Bold, strong, and looking fucking delicious in his perfectly tailored suit.

He has the kind of flawless face that makes you stop in your tracks. The kind of tousled dark brown hair that causes car accidents when he walks down the street. The kind of smile that makes you hate your life because he's not in it. The kind of catastrophic emerald green eyes that make you think you died and went to heaven.

Simply said, he's beautiful.

The lines around his eyes become visible as he smiles at me. I give him my shoulder before he can see my blushing cheeks.

I'm here for *business*, not whatever he's here for.

The bartender lets out an audible sigh when he sees me and then shuffles over, looking like I just ruined his entire day. "What would you like?"

The man at the end of the bar is sliding over empty stools until he's sitting right beside me, smelling like hours waiting by the phone and tear soaked pillows.

"Whatever it is, it's on me," he says with a voice that feels like smooth leather.

"No, it's not," I say curtly, resisting the urge to look over at him. "I can pay for my own drink."

"Ralph," the man says to the bartender, ignoring me. "Put it on my card."

Ugh. This is why I don't come out to bars.

"What do you want, lady?" Ralph the bartender asks, looking annoyed that I'm making him perform his job.

"A white wine spritzer, easy on the white wine. In a martini glass, please." The white wine spritzer is for me. The martini glass is for Emily. I'll tell her it's a strong cocktail to get her off my back.

"A white wine spritzer?" the man beside me says with a chuckle. "This is Vegas, not Disney World."

"Why does everyone keep saying that?" I snap, finally turning to him. *Wow.* Those eyes are from another planet.

He grins now that he has my attention. "Because Vegas is a place to let loose and have fun."

"I'm loose," I say, trying to look casual. *Damn, I never know what to do with my arms.* He chuckles as he glances down at them sticking out awkwardly like the stiff arms of a broken manikin.

"I'm having fun," I lie. My cheeks burn as his eyes inappropriately wander up and down my gray pantsuit.

"Let me show you how to have fun," he says, meeting my eyes again.

"Are you going to jump out the window?" I ask, throwing a smirk back at him. "Because that would be really fun for me."

He chuckles as he turns to the bartender, and my lips curl up into a smile at having made him laugh.

"Ralph," he says as the bartender is about to pour my drink. "Scrap the white wine spritzer. Give us two Lucky 7s."

My chest tightens. Why can't he just leave me alone and let me get my drink? The sooner I'm out of this bar, the better.

"Want to get lucky?" he asks with a heart-stopping smile.

I stare him dead in the eyes with a blank expression. "No, I want to get out of here."

He chuckles. "Back to all that fun you're having?"

I roll my eyes. It seems like all of Vegas won't leave me alone until I have a drink. *Fine, Vegas. You win!*

"What's in a Lucky 7?"

"Yes," he says, rubbing his hands together in excitement now that he finally broke me. "It's always different."

"Huh?"

He points to the top row of bottles and my eyes fall onto his thick forearms that are creeping out of his suit. They're covered in tattoos.

Good thing he's not my type.

I lean against the bar so that my legs don't give out on me.

"Count seven bottles from the left," he says as Ralph the bartender grabs it. "Now on the second shelf, you count seven bottles from the right. Last shelf seven bottles from the left again. Mix them together and you have Lucky 7s."

"I'll be lucky if I don't puke it up," I say, crinkling my nose up in disgust.

He laughs. "It won't be that bad. Probably. Ralph, what do we have?"

The bartender places two bottles in front of us as he quickly dusts off the third bottle. "Scotch," the hot guy beside me says, reading the label. "And Kiwi Schnapps. Ew. What the hell is that?"

Ralph places the third bottle on the marble bar with a clunk.

"What the hell is *that*?" I ask, staring at it with wide terrified eyes.

"Insane-O Worm-O Tequil-O," the man says as he picks up the old bottle and rolls it around in his hands. "I think the last time they served this was to celebrate the end of the Civil War. Where's the worm?"

"He probably moved back to Mexico," I say, leaning away from it. "I would too if I had to live in that bottle of acid."

The man hands the bottle back and grins to Ralph. "Mix 'em up!"

"No, thank you," I say as Ralph opens the bottles. My eyes immediately start watering as soon as the bartender opens the Tequila. Even Ralph jerks his head back in surprise. "I'll stick with my white wine spritzer."

"Come on," the man says at the bartender pours a shot of each bottle into two glasses. The color looks like raw sewage but doesn't smell nearly as good. "You're going to let me go to the emergency room all by myself?"

Ralph slides a glass in front of him and one in front of me.

"Ugh," I say, jerking my head to the side to get away from the toxic fumes.

"It's a good luck drink," the man says as he lifts up his glass, grimacing as the smell hits his perfectly shaped nostrils. "I know you need some good luck."

My meeting with Mack McMillan tomorrow morning flashes into my head. "How do you know I need good luck?"

"Everybody in Vegas needs good luck."

I raise an eyebrow as I look down at the drink, sitting there full of future regrets. *I do need some good luck.*

"It's called Lucky 7s for a reason," he says, holding the glass up to me.

"Fine," I say with a sigh. If anything, it may get Emily off my back. Hopefully she believes me about all of this, which she probably won't.

He taps my glass with his and smiles as he looks me in the eyes. "Asses up."

A river of burning lava scorches my throat as I gulp down the huge shot. "*Geez!*" I say, coughing like a first-time smoker as my eyes start watering like a broken fire hydrant.

I frantically wave my hand in front of my open mouth, hoping that some of my tears will drip into my mouth to soothe the intense burning. "So, that's what a Molotov cocktail tastes like," I say, gagging as it threatens to come back up.

The man isn't faring any better, I'm happy to say. He's wiping his watery eyes with the back of his hand as he takes a sip of his scotch to get rid of the horrible taste.

"It feels like a demon just blew a load in my mouth," he says, sticking his tongue out as he coughs.

"See?" I say when the worst of the burning has settled. "This is why I'm anti-fun."

"At least now you'll have some good luck," he says, waving the bartender back over. "Can you get the pretty lady a white wine spritzer? Actually, make that two. I need something to soothe my throat."

"In a martini glass," I call out to Ralph's back.

I close my eyes as my stomach starts to gurgle. That shot was a bad idea. It's time to go back to my room before it hits. I'm not used to drinking, and a shot like that might be enough to get me tipsy.

And I really don't want to be tipsy in front of my boss. Mr. Wallace sees me as the model of self-discipline and control, and I'm *never* going to do anything to ruin that image he has of me.

"Two white wine spritzers in martini glasses," Ralph the bartender says, handing over the drinks. "Now, who's paying?"

"He is," I say, pointing at the man sitting next to me. "You can pay for my drink now for putting me through that."

He smiles as he pulls out a wad of cash, slides off two bills, and hands them to the bartender. "I never got your name," he says as I take my drink.

I smirk at him as I walk away. "I know."

He turns on the stool as I walk back to my table. "You can at least give me your name. You're going to get lucky tonight, and it's all because of me."

I snort out a laugh. "Yeah," I mutter to myself as I walk away from him. "Like *that's* ever going to happen."

7

Ralph the Bartender

STILL THREE NIGHTS AGO...

"CAN I GET A GLASS OF BEER?"

You can get a glass of shut the fuck up.

"Sure," I say, giving the guy at my bar a wide smile even though I would rather throw the beer in his face. I'm on hour nine of a ten-hour shift, and my boss has been up my ass the entire time.

I just want to go home, smoke a joint, and play Call of Duty until I pass out in a pile of Cool Ranch Dorito crumbs.

I take a deep breath as I grab the beer from the fridge and hand it over. "Eight dollars."

The guy peels off a ten from his fat wad of cash and slides it across my bar. I grab the bill and wait a few awkward seconds, hoping that he'll say keep the change, but he just stares at me with big stupid eyes.

Ugh. I hate this job.

"Here's your change," I say with a big smile as I give him his two dollars. He reaches into his pocket and pulls out a quarter and a dime. He tosses it on the sticky bar and leaves with his beer without saying another word.

"Asshole," I mutter under my breath as I grab the shitty tip.

Just when things are going bad, my boss comes over to make it even worse.

"Can I get cut?" I ask, staring at him with hopeful eyes.

He rolls his eyes as he walks past me, ignoring my question.

"Asshole," I mutter again when he's out of earshot.

He stops and turns. *Uh-oh.* It's never a good sign when his shoulders tense up like that.

"What's this doing here?"

"Huh?" I turn to see where he's pointing and take a breath of relief. For a second, I thought he found my stash of weed that's hidden behind the bar.

"What's that bottle doing out?" He walks over to the shelves of alcohol and grabs the old dusty tequila bottle off of the counter.

"I was just cleaning up," I say with a shrug. I can't tell him the truth because I pocketed the cash for the two Lucky 7s.

He holds the bottle up to the light and inhales sharply.

"What's the matter?" I ask, feeling my heart start to race. I hate this job, but it's all I have. I really don't want to get fired.

"This expired four years ago," he says, turning the bottle of Insane-O Worm-O Tequil-O around in his hands. "Look, the worm disintegrated. It turns into a narcotic and becomes toxic when it decomposes. It can really fuck someone up. Did you serve this to anyone?"

I swallow hard as I look down the bar to the place where the good-looking guy who left me a huge tip was sitting. The stool is empty.

"No."

My eyes dart across the bar to the hot girl who was dressed like a sexy librarian—the uptight one with the fax machine up her ass. She was with him and had a drink of that poison too. I gulp when I see her at a table full of corporate drones, throwing her hands in the air and singing show tunes.

"No one?" my boss asks, eying me closely.

I shake my head. "No one."

"Are you sure?"

I glance at her one more time and cringe when I see her with her shoe pressed against her face, talking into it like it's a phone. The people around her look very confused.

"I'm sure, boss."

He shakes his head as he takes the bottle and looks at the dusty shelves. "Go through the rest of the bottles and see what else is expired. I told you to do that last week."

He walks away mumbling something about how nobody listens to him or something like that. I'm not really listening.

I'm too busy watching the librarian chick as she runs out of the bar with one shoe on her foot and one shoe on her ear.

Oh, well. I hope she doesn't die.

I crack open a beer when my boss heads in the back and then duck down behind the bar to take a sip.

One hour to go.

Fuck, I hate this job.

8

Dahlia

"I WONDER which one I'll pick," I say, grinning as I walk down the row of shiny new Ferraris.

Tyler grins beside me. "How about that one?" he says, pointing to a cardboard cutout of a Ferrari that's on display.

"Not expensive enough," I say with a smirk as I turn to him. "So many to choose from. Maybe I'll get one in each color."

"Ferraris are so last year," he says, shaking his head as he stuffs his hands into his pockets. "Hyundai. Now that's what all of the elite are buying this year. I can see you driving a nice *used* Hyundai Accent."

I narrow my eyes on him. "And I can see you explaining to your parents why they're not getting any grandkids."

He gulps.

"Yeah. You're not getting out of this one."

I don't even want a Ferrari. I just want to watch him squirm.

What am I going to do with a Ferrari in a small town like Summerland? Park it at the only diner in town next to a tractor?

This is all just to mess with him like he's messing with me.

"Hello, Mr. McMillan," a salesman says as he rushes over. He looks like he should be in a used car dealership—not a Ferrari dealership—with the white powder from his donut still stuck to his clip-on tie. At least I hope it's icing sugar and not nose sugar, but this is Vegas after all, so you never know.

"Your father said you were going to be stopping by."

Tyler shakes the man's hand. "Nice to see you again, Harvey. I'm looking for a wedding present for my hot new wife."

Harvey turns to me with a warm smile. "You definitely came to the right place. What are you driving now?"

"A bike."

He laughs. He thinks I'm joking, but I'm not. It's yellow and it has a big basket on the front. I love it.

Harvey smiles as he points to a sleek red Ferrari that's raised above the others on a stage. "Let's see what we can upgrade you with."

I grin at Tyler as I hook my arm around Harvey's. "Yes. Let's go see."

Tyler shuffles behind us as I look around with my chin in the air. "I need something with a large trunk. I'm going to be doing a lot of shopping now that I'm Mr. McMillan's wife, and I need something that can carry my many bags."

"How many bags are we talking?" Harvey asks.

"Yeah," Tyler grunts from behind us. "How many bags are we talking?"

I glance back at him over my shoulder and grin. "A lot."

Harvey slides his arm out of mine and darts to the front of the Ferrari parked on the stage. "This is our top model," he says, smiling widely. "The GTB engine has six hundred and sixty horsepower at eight thousand rpm."

"I don't care about all of that," I say, waving a hand at him. "I need trunk space for my *daily* shopping trips now that I'm Tyler's *hot new wife*."

Tyler steps up beside me as Harvey pops the trunk open. "As you can see it has *plenty* of space," Harvey says, waving his hand into the empty trunk. "Even enough for a middle-aged man who likes to eat too many donuts."

I laugh as he climbs in, happy that it is only icing sugar on his tacky tie.

"See?" he says, laying down inside the trunk. "Tons of room for bags. Enough for Armani, Gucci, Michael Kor—"

Tyler closes the trunk with a bang, interrupting Harvey's sales pitch. I feel guilty for laughing at poor Harvey who's locked in the trunk, but it doesn't stop me from bursting out in giggles.

"You're killing me here," Tyler says, looking at me with narrowed eyes.

I clasp my hands together while I kick my leg out behind me and bat my eyelashes like I'm in an episode of *I Love Lucy*. "All in a day's work for a pretty little wife."

Harvey starts banging on the inside of the trunk. His muffled voice comes through between thumps. "Excuse me."

"Are you going to let him suffocate?"

Tyler stares me down. "Are you going to let me go broke?"

"Are you going to make me break your mother's heart?"

We stare each other down for ten heated seconds before he reaches down and pops the trunk back open.

Harvey climbs out, laughing nervously. "So, that's the trunk."

I keep my eyes locked on Tyler. "Good to know that I can fit a dead body in there. I might have to before this is all over."

He smirks. "It's not nice to threaten to kill your husband." He turns to Harvey and nods his head. "We'll take it!"

Harvey's face lights up with a wide smile before he sprints away to get the paperwork.

A heaviness settles in my stomach as guilt crashes down on me. "Tyler, no," I say, shaking my head. "I was just messing around. It's too much."

Tyler shrugs. "It's only half a million dollars."

"I don't need a car," I say, feeling both awful that he thought I was serious and honored that he's willing to spend that much money on me. "And I *certainly* don't need a Ferrari."

"Well," he says with a smirk as Harvey runs back, clutching the contract to his chest, "you're getting one."

I try to convince him otherwise, but he just ignores me as he signs the contract on the hood of the car and hands over his American Express black card.

And just like that—I own a Ferrari.

"I TOLD you I didn't want it."

Tyler just smiles as he shoves the new key into my hand.

"You told me you didn't want the drink when we first met, but that didn't stop you from taking it."

"Yeah," I say with a laugh. "And look how that turned out. How do you keep making me do things I don't want to do?"

"My charm? Good looks? Winning personality?"

I shake my head slowly as I study him. "No. That's not it."

"You can't control yourself around me," he says, walking around to the passenger's side of my brand-new unwanted Ferrari. "Just admit it."

I shake my head, but that must be it. What else explains me waking up naked in his bed? As much as I hate to admit it, Tyler does something to my body. He has some kind of control over it on the most basic primitive level that my sane, conscious mind can't reach.

But once I figure out how to turn it off, *I'll* be back to being in control.

"Get in," he says before his head disappears under the shiny red roof.

I take a deep breath and open the door of the car. *Wow*. This is not a car. A car is what I drove around town until the bumper fell off in front of the barber shop. This is a *Ferrari*. It's a driving *machine*.

I'm surrounded by smooth leather as I slide into the bucket seat, moaning as it massages my ass cheeks like a master masseuse. My breath quickens as I glide my palms over the sleek red steering wheel. This is what heroin must feel like to a junkie. It's what boobs must feel like to a teenage boy. Is it possible to have a love affair with a car? Because I'm in love.

"I told you," I say, my words coming out in a breathless

mess as I look around the interior of this dream machine, "I don't need a—"

The words drop out of my throat when I see Tyler sitting next to me looking gorgeous in the beautiful car. He looks like this car was made for him as he leans back in the bucket seat, grinning as he watches me. He's wearing ripped up jeans with a black polo that rides up high on his muscular tattooed arms. I wonder what I look like beside him. Can I pass as his wife, or do I look like his overworked maid? I guess we'll find out at the party tonight.

"Just start the car," he says, pulling out his sunglasses. God, he looks even hotter with sunglasses on.

"Fine," I say as my finger hovers over the start button. "But I'm not going to change my min—"

The Ferrari rumbles to life when I push the button. It purrs like a wild tiger, sending heat rushing through me. My cheeks redden, and my body tingles as the seats vibrate under me, making the heat settle between my legs.

Yup. I'm definitely in love with this car.

"See?" he says, turning to me with a knowing smile. "What do you think?"

"I think you're crazy if you think I'm keeping this car." *Please let me keep this car. How can I go back to riding my old, squeaky bike after sitting in this beast?*

"You're keeping it," he says casually as he opens the window. "Hey, Harvey. Can you have someone drive my car back to my pop's place?"

"Definitely, sir," Harvey says as Tyler tosses him the keys. "I'll have someone drive it over right away."

My heart is beating so fast as I slowly pull out of the parking lot, terrified that a bird is going to take a dump on the hood or that I'll roll over a wad of gum.

Adrenaline surges through my veins as I pull onto the

street, going as fast as the elderly couple shuffling down the sidewalk beside me.

"This is a Ferrari, not a baby stroller," Tyler says with a laugh. "You're going to have to push on the gas with your foot."

My head flies back into the seat as we surge forward, *way* too fast.

"Not *that* hard," Tyler says, laughing. "Just relax."

It takes about ten minutes of driving around the back streets before I'm comfortable enough to head onto the busier roads.

"Everyone keeps looking at us," I say, feeling self-conscious as people on the sidewalk take videos of us as we drive by.

Tyler chuckles. "They want to see who's behind the wheel of a Ferrari. You better get used to it."

"I feel like a queen," I say with a giggle. "Move aside peasants. A rich bitch is coming through."

I turn down a road that I've never been on and gasp when I see what's ahead: A huge blinking sign with a large pineapple on top.

The Pineapple Chapel.

My stomach turns rock hard as we approach it. Tyler's knee is bouncing up and down like a basketball as he looks at it through the windshield.

"The scene of the crime," he mutters. "Should we go renew our vows?"

I don't know why I turn into the parking lot, but I do.

"What are you doing?" he asks.

My mouth is so dry as I pull into a parking spot. "I have to go in and see if I can remember what happened."

Tyler doesn't say a thing. He just nods, takes off his seatbelt, and steps out of the car.

The chapel is even tackier than I imagined it would be. It's the marriage equivalent of fast food, complete with a drive-through.

It's a place where mistakes are made, vows are broken, and plastic pineapples are admired. I can't help but wonder how many families were disappointed by this place as I turn the pineapple shaped doorknob and walk in.

"Wow," Tyler says, looking around at the tacky pineapple wallpaper and carpeting. "It's like Disney World for people who really love pineapples."

"I wouldn't want to meet *those* people," I say, cringing as I look at a gaudy pineapple centerpiece on the reception desk.

"We're *those* people, apparently," Tyler mutters as he picks up a Bible off the table. It has a pineapple stitched onto the cover.

The small reception area is empty, and no one has come to see us. "Where is everyone?" I ask, looking around. "You'd think they'd have someone to greet us considering this is business hours."

Tyler laughs. "I don't think they have people getting married here during the day."

"In here," I say, waving him over when I pop my head into a doorway. It's the small chapel room where we must have gotten married. There's about six folding chairs spewed around the room in no particular order, a dozen pineapple-themed slot machines lining the walls, and the podium in front which, of course, is shaped like a pineapple. There's also an Asian man dressed up like Elvis sleeping on the floor. In other words: it's classy as fuck.

"Wow," Tyler says, chuckling as he walks in. "We really went all out for our wedding."

"Out of our minds," I mutter as I walk over to Asian Elvis, holding my nose as I bend down to wake him up.

"I wonder if his singing sounds any better than his snoring," Tyler says, walking up behind me.

I shake his rhinestone-covered shoulder, but he doesn't wake up. He's in a whiskey coma.

"Let me try," Tyler says, clearing his throat. "And now, put your hands together for the one true King of rock and roll: Asian Elvis!"

The man springs up into a sitting position, wiping his eyes as he gives us a "thank you very much" in a thick Chinese Elvis accent. He looks around in confusion for a minute and then frowns when he sees us and not a huge crowd of Asian Elvis fans (if such a thing exists).

"Your shit is over there," he says, pointing behind me as he lies back down on the pineapple carpet.

I clear my throat as I stare at him. "Our *shit*?"

He sighs as he takes his golden sunglasses and puts them over his bloodshot eyes. "Your mugs, lady. Your tacky plastic mugs."

I glance back at Tyler and scoff. I can't believe this guy's rudeness. This is a business after all.

"That's really rude," I say, turning back to him. Elvis would be rolling in his grave, if he is actually dead. "I'm a paying customer!"

"You *were* a customer," he corrects. "We don't get repeat customers."

I snort out a laugh. "So, you're telling me that no one who gets married here gets a divorce?"

"That's great news," Tyler says from behind me. The nasty look I shoot him shuts him up real fast.

"I find that hard to believe," I say to the sleeping King.

He sighs. "They may get divorced, but they're not stupid

enough to marry some random stranger in Vegas, *again*. That's one mistake you only make once in your life."

I stare at him, speechless, although he does have a point. I know I definitely won't be returning here (hopefully).

"Stuff is over there," he says, pointing behind me with his eyes still closed. "No refunds. The videos have been mailed."

I nearly choke. "Videos?"

"Wedding videos you ordered," he says. "They have been mailed."

"To who?" I say, nearly having a panic attack.

"I wouldn't worry about it," Tyler says with a shrug. "We were probably so drunk that we scribbled nonsense on the envelopes."

God, I hope he's right.

Tyler makes his way to the back, and I get up to follow him. There's a cardboard box on the counter stacked full of cheap plastic mugs.

"Wow," Tyler says when he pulls one out of the box. "I can't wait to show this wedding photo to our grandkids."

I grab the mug out of his hands and stare at it with disbelieving eyes. "What the hell happened that night?"

My hands can't stop shaking as I stare at the photo. *So, it's true. We're married.*

In the photo, I'm wearing a white plastic dress with a pineapple bra on the outside, looking like the crackhead version of the little mermaid. Instead of sea shells on my boobs, I have pineapples. I wish that was the worst part of the photo, but it's only the beginning. Tyler has a ball gag strapped in his mouth, like he's in a scene out of Pulp Fiction, and I'm holding up a leather whip.

Our twisted, fucked up faces make the photo look more like a mugshot than a wedding photo. The picture looks like it should be on the evening news over a heading of: *Wanted For Arrest! Crystal meth drug dealers. Call if you have any information*, instead of on our fireplace mantel.

My stomach hardens as the cruel realization that this is actually me settles in.

"A ball gag? A whip? Where did we get all of this stuff?" Tyler asks, staring at another mug.

"I need some air," I say, feeling like I'm going to be sick. I toss the mug into the box and rush out of the chapel, taking big gulps of air once I'm back in the parking lot.

Tyler comes out a minute later, holding a mug in his hand.

"What's that?" I shout, pointing at it like it's cursed. "Why are you taking one?"

His face softens as he stands in front of me. "We got married, Dahlia," he says after taking a deep breath. "Even if we were drunk or drugged or whatever, we still loved each other enough to get married. Even if it was for only five minutes, and even if we can't remember it now. It still happened. We loved each other enough to say those eternal vows."

My heart skips a beat as he adoringly looks down at the mug in his hand.

"I don't know what happened that night, but I do know that I would never marry someone who I didn't love completely. We may not remember it, or want to believe that it happened, but it did. Why wouldn't I want to keep a memento of that night? Of that moment? It's part of my life now, and I want to remember it."

I take a few deep breaths then storm back into the chapel, coming out a few seconds later with a mug of my own.

Tyler smiles when he sees the mug in my clenched

hands. He opens his mouth.

"Don't say *anything!*" I snap, charging past him to my new car.

He just grins as he follows me in.

"*Anything!*"

Once we're back on the road, he turns to me. "I only like it because your eyes are all squiggly," he says, cutting the tension.

I laugh, feeling better than I have since I first pulled into the chapel. "Ugh," I say when I glance down at the mug in his hands. "They are all squiggly."

"They're not that bad," he whispers, smiling as he looks down at the photo.

I shake my head as I giggle. "We're going to have kids with tattooed arms and squiggly eyes."

Tyler laughs for a moment, and then his face drops. "Wait," he says, jerking his head toward me. "Are you pregnant?"

"No," I snap back. "Definitely not. I know my body, and I can tell with a hundred percent accuracy that I'm not."

I turn to the side window so that Tyler can't see my panicked face. *Oh, God! Please don't let me be pregnant!*

It's then that I remember the almost empty box of Magnum condoms in my purse. Hopefully, we used protection.

Chances are, I'm not pregnant. That should be a good thing. But for some reason, it just leaves an empty feeling in me.

Is it bad that a small part of me wants more than a cheap plastic mug as a memento of that night?

I cringe when I look down at the photo once again. *Yes, it's bad, Dahlia. Those two cracked-out people should definitely not be having kids!*

9

Dahlia

"ARE YOU NERVOUS?" Tyler asks as we're about to walk out into the backyard.

"No," I say, shaking my head as my heart pounds in my chest. I shake out my hands and then try to place my arms naturally, but any position I put them in seems anything but natural.

"What are you doing?" he asks, looking at me with a raised eyebrow. "You look like you're playing with an invisible marionette."

"I don't know!" I snap. My palms are so sweaty. This dress is so tight. "I'm freaking out!"

"It's just a party," he says in a calm voice. "Just try to have fun."

"A party with a hundred people I don't know," I fire back. "And they're all expecting me to be your perfect new wife."

He smiles as he looks me up and down in my new red dress. "You definitely look the part. That dress looks fucking perfect on you."

I feel like I'm going to puke. This can't be happening. Over a hundred of the most powerful people in the country are in the backyard waiting to meet Tyler's new wife. Waiting to meet me.

I'm not prepared for this. I *hate* being unprepared.

"I'm leaving," I say, turning to the front door as panic starts to settle in.

"Whoa, whoa, whoa," Tyler says, grabbing my hands before I can bolt. He bends his knees until our faces are level. "It's going to go great," he whispers in a soothing voice. I can already feel my nerves going away as I stare into his bright green eyes. "I'll be beside you the entire time. Everyone is going to love you."

"You don't understand," I say, gulping down panicked breaths of air. "I'm not good with people, and I'm *definitely* not good at parties."

"You don't give yourself enough credit. You're fun to be around. Just be yourself."

I shake my head out, trying to get rid of the migraine that's raging forward, and take a deep breath. I have to do this. If I don't, Mr. McMillan will still be in charge of the company and will surely close down the factory in Summerland.

I squeeze my eyes impossibly tight, thinking of the park in the small town of Summerland where all of the families gather on Sunday afternoons for a huge communal barbecue in the summers, and the little elementary school that puts on the most adorable plays at Christmas time. *I have to do it. For them.*

"Okay," I say, opening my eyes and slowly exhaling as I look at Tyler. "Let's just go."

He nods and then turns to the door. My eyes glide over his body, admiring the fitted suit he's wearing. It's a gorgeous dark blue with a light blue collared shirt underneath. He's not wearing a tie, and the first few buttons are open, giving me a mouth-watering glimpse of the tanned skin of his muscular chest.

He takes my hand and gently pulls me to his side. I catch our reflection in the mirror on the wall and gasp at how good we look together.

It's all pretend, Dahlia. Don't forget that.

The next thirty minutes are a blur as I'm whisked around the McMillans' spectacular backyard, meeting dozens of people. I smile and nod as Tyler introduces me to cousins, business associates, family friends, neighbors, and on and on and on.

"This is my cousin, Jason," Tyler says, smiling as he introduces me to a handsome young man in a sports jacket and jeans. "He's the real brains behind McMillan Worldwide."

"Nice to meet you," I say, shaking Jason's hand. "I was wondering who the real brains of the company was. I knew it couldn't be this guy," I say, pointing at Tyler.

"I'm more like the cock of the company," Tyler says with a grin.

"You sure are," Jason says with a grin. "You're always good at fucking things up."

We all laugh and then chat easily for a few minutes. Jason seems like a nice guy, and I'm glad I'll have a friend at the new corporate office and in Tyler's family.

"I like him," I say when we move on.

"He's the good cousin," Tyler says with a nod. "His older brother Nick, on the other hand, is the asshole of the company."

We walk around the lit up inground swimming pool and slowly make our way to the grass, ducking under the tall maple trees with beautiful lanterns hanging from the thick branches. My head is spinning with a million names that I'll never remember when I finally get a break.

"That was... something," I say when Tyler comes back with a beer for him and a white wine spritzer for me. I down half of it in one gulp.

"You did great," he says, watching my lips as I take another sip. "Everyone believed that you were my wife."

I take another long gulp as my heart finally stops pounding. Mack McMillan has very powerful friends, and I just met dozens of owners and CEOs of the nation's biggest companies. Every time I shook a hand of a CEO, I saw it as another company that I won't be able to work for once this all blows up in my face.

"Oh, fuck," Tyler mutters, rolling his eyes as he looks away from the smug-looking guy who's approaching us with a smirk on his face. "I was hoping he wouldn't come."

"Cuz!" the man says, opening his arms as he arrives.

Tyler gives him a quick hug that lacks any real emotion.

"Dahlia," Tyler says, sliding a protective arm over my shoulder, "this is my cousin, Nick."

Nick gives me a warm smile as he shakes my hand. I can feel Tyler's body tighten beside me, and it only eases up when I get my hand back from Nick.

"It's nice to finally meet the woman who locked down my cousin," he says with an easy smile. He looks similar to Tyler but is not nearly as good-looking and definitely doesn't have the same *je ne sais quoi*. His nose is thicker, and his eyebrows are starting to look like scary caterpillars the more I look at them.

Stop staring at his eyebrows!

"So, Tyler kept you hidden from us for two whole years?" he says, glancing at my breasts. "I can see why. He must have been worried that I would steal you for myself."

"I don't think that would have been a problem," I say, staring him dead in the eyes. I know Tyler doesn't like this guy, and after thirty seconds with him, I can see why. The arrogant looks, the condescending tone, the sinister eyebrows-it's all turning me off faster than being on a date with a guy who can't stop bitching about his ex.

He laughs it off. "You're the one from the Summerland factory," he says. "Don't worry, we'll be sure to have a job for a wife of Tyler's in the company once we close the plant down."

I whip my head around to glare at Tyler with accusing eyes. The whole reason I'm here is because he promised that the factory would remain open. I wasn't aware they had already made plans to shut it down.

"That decision is not final yet," Tyler says, raising his chin as he stares his cousin down.

Nick shrugs. "It's only a matter of time. That was why we bought it in the first place."

My heart is thumping in my chest. *That's why they bought it in the first place? What the hell?*

"Oh, really?" I say through gritted teeth as I try to melt Tyler with my eyes.

"Would you excuse us, Nick?" I say without taking my eyes off of Tyler. "My new husband has a lot of explaining to do."

Nick cringes and then leaves, laughing to himself at the trouble he's caused his cousin.

I cross my arms over my chest as I glare at Tyler with hard eyes. "Explain."

"I told you," he says, looking exasperated.

"The truth. I want the *truth* or I'll scream out that this whole marriage is a sham."

"Dahlia, I told y—"

"Three."

"Dahlia..."

"Two."

"Okay, okay," he says in a panic. "I'm not the only consideration for the top position at McMillan Worldwide Inc."

I want to skin him alive.

"Just wait," he says, looking jittery when he sees my furious face. "I'll explain everything. My father is also considering my cousin Nick for the spot."

My arms drop to my sides as an empty pit forms in my stomach. "And Nick wants to close the factory?"

Tyler nods his frustratingly beautiful head.

"I told you the truth," he says, running a hand through his hair. "If I become the boss, I give you my word that I'll keep the factory open in Summerland."

I raise an eyebrow at him. "And how can I trust you?"

"Because you scare the shit out of me when you're like this," he says with a laugh.

My stomach is rolling with nerves as I quickly think it through. I didn't know there was another person in the running for the job. Now I really have to make sure this sham of a marriage works. It's crucial that we pull this off.

"All right," I say, taking a deep breath as my nerves start to settle.

"All right, what?" Tyler asks, gulping as he watches me.

"All right, you'll help me, or all right, you're going to tell everyone the truth?"

I stare at him for a few seconds letting him stew nervously. "All right, I'll help you. Nick can't become the boss."

Tyler exhales long and hard. "Thank you," he says, looking relieved. "You must really like that town to stay married to me."

"I do," I say, nodding. How can I explain to him what the town really means to me? I grew up in chaos, living in vans and trailers, moving from one hippie commune to another every few months, all while my parents loafed off all day and let me handle the important stuff like making food, money, and paying the bills.

The town of Summerland was the first place that ever felt like home to me. I had moved there by myself in my late teens and had immediately fallen in love. It was stable and sweet and loving and just *normal*-something I had always dreamed of growing up.

I'll die before I let it be destroyed.

Tyler's mother Kirsten rushes over, barely able to contain her excitement. "Eeeee!" she squeals, grabbing my hand and squeezing it so hard that I let out a whimper. "I have a surprise for you!"

I should be happy. Getting a surprise from a billionaire is usually a good thing, but for some reason, a cold chill is snaking down my back, and I feel like I should be running in the opposite direction.

I just hope it's not what I'm worried it is.

"Mom," Tyler says, stepping forward. "Dahlia doesn't really like surprises."

"Yeah," I say, shaking my head. "I hate them."

"Not this one," she says, squealing as she yanks me in

the direction she came. She drags me across the lawn and through the crowd of guests, only stopping when we're on the stairs leading into the house where everyone can see. I have a really bad feeling about this.

"Excuse me," she yells, waving her hands in the air to get everyone's attention. The DJ stops the music, and every head in the enormous backyard turns to look up at me.

Luckily for Tyler, he steps up beside me. I would have killed him later if he would have left me all alone up here.

"I just want to welcome Dahlia to the family," she says, smiling warmly at me.

Ah. It's so genuine, which is making it really hard to hate her right now.

"But when my son got married, our family grew by more than just Dahlia," she says, getting the giggles.

No.

My stomach hardens as the painful realization hits me like a punch in the face.

"We also got Dahlia's *parents!*" Kirsten spins on her high heels as she points to the door.

Oh, God—No!.

My blood pressure goes through the roof as my parents appear behind the glass doors, looking like they just walked out of Woodstock, stepped into a time machine, and arrived in the McMillan's kitchen.

The whole backyard is silent, so everyone hears my mother swearing as she can't figure out how to open the sliding glass door. The. Sliding. Glass. Door.

How the hell does someone get to be in their fifties and still not know how to open a sliding glass door? Hundreds of LSD hits, that's how.

Kirsten rushes up the stairs and easily slides the door open for them.

"Hi, Rainbow!" my mother says, waving her hand over her head as she steps through.

I cringe as I hold onto Tyler for support. "Please tell me there's a rainbow in the sky behind me," I say, staring in disbelief as the last two people on the planet I would want here walk out.

Tyler looks back and shakes his head. "Sorry. No rainbow in the sky tonight."

I grit my teeth as they walk down the stairs, smiling from gauged earlobe to gauged earlobe. They know how much I hate my real name, but they still refuse to call me anything but Rainbow Solstice the First, or Rainbow for short.

My body stiffens as my mother throws her arms around me, and a whiff of stale weed hits my nose. The smell always reminds me of my childhood.

"You look so great!" she says, pulling away to look me up and down. "A little mainstream for my tastes, but you still look good."

"You look good too," I lie, looking her up and down. "Is that a new burlap shirt?"

She nods proudly. "I made it out of a sack of potatoes."

I exhale long and slow. "You can't tell at all."

"Rainbow!" my father says, pushing past my mom to give me a hug. His long gray hair tickles my face as he squeezes me. "It's good to see you again! What has it been? Four months? Five?"

"Six years," I say, cringing as I start to hear whispers and giggles behind me.

The only way these two people would look more out of place is if they sprouted a second head.

"Great party!" my father says, looking around with a nod. He waves to someone near the pool. The man doesn't wave back. "I brought rolling papers if you guys have weed."

My mother slaps his arm. "This is a *fancy* party, Echo. Get the bong from the van."

My father Bill, or Echo as he likes to be called, turns to head back to his van, so I grab his tie-dye shirt, and yank him back. "No bongs," I warn him.

He shrugs as he turns back to us. "Good thing I have this little guy," he says, looking down at the joint sticking out of his shirt pocket. I snatch it and crush it in my fist before he can spark it.

"No drugs."

Tyler steps in to introduce himself as I glare at the DJ, warning him with my eyes to turn the music back on. Luckily for him, he does, and the guests resume their conversations or begin gossiping about the two disasters that are my parents.

"Hello," Tyler says, offering his hand as he smiles at my parents. "I'm Dahlia's husband, Tyler. It's so nice to meet you."

"Nice to meet you too, young man," my father says, trying to act like normal people act but failing miserably. "I'm Echo, and this is my wife, Essence."

"He's actually named Bill," I interrupt, "and her real name is Carol."

My father looks at me funny. "And your real name is Rainbow Solstice the First."

"Don't remind me," I say, rolling my eyes. "I'm reminded of that every time I have to pull out my passport and the people reading it start laughing."

"She was always this difficult," my mother says, smiling at Tyler. "Rainbow always had this extreme need to follow the rules."

"They're called *laws*, mother," I say, glaring at her. "And they're what keep society functioning."

She just shrugs. "I have a different view on how the world should work."

"An *insane* view," I mutter as I look away, feeling an irresistible urge to make a run for it.

"So, what do you do for weed money?" my father asks Tyler.

Tyler chuckles. "I run an international corporation that acquires companies to restructure and optimize to enhance production rates and profits."

My father just stares at him with a blank expression on his wrinkly face. "Sounds like you can buy a lot of weed."

Tyler laughs. "I guess I could."

My father scratches his temple as his face twists up. I can tell he's trying to think up something intelligent to say. "Do you work at the computer-net?"

"Dad," I say, interrupting him. "You mean the *Internet*."

"Yeah, that's the store," he says, pointing at me. He looks down at the old worn out tie-dye shirt that should have been thrown out in the 70s. "I make these shirts," he says proudly. "My friend Tree Dancer is going to get me into the Internet store to help me sell them."

My mother nods as she listens. "That's going to be for our retirement fund."

To my horror, Kirsten and Mack come creeping over. "Sorry to intrude on the reunion," Kirsten says, smiling happily. "But I have to meet my new family!" She squeals again. "Dahlia, were you surprised?"

"Surprised doesn't begin to explain what I'm feeling right now."

She grabs my arm and squeals again as she squeezes it. "Good. I'm so happy!"

I sigh as she clings onto my arm like a needy toddler.

She's lucky she's so nice. It's the only thing stopping me from pushing her down the stairs.

Mack shakes my father's hand, and the sight of my new boss *and* father-in-law meeting my dad makes me want to light my hair on fire just to create some kind of distraction.

"Nice to meet you, Echo," Mack says. "That's such an interesting name. What does it mean?"

"It means when you yell and the sound repeats," my father says, nodding.

My cheeks burn red. "I think Mr. McMillan knows what an echo is, Dad. I think he was asking *why* it's your name."

"Oh," my father says, looking confused. "Once I was high on acid and my echo started talking back to me. It was incredible. A real life-changing event."

"Your echo started talking to you?" Tyler asks. I shoot him a dirty look. I don't want him encouraging my father like this.

My father nods. "I would say something, and my echo would respond."

"Are you sure it wasn't someone talking to you?" I ask, folding my arms over my chest as I glare at him. My heart is beating so rapidly in my chest that I'm worried everyone can see it thumping away in embarrassment.

My father tilts his head to the side as he thinks about it. "Maybe," he says with a furrowed brow. "I was in a Walmart at the time."

Our pathetic little group goes silent as we all marinate on my father's stupidity for a few seconds.

Mack breaks the awkward silence. "Dahlia got a new Ferrari today," he says, smiling at me.

"Really?" my father says, nodding like he's impressed. "Your mother and I had sex on a Ferrari once."

My chest tightens as my face, neck, and ears burn

impossibly hot. *No way he just said that.* My heart is beating so fast that it's going to stop working. I'm *literally* going to die of embarrassment.

"It wasn't ours, though," my mother clarifies in case anyone couldn't have guessed that the woman wearing a shirt made out of a burlap sack owned a Ferrari. "We saw it in the parking lot of McDonald's."

"All right," I say, stepping into the circle to break up this little party. "Mack. Kirsten. Is there anything I can help you with, inside?"

Both of my parents are already wandering off to the buffet table, muttering something about having the munchies.

"We're okay, dear," Kirsten says, following my parents with one eye as they walk through the backyard. "The caterers are taking care of everything."

After a few seconds of awkward silence, Mack and Kirsten wander off to talk to their guests, leaving Tyler and me alone.

I take a deep breath as I turn back to old Echo and Essence. The other guests are moving out of their way wherever they go, like the guests are afraid of catching my parents' poorness.

My stomach hardens as my father says something to Walter Rosendale, the eighth richest man in the country.

I turn to Tyler and bury my face into his hard chest. "I can't look," I whisper.

He wraps his arms around me and rocks me back and forth, making me feel a tiny bit better. "Want to get out of here?" he whispers.

I nod. "If it's anywhere closer than China, I'm not interested."

"It's not China," he says with a smirk. "But it's way cooler than here."

"An active volcano would be cooler than here," I say through gritted teeth.

Tyler laughs as he grabs my hand and guides me down the stairs. "Follow me. I know just the place."

10

Dahlia

"WHAT THE HELL IS *THAT*?"

Tyler laughs as he looks up. "A treehouse. Haven't you ever seen a treehouse before?"

"That's not a treehouse," I say, tilting my head back to look all the way up. "That's bigger than the shack I grew up in."

"You grew up in a shack?" he asks, looking at me funny.

"A shack would have been an improvement," I say with a sigh. "I lived in a van for most of my, well, what normal people would call a childhood."

"What do you call it?"

"Hell," I say, taking a deep breath. "Why do you look surprised? You just met my parents."

The huge treehouse is sitting in a large beautiful maple tree with wooden planks nailed into the thick trunk. It looks like it could be in a Norman Rockwell painting, if old Norm lived in the rich part of town.

Tyler helps me up first, which I initially think is nice until I'm halfway up and realize that he only let me go first so that he could see up my dress.

"Eyes on the tree," I say, frowning as I stare down at him, "and not on the *bush*."

He chuckles as he follows me up, keeping his eyes in front of him.

This treehouse is like something out of the Swiss Family Robinson after a home makeover. It has a freaking leather couch in it. "Are you kidding me?" I ask, looking around in shock. There are curtains over the windows, a rug on the floor, even a mini fridge that looks like it hasn't been plugged in for a while.

Tyler laughs as he climbs in. "You didn't have one of these growing up?" he asks with a smile.

"I lived in a tree for a week," I say, popping my head into the other room. *How many rooms does this thing have?* "But it was because our van was in the garage for repairs."

He's staring at me in shock. "You're kidding, right?"

I wish I was.

"It wasn't so bad once the squirrels accepted me as one of their own," I say, plopping down on the couch. I take a deep breath as Tyler sits beside me. "You don't know how happy I am to be here."

Tyler looks at me with a grin. "You're telling me you weren't enjoying the party full of my parent's stuffy friends?"

"Oh, my God," I say, cringing when I hear a tune being carried over with the nice summer breeze. That sound can only be one thing.

"What *is* that?" Tyler asks, tilting his head as he listens to it.

I drop my head into my hands. "A didgeridoo. My father is playing his *freaking* didgeridoo."

"Didgerie-what now?"

"You may recognize it as the long wind instrument played by indigenous Australians, but I recognize it as pure embarrassment from my teenage years."

"Wow," Tyler says, trying not to laugh at my horrible misfortune. "I thought I had it bad growing up."

"You had it bad growing up?" I say, staring at him in shock. "Yeah, it must have been so hard wearing thousand-dollar outfits and getting a brand-new Porsche on your sixteenth birthday."

He gives me a tight smile. "Money isn't everything," he says. "You try living in a house with my parents and their insanely strict expectations. This community is all about what you have and who you are. I always wanted to get away from it all."

I wave my arms, gesturing around to the treehouse. "You basically had an apartment to get away from it all."

He laughs. "Not like that," he says. "I always wanted to get away from these people. I always wanted to live in a place without so many expectations—a place where people can just relax and be themselves without trying to step on the person beside them to get ahead."

"It sounds like you would love Summerland," I say. My stomach drops just thinking about my cute little town where everyone knows my name. "Quick, go visit it before your company closes it down."

"*I* won't close it down," Tyler says.

"*You* might not be the one to make that decision," I say. "It seems like your cousin Nick has already made it."

Tyler grits his teeth together. "He's not getting the position."

"That's not what he said."

"That's what *I* say."

I don't want to say it but I have to. "You're going to need help. I can help you get the promotion."

He looks at me in shock. "You want to work together?"

I take a deep breath as I sink back into the couch. "I want to keep the factory open, and it seems like helping you is the only way to do that."

"Are you going to be able to pretend that you're my loving wife?" he asks.

My heart starts to beat a little faster as I watch him. He looks so gorgeous in his fitted suit and with his hair gelled to the side like that. It still blows my mind that he was inside of me.

"It's easy to pretend here in Vegas where you don't know anybody," he goes on. "But you'll have to pretend when you get back home. Everyone at work, in town, your friends— they'll all think we're married."

I try to hide my grin. I can't wait to see the look on everyone's face when I pull up in a shiny new Ferrari and walk out with this piece of man candy on my arm.

"I think I can handle that," I say. But I'm not doing this for the looks on people's faces. I'm doing this to save my town. "I'm all in. As long as you don't try any husband and wife stuff behind closed doors, we'll be fine."

"What kind of husband and wife stuff?" he asks with a raised eyebrow.

I give him a look. "You know what I'm talking about."

He grins. "All right. We're a team."

"A team?" I ask, rolling my eyes at him. "And is this our clubhouse?"

"It sure is," he says, starting to look around. He drops to his knees and looks under the couch, giving me a quick view of his nice ass. I can't help but wonder if he's wearing his red boxer briefs.

"What are you looking for?" I ask, watching him as he looks behind a loose wooden plank. "Invisible ink to write out our clubhouse rules?"

"That's a good idea," he says, putting the plank back in place, "but no. I'm sure I have a bottle of alcohol stashed somewhere up here."

I jump off the couch and start ripping up the couch cushions as he checks the other room. I could really use a drink right about now. I'm not sure what it is, but as soon as I hear my father playing his didgeridoo in public, I immediately need a strong drink.

When I yank up the last cushion, a dogeared nudie magazine falls to the floor. I laugh as I pick it up with my two fingers, holding as little of it as I can.

"Looks like alcohol is not the only thing you have stashed up here," I say. Tyler comes back from the other room and bursts out laughing when he sees what I'm holding. My mouth waters when I see a bottle in his hand.

"That was my favorite porn mag," he says, taking it from me. He flips through the naked pictures as he nods with a nostalgic smile on his face. "Ooooh, I remember her."

"Are you done looking at your porn?" I ask, still eying the bottle. It's Goldslick Vodka. Probably tastes like paint thinner, but I would happily drink paint thinner right now. I would drink anything that would drown out the sound of my father's didgeridoo. "I need a drink."

Tyler slips the magazine back under the couch and grabs the bottle. "Good, because I have just the thing."

I lick my lips as I stare at it. "Are those little gold flakes floating around in there?"

"Yup. Rumor has it that they slice the inside of your

throat on the way down, letting the alcohol get into your bloodstream faster to get you drunk as fast as possible."

"Sounds stupid."

He opens the bottle and offers it to me.

I need stupid right now.

Tyler laughs as I take a take a huge gulp until my eyes are burning and I'm coughing like crazy.

We pass the bottle around until it's gone down a couple of inches and I'm feeling a little buzzed. I like it up here in his treehouse away from the party.

"Congratulations," he says, smiling at me. "You're the first girl I've ever brought up here."

I turn to him in surprise. A hot guy like him should have had a line-up of girls waiting to come in here. "You never got any action up here?"

His eyes fall to where the porn magazine is hidden under the couch cushion. "Not with anyone else."

"Remind me not to come up here with a black light," I say, giggling.

He laughs. "I always wanted to have a girl up here."

"I'm your wife," I say, grinning at him. "Wives don't count. Plus, I'm not about to break your treehouse cold streak, so don't get any ideas. The only things that should be having sex in trees are birds and squirrels."

"And your parents," he says.

I burst out laughing. "My parents too."

"It's okay," he says, chuckling as he takes a sip from the bottle. "I left our ball gag at home anyway."

"What *was* that?" I ask, thinking back in horror at the ball gag strapped to his mouth in our lovely wedding photo. "Are you into that kind of BDSM stuff? Did we do *that*?"

"I don't know what we did," he says, handing me the bottle. Our fingers touch as he hands it over. With every pass of the Goldslick, our hands linger a little longer on each other. "I've never seen a ball gag in real life before."

"Where the hell did we get that?" I try hard to remember, but I can't. The memories from that night are gone for good. That's probably a good thing.

He just shrugs.

"Want any more?" I ask, offering him the bottle.

He shakes his head as he clutches his stomach. "I'm good. I think I drank an ounce of gold already."

We relax on the couch, enjoying the silence and the warm breeze wafting in through the open windows. I can hear the muted sounds of the party down below and take a breath of relief when I no longer hear my father's didgeridoo playing. My initial relief turns to panic when I realize that the silence means he's probably talking to people.

I close my eyes and swallow hard as I pretend that all of this isn't happening. This is all too surreal. I slept with this guy beside me. I don't do that kind of stuff.

One-night stands... They're not me. At all.

But the initial embarrassment and confusion are starting to wash away with every look he gives me. As much as I hate to admit it, I'm starting to feel curiosity and yearning now.

I'm curious about what happened, how it happened, how it felt.

And I'm yearning to experience it again.

I saw this man naked, and as sexy and stylish as his suits are, I can't help remembering what he looks like underneath that soft fitted fabric.

Lately, when I find myself staring blankly out the window and before I can get a handle on my brain, his long cock slides into my mind, penetrating my thoughts.

If I'm being honest with myself, I'm tempted. But being

dishonest is easier. I hate him. He's too privileged, he's too cocky, he's too goddamned beautiful.

But that dick...

I'm not that kind of girl. Really, I'm not. But when a rich, sexy, beautiful man makes it crystal clear that he wants to fuck you, even the straightest of straight girls can get a little curved around the edges.

And Tyler has made that strikingly clear. If I want his big dick, it's all mine.

I swallow hard, pushing down the naughty thoughts creeping up into my mind. I blame the Goldslick Vodka. Apparently, the gold flakes missed my throat and sliced open my horny center instead.

"We should get back down to the party," I say. I close my eyes, regretting it the minute it slides past my lips. "They're going to wonder where we went."

Tyler shrugs. "Let them wonder."

My cheeks start to heat up. "We're newlyweds in their eyes. They're going to think we're..." I can't say the dirty words in front of him.

"What?" he asks, turning to me with a grin.

"You know..."

"Playing Monopoly?" he asks with a smirk on his frustratingly sexy lips. "Yahtzee? Twister?"

"That's closer," I say with a chuckle.

He raises an eyebrow as he looks at me. "Naked Twister?"

I look away. I just wish he wasn't so hot. This would all be so much easier if he didn't look like he should be starring in the next Magic Mike movie.

He leans a little closer, and a whiff of his rich cologne has my head swimming. "I bet you would be really good at naked Twister," he whispers in a raspy voice.

"I would be," I say, feeling my heart jump into fifth gear. "But you'll never find out."

"Right hand, thigh," he says, placing his strong hand on my thigh. Warm shivers explode through my body, sending up goosebumps on every inch of my skin. Even the soles of my feet have goosebumps from this guy.

My chest is fluttering, and my head is as light as a helium balloon, but I take a deep breath and focus. This 'relationship' is already as complicated as Ikea instructions. We don't need to throw in sex to make it even worse.

"Tyler," I warn as he inches even closer.

My body is betraying me. My legs part, wanting his hand to slide down between them. Arousal courses through my body, making this even more difficult.

I'm getting wetter with every hard breath that I take.

His eyes are locked on my lips as he leans in.

My mouth waters as my breathing stops. He's my husband, and I'm his wife. I have the pineapple-covered marriage certificate to prove it. I should be able to kiss my husband if I want to. Right? Right???

"Left hand, waist," he whispers as he slides his hand over my waist, making my pussy throb.

My lips part, wanting to tell him to back off but the soft tickle of his breath on my lips has me forgetting what I want to say.

"Lips, lips," he whispers.

I jerk my head away at the last second. As much as I want to feel his soft lips on mine, I know it's a bad idea. We already did that once, and look where it got me.

"Right fist, nose," I say, clenching my hand into a fist and holding it up as a warning.

He laughs it off, but he looks disappointed as he moves

back from my personal space. I'm immediately struck with a strong sense of loss now that his hands are off of me.

It's for the best, Dahlia. He's your boss.

I take a mental cold shower, picturing abandoned puppies, port-a-potties after a weekend tournament, pink-eye, long toenails, turkey bacon.

Ah, that's better.

This whole situation is going to take pinpoint precision to pull off. We have to pretend that we're married in front of everyone we know, we have to get Tyler's dad to give him the promotion, and we have to save the factory from getting shut down.

The stakes are high, the whole town of Summerland and everyone in it is on the line, and it would be just plain irresponsible to complicate things with kissing, or sex.

As tempting as it is, it's just a mess that nobody needs right now.

"Let's go back down," I say, smoothing out my dress as I get up.

Tyler nods, looking disappointed as I head to the ladder.

He takes the bottle of alcohol and hides it behind the couch, probably out of habit from his teenage years. I take a quick glance at his ass as he bends over.

Bloody noses, squished cockroaches, old men eating apple sauce.

Nothing is stopping the dirty thoughts rushing forward, so I just turn away and climb down the ladder.

"Thanks for the break," I say when we're back on the perfectly manicured lawn. "I needed it."

"Anytime," he says, smiling at me. "You know where it is if you need it again. Normally there are no girls allowed, but you have boobs, so I'll bend the clubhouse rules just for you."

"I'm honored," I say, smiling as my cheeks heat up. Hearing him talk about my boobs is making me blush even more than usual.

We stand there awkwardly, so many unsaid words hanging between us. "I should go check on my parents," I say, looking back in the direction of the party. "Make sure they're not trying to sell any of the guests some weed."

Tyler laughs as he steps forward, sliding his hand on my lower back as we start walking. His hand feels good there, so I pretend not to notice.

"Shit," Tyler curses under his breath when he sees his cousin Nick approaching.

Don't stare at his eyebrows. Don't stare at his eyebrows.

"I'm taking off, cuz," he says, spinning an unlit cigar between his fingers. "This was cute, but I'm heading to a *real* party now."

Tyler puffs out his chest as his eyes narrow on Nick. "Don't let the door hit you on the way out."

Nick turns to me and smiles. "It was nice to meet you, Dahlia. When you come to your senses and leave this mutt, come see me."

I try to keep my eyes on his and not on the slow-moving bushy caterpillars that he calls eyebrows crawling on his face.

"It was nice to meet you too, Nick," I say, gritting my teeth. "And don't worry, we'll be sure to have a job for a cousin of Tyler's in the company once we take it over."

He laughs, jerking his head back in surprise. "You two take it over? That's cute, but I think you two would be better suited to taking over your father's tie-dye shirt empire. Leave McMillan Worldwide to me."

Tyler steps forward, looking like he's about to knock him out. "Don't talk about *my wife's* parents that way," he snaps in a tight voice. Possession is thick in the way he calls me his wife.

My skin is tingling as I watch him defend my honor. I want to break them up before the fists start flying, but I also desperately want to see that happen.

Nick cracks first. "I was just kidding," he says, laughing it off. "It's just a little playful competition."

"There's nothing playful about laying off fifteen hundred and ninety-two employees," I say, butting in.

Nick locks his eyes on me and scowls. "fifteen hundred and ninety-*three*," he corrects. The threat is clear. I'll be getting one of those pink slips if Nick gets the company.

"What was that?" Tyler rushes forward and grabs Nick by his collar, slamming him up against the tree.

A smile creeps across my face as I see Nick squirming nervously under Tyler's heated stare.

"Tyler!" a voice snaps from behind me. I spin around with my guilty heart pounding. "Let Nicholas go!"

Tyler releases his cousin when he sees his father charging over like an angry bull with Kirsten following close behind him. He takes a deep breath as Nick chuckles, slapping his back playfully.

"Thanks for the party, Auntie Kirsten and Uncle Mack," he says, pouring on the charm. "Unfortunately, I have to get back to the office to take care of something."

Tyler's parents say goodbye to Nick and then thankfully he leaves.

"What are you doing?" Mack asks his son, looking exasperated. "You're picking a fight with family?"

I'm about to butt in and help him out when Kirsten wraps her arm around mine, pulling me back to the party. I reluctantly go as I try to listen in on their conversation.

"You have to control your temper," Mack says, sounding

disappointed. "How can I trust you to take over an international corporation if you can't get through a family party without knocking your cousin's head off?"

I gulp as Kirsten drags me out of earshot. If we're going to be a team, we have to work better than what we're doing. We have to play smart if we're going to outplay the evil caterpillar whisperer Nick.

"We were looking everywhere for you two," Kirsten says, squeezing my arm.

"I'm sorry," I say, trying to get back on her good side. "There were so many people, and I just got overwhelmed. Tyler took me away for a little break."

I look back over my shoulder where Tyler and his father are having a heated conversation.

"I hope I didn't get him into trouble," I say, wishing I could hear what they were saying. "Nick was being a bit of a jerk, and Tyler stepped in to save me."

Kirsten waves her hand dismissively. "Those two have been at it since they were in diapers. One day they fought over a rattle, and they haven't stopped since."

We continue toward the pool where the party is happening, and I look around for my parents with an empty feeling in the pit of my stomach. "Do you know where my parents are?"

Kirsten bites her bottom lip nervously. "I'm not sure…"

"Kirsten," I say, tilting my head as I stare at her.

She looks uncomfortable as she looks around the yard. "I believe they were taking a nap in the hammock over there."

A group of teenagers are giggling near the hammock. One of the braver guys is holding up his phone, videotaping my parents doing I-don't-want-to-know-what.

"I'm sorry about them," I say, feeling my neck get hot

with embarrassment. "They shouldn't be allowed out in public."

Kirsten wraps her arm around me and pulls me into her. "They may be a little rough around the edges," she says with a warm smile.

"They're like broken glass around the edges," I say, laughing.

"But they brought you into the world," she says, smiling at me, "so I'm eternally grateful to them."

I drop my eyes to the grass as a thickness settles in my throat.

"I've never seen my son so taken with a girl," she says, grinning at me. "You're the first girl he's ever introduced us to."

My heart flutters at her words. If this was real, it would be a huge compliment, but it's not real. None of this is real. I have to remember that no matter how real it feels.

"I'm so happy you're part of our family now," she says with her eyes sparkling. It's so genuine and real that the guilt weighing down on me feels heavier than ever. "I've always wanted a daughter, and I can already tell that we're going to be *really* close."

I cringe as she pulls me in for a warm hug.

I'm the worst person alive.

11

Dahlia

"THANK YOU FOR THE PARTY," I say, smiling at Kirsten when the last of the guests finally leave. "It was wonderful. I'm really tired and am just going to head back to my hotel for the night."

Tyler's mother shakes her head so hard that I'm worried it's going to fly off. "No, you're not."

"I'm not?"

"You're family now," she says, looking dizzy. "You're staying over."

I glance up at Tyler who's standing next to me. He just shrugs.

I guess I'm staying over.

My parents are still in the hammock—I can hear their snoring from here—so I guess I should stay and keep an eye on them. I have to make sure they don't go skinny dipping in my new in-laws' pool in the morning.

Kirsten brings us into the house and shows us to a guest room that she set up.

"Mom!" Tyler shouts, looking around in disbelief when he steps into the room. If there was a camera set up in the corner, it would look exactly like the set of a soft-core porn movie. There are lit candles on every available surface, a bottle of lube on the nightstand, and an R. Kelly mix-tape playing softly over the speakers.

I'm guessing Mrs. McMillan wants grandchildren.

Badly.

Thankfully, Tyler doesn't want to give her any. "Mom, can you be a little more subtle?" he asks, staring at her in disbelief.

"I want grandkids!" she whines. "I want sticky fingers and cute tiny toes and grandma kisses and little scraped knees that I can put adorable little band-aids on. I want to relive the magic that only a toddler can bring."

"Sounds like you should start your own babysitting business," Tyler says.

Kirsten shoots him a warning look. One that only a mother can give.

She turns to me, looking for an accomplice for her evil plan to bring a baby into our lives. "You want kids, don't you Dahlia?" The look on her face is so full of hope that I feel horrible that this is all fake.

"Someday," I say, glancing quickly at Tyler. And it's true. Since my family life growing up was a complete disaster, I've never thought that I would ever have a family, but sticky fingers and scraped knees are starting to sound kind of appealing. Especially if the little ones running around have Tyler's smile.

I'm beginning to think that one day I'll be ready for kids, but that's still a long way away. I'm not getting impregnated tonight, no matter how many guilt trips Kirsten throws at us.

"Great!" Kirsten says, clasping her hands together as she grabs the door handle. "There are toys in the nightstand and some outfits in the closet."

"What?!?" Tyler shouts, whipping his head around. His mother just smiles maniacally as she closes the door, leaving us inside.

"Is she going to lock us in here?" I wouldn't be surprised if she had installed a lock on the other side of the door to keep us in here until my belly is swollen.

"I'm sorry about this," Tyler says, heading over to the nightstand. "My mother can be so embarrassing."

"*Your* mother?" I say with a laugh. "At least her clothes don't smell like potatoes. If anyone is going to win the argument of most embarrassing mom, it's me."

Tyler's back tightens as he opens the drawer of the nightstand. "Look in here before you say that."

I'm giggling as I rush over and peek over his shoulder. It looks like a mini sex shop stuffed into a drawer.

All of the color has been drained from Tyler's face. "Dildos, vibrators, handcuffs, anal beads, Jesus Christ, what the hell are my parents into?"

I can't help but laugh. I'm loving it that my parents aren't the only freaks. "They're not as bad as their son," I say, grinning at him. "I don't see any ball gags or whips."

He shakes his head. "We haven't looked in the other nightstand yet."

"Or the closet," I say, skipping over. I open the large double doors and start laughing when I see a row of seethrough pieces of lace lingerie hanging up. "Your mother really wants grandkids," I say, staring at the wicked wardrobe in shock.

Tyler is walking over with his jaw hanging open in shock. He grabs a lacy pink piece and pulls it out. "Maybe she's not so crazy," he says, holding it against my body. "This would look fucking spectacular on you."

My breath quickens with his hands so close to my body, holding up the sexy outfit against me. His eyes look hungry, like he's picturing what I'd look like in it.

I give him a few seconds to eat his heart out and then I push his hand away. "Don't get any ideas," I say, giving him a look. "Your mother picked this out, remember?"

No matter what the heat swirling between my legs is saying, I'm not going to have sex with Tyler, especially with his parents sleeping down the hall. There's too much on the line for both of us, for the town, to complicate things with sex.

"I'm disturbed at how well my mother knows me," he says, still gawking at my body as he holds the lingerie in his hands.

"Maybe she found your porn stash and knows what you're into."

He grins.

It's time to shut whatever he's thinking down for the night.

"Do you think your mother tried them on?" That should do it.

He squeezes his eyes shut as his face twists up into a look of disgust. "Ugh," he says, crinkling his nose up. "Why would you do that?"

"I bet she looked great in that one," I say, pointing to the lacy number in his hands. He throws it on the ground like it's made of acid and leaps for the door.

"This is too fucking weird," he says, swinging it open.

"Agreed," I say, following him into the hall. The lights

are out and the house is quiet. All I can hear is Mr. McMillan's snoring mixed with the soft bragging of R. Kelly, post-peeing incident.

"Come," Tyler says, waving me over. "I know just the place where we can crash."

I cross my arms over my chest, standing my ground. "It's not another sex room, is it?"

He shakes his head.

"Another treehouse?"

"Better."

I don't know what to expect, so I just follow him down the hall. He opens a door, and I smile when I see that it's his old room.

I chuckle under my breath when I walk inside and see an N'Sync poster hanging on the wall. "I bet you never had a girl in here before either."

He just laughs. "What gave you that idea?"

"The kiss marks on Joey Fatone's face," I say, giggling.

"I've always been a sucker for frosted blonde tips and glasses with yellow lenses," he says as he closes the door behind us. "Don't judge me. It's only up there because I lost a bet."

"*Sure*," I say, laughing at him.

"It's true!"

"Mm-hm," I mumble as I walk around his room, looking at all of the teenage boy stuff. His dresser and desk are littered with CDs, football trophies, comic books, and old school books. It's like I stepped into a time machine and went back a decade to become Tyler's fake girlfriend instead of his fake wife.

Real wife.

I keep forgetting that we're actually married—at least according to The Pineapple Chapel we are.

"Any more nudie magazines in here?" I ask as I rifle through some Wolverine comics.

"No," he says, shaking his head. "Just don't look in the closet in the box under my baseball cards."

He sits on his bed and watches me as I look through his things. He seems more amused than annoyed at my complete lack of giving a shit about his privacy.

"What the hell is this?" I ask, holding up a whoopee cushion. "What are you fourteen?"

"I was when I got it."

I just shake my head as I toss it back onto his desk. "I'll never understand boys."

"It's funny," he says with a laugh. I roll my eyes.

"So?" I say, crossing my arms as I lean on his desk. He looks so sexy sitting on his bed in his perfectly tailored suit. His hair is swept to the side, his jade green eyes locked on me. Even the Spider-Man bedspread he's sitting on isn't killing my arousal. "Where am I sleeping?"

He scoots to the side and slaps the bed beside him. "On Peter Parker's face."

I'd rather sit on Tyler McMillan's face. But that's not going to happen.

I glance at the closed door and then settle my nervous eyes back on him. I should have insisted on leaving earlier. I should have insisted on the annulment. I should have picked an uglier guy to marry.

"Is that a good idea?" I ask, feeling my voice crack.

His beautiful face softens. "I won't try anything, if that's what you're worried about. If I was planning on trying anything I wouldn't have run out of the sex room that my mother so creepily prepared for us."

"This room is even worse," I say, glancing up at the

N'Sync poster on the wall. "Mr. Timberlake is getting me so hot."

"Works every time," he says with a sexy laugh.

"Fine," I say, raising my chin. "We can sleep in the same bed, but there will be no touching, no clutching, no feeling, no moaning, no groaning, no nudging, no groping, no talking, no licking, no kicking, no poking, no stroking, and definitely no nudity."

"But can we have sex?"

"No contact of any kind. You understand me?" I ask, staring him down with my fiercest stare.

"Got it," he says, giving me a sexy salute. "No fun, whatsoever."

"That's right." I push off the desk and look around. "I can't sleep in this dress."

"I was hoping you'd say that."

I narrow my eyes on him. "I'd like to borrow some pajamas."

He jumps off the bed. "Avengers or Batman?"

"No N'Sync pajamas?" I joke.

He shakes his head. "Those are for me only. I don't share them with anyone."

"All right," I say, laughing. "I'll take Batman."

He rifles through his dresser and pulls out some comfy pajama pants with the Batman logo plastered all over it. "Batman pants," he says as he hands me the pants and then opens another drawer. He pulls out a t-shirt and drops it into my hands. "And a Sum 41 T-shirt. Anything else?"

"Some privacy?"

He steps back and curses under his breath as he takes one last look at me in my dress, looking me up and down slowly. "You really are beautiful, Dahlia."

His words bring a mild pain in my chest, and I have to

look away so he doesn't see my pink cheeks. "Wait until you see me with no makeup on in your old pajamas."

He smiles. "I can't wait."

My heart is pounding as he gives me a little wink and leaves the room, bringing some old clothes for himself.

I quickly get changed then crawl under the covers of his bed, pulling the blankets up to my chin while I wait for him.

He comes back a few minutes later wearing plaid pajama pants and a tight Pearl Jam t-shirt. The shirt is snug around his muscular frame and large arms, showing off every delicious curve of muscle. He must have filled out a lot since the last time he's worn it. Mine, on the other hand, is huge on me.

But it's wrapped in his essence, so it's not that bad.

"This is weird," I say, watching him as he walks to the other side of the bed.

He shrugs. "We've done more than this. *A lot* more."

"But we can't remember it," I remind him. "It didn't happen if we can't remember it. Remember?"

He chuckles as he slides under the covers beside me, making my skin tingle. "I don't have to remember," he says as he settles in beside me. "I have the souvenir mug to commemorate the evening."

I close my eyes, screaming in my head to shut out the embarrassing thoughts like I always do when I picture our lovely wedding photo.

"I still can't believe that happened," I say, staring straight ahead. "You may do things like that all of the time, but I never do."

"Wake up with a ball gag in my pocket and no memory of getting married the night before?" he says, looking at me funny. "I can't say I've done that before."

"I meant the sex," I say, feeling embarrassed. "One-night stands. It was the first time I did that."

"It never happened," he says, turning off the lamp beside him and plunging the room into darkness. "Remember?"

"Yeah," I whisper, suddenly disappointed that he finally agrees with me. "But it kinda did."

"I know," he whispers back, turning to look at me. His flawless face is even more gorgeous in the soft darkness with only the moonlight creeping in through the blinds lighting him up. His muscular arm is over the sheets, his tattoos looking dangerously sexy.

"Think back," he says, watching me. "We had the drink, then what?"

I try hard to remember but there's a long deleted scene in my brain where the memory should be. "My friend Emily said that I was dancing in a fountain and then she lost me. Next thing I remember is waking up with you."

"Naked."

"Yes," I say, cringing as I remember that morning. "Very naked."

He smiles as he gazes into my eyes. "Maybe if we recreate the moment now, the memory will pop back into our heads."

"Do you have a ball gag?" I ask.

He shakes his head with a smile on his lips.

"Damn," I say, turning over. "Then next time."

"Next time," he says, turning away from me. "Goodnight, Pumpkin."

He can't see my face so it's safe to smile.

"Goodnight, Tyler."

I think we'll just have to face the fact that we'll never know what happened that night...

12

Big Doc

The night...

"Look at that drunk chick," I say, laughing as I point to a cracked-out girl who's standing in the fountain in front of the Olympus hotel. The water is up to her knees, and she's making out hard with the stone statue of Poseidon.

This is what I love about Vegas. Taking a smoke break always comes with a hell of a show.

My tattoo shop is set up on the strip, so I see all kinds of shit from the corporate sheep like the fountain-kisser over there who can't handle Sin City. It's like they leave their inhibitions and common sense at the McCarran baggage claim, doing things they would normally never do in public. But somehow, it's okay because they're in Vegas.

"Wait until security comes," my assistant Jess says,

giggling as she watches. "Paul is going to pepper spray her for that."

"You think?" I ask, taking a drag of my cigarette.

She looks at me with her tattooed forehead wrinkled up. The ink roses on her forehead kind of looks like a pussy when she furrows her brow like that, but I shouldn't make fun of her. I'm the one who tattooed it on her after all.

"Come on, Big Doc. Have you ever met Paul?" she asks, grinning at me.

I nod. "She's getting pepper sprayed."

The girl's cute friend is laughing at her, telling her to suck Poseidon's stone dick when Paul finally comes out, clutching the pepper spray that's strapped to his belt. The cute friend takes off running when she sees security coming, leaving the drunk girl all alone with her new stone boyfriend.

This scene is going to be so good that I no longer care that I have no clients for the night. My tattoo shop has been empty for too many nights in a row, and I'm lucky if I'll be able to pay the bills for the month. At least I have a show to distract me from my money problems.

"Miss!" Paul shouts, standing on the edge of the fountain. "This is private property. Get out of the water—now!"

"Pepper spray her!" Jess shouts.

Paul turns to us and rolls his eyes. "Miss," he repeats, turning back to the crack head. She's not listening. She's too busy trying to stick her hand down Poseidon's stone pants. "I'm giving you to the count of three to get out or I'm coming in."

The woman turns to him, seeing him for the first time, and covers her open mouth with her hand. "Oh, my goodness," she says with wide wild eyes. She keeps jerking her head from side to side, and her hand keeps twitching beside her. She's pretty fucked up. I should get the name of her dealer.

"You have a rainbow growing out of your forehead," she says, staring at Paul in wonder. He steps back as she approaches him with her arms out like a zombie. "Rainbow," she whispers.

Paul, who definitely doesn't have a rainbow growing out of his forehead, backs up, looking more nervous than ever.

The girl's hair is a wild mess as she climbs out of the fountain and walks up to Paul with pure wonder in her bloodshot eyes. "Are you magical?"

"Miss," Paul says, stepping backward. "Stay back."

She tilts her twitchy head to the side as she walks up to him, ignoring his warnings completely. "Can I touch your rainbow?"

Jess is giggling beside me. Her cigarette is finished, but she's lighting another one. We're not going anywhere until this show is over. "She's getting pepper sprayed."

"Yup," I say, watching.

Paul struggles to yank the pepper spray off his belt but can't get it unhooked. His eyes widen in panic as she lunges forward with her hands out. He spins away and sprints back to the hotel, looking over his shoulder as he runs away from her.

"Pirate's gold!" she yells before leaning over the ledge of the fountain and grabbing handfuls of wet pennies. She stuffs them into her purse like they're priceless treasures.

Just when we think the show is over, a guy in a disheveled suit comes running out of nowhere and wraps his arms around her. He looks just as fucked up with his wide, twitchy eyes and a business tie wrapped around his forehead like a corporate Bruce Lee.

"Bar girl!" he shouts, staring at her with crazy eyes. He

must have the same dealer because he looks equally fucked up.

"It's you!" she shouts back, smiling widely at him. "I've been looking for you *everywhere!*"

"I was riding on a unicorn!" the guy says, bouncing from foot to foot. He can't seem to stay still.

Neither can she.

"Wow," she gasps, staring at him like his drunken face is made of pure energy. She reaches up, touches his cheek, and then just like that, they're making out.

Heavily.

I mean tongues dragging across cheeks, hands dug into matted hair, teeth crashing together. At one point, I'm worried that she's eating his face.

I really have to get the name of their dealer. For a friend...

"This is the best night of my life!" the man says when they finally pull away.

"Oh, shit!" the girl says, looking back at the statue. "My boyfriend is going to get jealous."

"Fuck that guy," the drunk man says, grabbing her wrist. "You're my girl now."

"Okay," she says as he pulls her toward us.

"Brace yourself," Jess says as they lock eyes on us.

I take one last puff of my cigarette and then crush it under my foot. These two look high as fuck, and high as fuck people are always insanely unpredictable.

"Is this an apple pie store?" the man asks when they arrive.

Jess looks up at me and giggles.

"No," I say, standing with my back straight, ready for anything. "This is a tattoo shop."

They both look confused. The strong drugs burning through their brains like acid probably aren't helping.

"We should get matching tattoos!" the girl says when my words finally get through the hazy fog in her head. "We're soulmates."

"Definitely," the man says.

"We don't serve people in your condition," Jess says, taking a drag of her cigarette.

The man reaches into his dirty jacket and pulls out a wad of money. My eyes turn into dollar signs as I stare at the thick pile of Benjamin Franklins in his hand. That could pay my personal and work bills for the next two months.

So what if they're a *tad* fucked up? If they want a tattoo and are willing to pay for it, then I should give it to them. Otherwise, they're just going to go to another shop down the street.

Why shouldn't I take their money? Sure, it's a tad unethical, but I really need the cash.

When he stuffs the wad of bills into my hand, my ethical dilemma vanishes.

"What can I get you and where?" I ask, slipping the money into my pocket.

"I want her name," the guy says, wrapping his muscular arm around his deep-fried girl. "What's your name?"

The girl looks up at the sky for a second. "I think it starts with a D. I want your name tattooed on me too, on my forehead like hers," she says, pointing at Jess.

I swallow hard. I'll take their money, I'll give them tattoos, but I'm not tattooing their faces no matter how much they beg me for it.

So what if they don't even know each other's names and are likely to regret it in the morning? This is Vegas. This town was built on regrets.

Who am I to deny this nice couple their true Vegas experience?

They both pull out their drivers' licenses and are trying to read them. The chick has hers upside down.

"Let me help you with that," Jess says, slowly taking it from them. "Tyler and Dahlia."

"That's it!" Tyler says, pointing at Jess. "We're soulmates."

"Awesome!" I say, taking a deep breath as I open the door. "Then let's go get some tattoos!"

13

Tyler

"Why is your father-in-law swimming naked in my pool?"

That's the first question my mother asks when I walk down in the morning. Thankfully, Dahlia is still sleeping upstairs. She would absolutely die if she knew this was going on right now.

"Is that coffee I smell?" I ask, looking over her head into the kitchen. This whole situation is going to go a lot better if I have a cup of coffee in my hand. It's too early for saggy old penises before a hit of caffeine.

"Tyler," she grits through a clenched jaw. I haven't seen that angry face since I was a teenager. "I said there's a naked man *in my pool!*"

I sigh as I walk over to the back doors, dreaming of a steaming cup of coffee. "Where's Dad?"

She looks even more pissed now. "He's out back doing yoga with *that woman!*"

"You mean Dahlia's mom?"

My mother crosses her arms over her chest and huffs out a breath. "They smoked marijuana cigarettes!"

"Dad did?" I ask, staring at her in shock. "Mack McMillan?"

Her nostrils are flaring as she stares at me. "He liked to hit the reefer in college, but I made him promise to give it up forever when I married him."

"Dad?" I say, still staring at her in shock. The father I knew would never have touched the green stuff. Lord knows, he's needed it over the years.

"Yes, your father," she says, placing her palms on my arm. She pushes me with all of her might, but she slides backward and I don't move. "Now, I have been very nice to those people, but I don't want that man's penis in my pool!"

"All right," I say, running a hand through my hair as I walk outside.

Sure enough, Dahlia's father Echo is doing laps in the pool naked, looking like the world's ugliest merman with his long gray hair trailing out behind him.

He flips on his back and pushes off the wall of the pool, doing a backstroke while showing off his free willy.

"See?" my mother says, marching up beside me.

"Unfortunately, I can," I say, taking a deep breath. *What the hell did I marry myself into?*

I look down at my mom and shrug. "At least his penis is out of the water now."

She stomps her foot with a huff of breath and storms back into the house.

"Good morning, Echo," I say when he stops for a breather at the other end of the pool. "Can I loan you a bathing suit?" *Before my mother has a shit fit?*

His long gray hair is plastered to his head, making him

look like the creature from the hippie lagoon. "I'm perfectly zen like this, Tyler. Nothing invigorates me sexually like a naked swim in cool refreshing water."

I take a deep breath, trying to figure out the best way to deal with him. "I'll buy five of your tie-dye shirts if you put on a bathing suit."

He jumps out of the pool with a huge grin on his face. "You won't be disappointed," he says as he grabs the towel and wraps it around his tanned wrinkly body.

"I'm already not disappointed," I say, taking a breath of relief now that his mini Woodstock is covered with a towel. "Just stay like that, and I'll go get you a bathing suit."

I glance over to where my father and Dahlia's mother Essence are practicing yoga on the grass. My dad is giggling as he tries to bend his legs into the shape of a pretzel.

His eyes are bloodshot and half-closed, but I'm still having a hard time believing that he's stoned.

I hurry into the house, passing my mother who is wiping the counter so hard that I'm worried she's going to crack the thick granite. She always cleans when she's pissed.

"He's out of the pool and covered up," I say as I rush past her.

She glances out the window and scowls. "Remind me to burn that towel after."

I race up the stairs, surprisingly excited to see Dahlia. I had a lot of fun with her last night, and I'm actually grinning to myself now that I get to see her again.

I slowly open the door to my bedroom in case she's still sleeping. She moves her head on the pillow when I walk in and looks up with tired groggy eyes.

The sight is so beautiful that my heart skips a beat. I take a step back as I watch her sit up in the bed with my skin tingling. Her hair is a wild mess, but I fucking love it. Long curly strands of brown hair that are finally let loose by their strict owner cascade over her shoulders and over my favorite Sum 41 t-shirt.

The lucky shirt is too big and hanging off her body. The hole for the head has fallen over her shoulder, giving me a tempting view of her soft skin.

I thought she looked stunning last night in her gorgeous red dress, but she looks absolutely mesmerizing now, waking up au naturale with no makeup on in my shirt and in my bed.

This girl is starting to get to me. I'm starting to have feelings.

I wanted her last night. Having her in my bed and not trying to make a move was pure torture, but I can tell that Dahlia is the type of girl who needs to take things slow. With parents like hers, I can see why.

But this thing between us is already complicated enough without throwing feelings into the mix. My priority has to be the company. Nick can't be the one to run it. He would ruin everything my father worked so hard to build.

And he just might be the one to get it if our marriage is revealed as a sham, or if this thing ends up in a disastrous fight. We have to stay civil and remain on speaking terms.

That means I have to shut down these feelings.

Feelings can come after I get the company. Nothing is more important to me than that.

But that doesn't mean we can't enjoy each other's bodies again if we can somehow keep our messy feelings out of it.

I just know that I won't be able to resist trying when I see her in the office on Monday morning. We can still play some games without getting any feelings involved. If I ramp up the sexual tension at work, maybe we can have another go before she leaves—a night to remember with absolutely no feelings involved.

Monday morning, it's on.

"What are my parents doing?" she asks, rubbing her eyes. It's the first thing she asks.

I smile as I walk over to my dresser and open a drawer. "Your mother is doing yoga with my father, and your father is swimming."

Her back straightens as she looks at me with terror in her eyes. "Is he wearing a bathing suit?"

I pull one out of my drawer and hold it up. "He will be now."

"Oh, God," she says, dropping her head back down on the pillow. Seeing her lying in my bed is getting me going. I'm starting to harden in my shorts as I picture crawling on top of her and giving her a proper good morning.

"Why would your mother invite them?"

"It's going great," I lie. "It's a beautiful day out. Why don't you join your dad for a swim before breakfast?"

"A swim does sound nice," she says, staring up at the ceiling.

It sounds perfect. I would love to see her hot body in a tight bikini.

"But, I don't have my bathing suit here."

I grin, already prepared. "I figured my mother would make you sleep over, so I went bikini shopping."

She sits back up with a look of disbelief on her face. "You bought me a bikini?"

I grin as I head to my closet and pull out a bag from Bikini Boutique. "Of course! I'm your husband. I've got you covered."

Her face hardens as she stares at the bag. "How covered? I'm afraid to see the size of that thing."

"I made it out of dental floss," I say with a chuckle as I pull it out of the bag and toss it onto the bed. "Try it on."

She holds it up and my dick hardens just picturing what she would look like in it.

"It's a little small," she says, holding the top against her chest.

"At least it's not see-through," I say with a grin.

She stuffs it back into the bag. "I don't think so."

I have to pull out the ace in my sleeve. She's making me do it.

"No bathing suit for you, no bathing suit for your father."

Her face drops as she glares at me. "You can't be serious."

"Try me," I say, holding Echo's bathing suit over the open drawer. We stare each other down for a few seconds, me smirking, her glaring.

"Fine," she says with a huff of breath. She grabs it and gets out of bed. "But if it's too small, I'm not coming out."

"That's okay," I say as she shuffles to my en suite bathroom. "I have cameras in there anyway. Kidding," I say when I see her face.

Note to self: Install cameras in my bathroom.

She closes the door, and I start pacing around my room like a hungry tiger. The anticipation of seeing her in only the bathing suit I bought her is killing me and making my dick ache. I purposely bought it a size too small so I can see every single one of her curves.

"Did you buy this in the kids' department?" she asks through the closed door. "This thing is miniature."

"I'm sure it's fine," I say with my heart racing. "Open the door and show me."

"No way."

"Okay," I say, smirking to myself. "I'll just go tell your dad that he can swim without a bathing suit."

I hear a muffled *'ugh'* from the other side of the door before the handle starts turning and the door slowly opens.

My breath quickens and the smile on my face vanishes when I see her. She's perfect.

The tight blue bathing suit is clinging to her body, showing me everything except the very best parts.

She's standing there shyly as she slowly moves her eyes from the tiles under her feet up to mine. It takes everything I have not to pounce on her.

"Too small, right?" she asks, covering her perky little breasts with her arms.

I just shake my head, staring at her like she's the most beautiful thing I've ever seen, because she is.

"Say something."

"Wow."

"Shut up," she says before turning to grab my Sum 41 shirt off the counter. My eyes immediately fall to her ass as she turns, and I snap my head back in surprise when I see a bit of ink on her butt cheek, peeking out from under the bikini bottom.

I can only see the tip of her tattoo but the sight makes my body flood with warmth. *Fuck, I want to see the whole thing.*

"I didn't picture you as the type to get a tattoo," I say as she shakes out the shirt.

"That's because I would *never* get one."

"Then what's that?" I ask, pointing at the nicest ass I've ever seen.

"What's what?" She twists around, trying to see her butt but she can't see the tattoo from her angle.

"Stop messing with me," she says, straightening back up.

"I'm not going to take my bathing suit off."

"There's a tattoo back there," I say with an unflinching voice. *And I desperately want to see it.*

She rolls her eyes and then steps up onto the ledge of the bath so she can see her ass in the mirror. "*What the fuck?!?*" she screams when she sees the tattoo.

She yanks the fabric to the side and gasps when a brand-new tattoo is revealed on her right butt cheek.

I walk over, narrowing my eyes to see better. "Does that say—"

The words disappear from my throat when I see my name branded on her formerly flawless ass. TYLER is tattooed on her goosebumped skin in big block letters.

This is too perfect. Her ass is mine forever.

"That's my name," I say, trying not to laugh as she freaks out. "Your ass is officially mine."

"What the fuck?!? What the fuck?!? What the fuck?!?" she screams, shaking her head like a madwoman as she stares at the reflection of her ass in the mirror. "How did this happen?"

I can barely contain my grin. The marriage certificate wasn't permanent, but this is.

"This is the first time you've seen it?" I ask.

She jumps off the ledge of the bath, rips the Sum 41 shirt off the counter, and yanks it on. "Yes, it's the first time I've seen it! I don't look at my ass in the mirror every day!"

"You should," I answer. "If I had that ass I'd be staring at in the mirror *all* day."

The heated look she gives me makes me take a step back and gulp.

"Wait a minute," she says when something dawns on her. She pulls the shirt back up, licks her thumb, and tries to wipe the tattoo off her skin. It's not going anywhere. It's real.

"Shit!" she curses, yanking her shirt back down. Her jaw is clenched tight as she looks up at me. "Where's yours?"

My face drops. I didn't think of that. I was there too on that crazy night, so if she has my name tattooed on her ass, I probably have her name tattooed on mine.

I slide down the back of my shorts and check out my ass in the mirror. There's nothing there.

"Fuck you," she says, elbowing my ribs as she storms past me into my room.

I swallow my laugh as she stomps into the hallway. I follow her downstairs with my eyes locked on her round ass, which is now officially mine.

"Look at all of these seeds," my father says, staring in wonder at the strawberry in his hand. "Will a strawberry tree grow in my stomach if I eat this thing?"

My mother rolls her eyes and turns away from him, looking disgusted. Yup, he's still high as fuck.

I glance over at Dahlia, who still hasn't looked at me since the incident in the bathroom. We're eating breakfast with all of our parents outside, and to say it's awkward is a massive understatement.

My mother is pissed at my dad, Dahlia is pissed at the world, my father is soaring through another dimension, and my new father-in-law is trying to get me to buy into his new business venture.

"I'm offering to get you in on the ground level of this enterprise," Echo says, talking with his mouth full. "You're family now, Tyler, so I want to offer you this great opportunity."

"Do people still wear tie-dye shirts?" I ask, staring at the half-chewed bagel in his mouth.

"They will when they see *our* shirts," he says, nodding. "But joining in won't come cheap. I need you to invest some big money to get in."

"Maybe I'll turn into a strawberry," my father says, still mesmerized by the piece of fruit in his hand.

"What kind of big money?" I ask, already trying to figure out how I'm going to turn him down. I'm happy to help out my new in-laws, but I'm not about to invest six or seven figures on a hippie t-shirt company.

Echo inhales sharply. "It's big money," he repeats. "A full six hundred dollars."

Dahlia rolls her eyes. "Can we talk about something else?"

"Like strawberries," my father says. He brings it to his mouth to take a bite but then gasps and throws it on the ground instead while looking panicked.

How much did he smoke?

"Sure," I say, taking a sip of my orange juice. "I can invest six hundred dollars." Ending this conversation would be worth six hundred dollars alone.

"That's six hundred dollars you'll never see again," Dahlia mutters under her breath.

"Unless my wife wants to spend it on something else," I say with a grin. "Maybe a back tattoo of her husband's face?"

She stabs a piece of sausage with her fork as she glares at me from across the table.

"So," my mother says, turning to Dahlia. "Do you want to have kids?"

"Mom!"

Dahlia's mother Essence scoffs. "Ew. Don't have kids. They're such a bummer and will ruin your life."

"Gee, thanks, Mom," Dahlia says, rolling her eyes.

My father picks up a strawberry and throws it over the fence into the neighbors' yard with a grunt. "It was an evil strawberry," he says, looking around nervously.

"Maybe you should go take a nap, Dad," I say, watching as he picks up another strawberry and slowly cuts it with a knife and fork.

My mother is staring at him in complete disgust. "I've never been less attracted to you."

This whole breakfast has been a complete disaster. I'm just glad my dad is too fucked up to notice.

Dahlia looks at my mother now that my dad is silent as he eats the evil strawberries. "Yes, I would like to have kids."

My mother smiles for the first time today.

So do I. I would love to see Dahlia pregnant with a child. Preferably mine.

"Just don't raise your kid in that uptight community you live in," Essence says, crinkling her nose up. "When are you returning to Winterland anyway?"

"*Summer*land," Dahlia corrects, glaring at her. "And I'm not sure. That's up to my new boss."

Her eyes dart over to mine, and my heart speeds up when I realize that I get to spend all week with her. I'm her boss and can order her to be where I want, when I want.

"You'll be able to return to Summerland soon," I say, swallowing hard as I stare back at her. "I was planning on keeping you at the McMillan Worldwide corporate office this week to introduce you to everyone and to how we do things at the company. What do you say?"

"Really?" she says, perking up. "I'd love to."

Good. Because I want to show off my hot new wife and her ass that's now all mine.

14

Dahlia

"ARE you Mr. McMillan's new wife?" a woman asks as she shuffles over, clutching her coffee mug to her chest. The mug says, *A Fun Thing to do in the Morning is Not Talk to Me*, but the way she's staring at me with lit-up, excited eyes tells me we're about to do *a lot* of talking.

I take a step back as she rushes toward me, waving two other ladies over along the way. "This is Tyler's new wife," she says, already introducing me to the two women flanking her sides even though we haven't even been introduced. "The surprise wife from Hospitech in Summerland. I'm Susan, and this is Ashley and Beth."

Susan the office gossip. Every office has one, and lucky for me she found me as soon as I walked through the doors of the McMillan Worldwide Inc. head office.

"I'm Dahlia," I say, nodding uncomfortably as they stare

at me like I'm some kind of abstract art exhibit that they can't quite figure out.

"Tell us how you locked down Tyler," Beth (or was it Ashley?) asks.

"He's so hot!" Ashley (or no, that one is definitely Beth) says.

I just shrug. "He's okay."

"Okay?!?" Susan says, staring at me in shock. "He's definitely the hottest guy I've ever seen."

"Me too," Ashley and Beth say at the same time, nodding like chickens.

"Is that the ring?" Susan asks, grabbing the wedding ring that's hanging from my necklace and nearly ripping my head off as she yanks it toward her. "It's beautiful! Two karats?"

"I don't know," I say with a shrug.

"Why are you wearing it around your neck?" Beth asks, leaning over Susan's shoulder to see.

"It's too big," I say, forcing out a smile. "We still haven't gotten it resized."

Susan finally lets it go and I take it in my hand, twirling it in my fingers. It is too big, and I'm glad that it is, because it provides me with the perfect excuse not to wear it on my finger. But in a messed-up way, I do like having it on me.

Susan shows me around for the next twenty minutes, giving me the dirty lowdown on all of the employees, including Carl who has an open relationship with his wife and is trying to get with the new receptionist Mandy, but she is only into black guys, and Malcolm whose teenage son just got his girlfriend knocked up. By the time we get to the executive offices on the top floor, my head is dizzy with office gossip, and all I want to do is get the hell away from Susan.

"That's your husband's office," she says, pointing to a

huge corner office with insanely high ceilings and a gorgeous oak door that's open just a crack.

My heart speeds up as I stare at it. I've seen Tyler naked, in his pajamas, in his childhood treehouse, but this is a side to him I haven't fully seen: Big powerful boss. His name is stenciled in white block letters on the window in front of the closed blinds.

The McMillan Worldwide Inc. skyscraper is a big one. It's packed full of employees of all sorts, but nothing is like the top floor where Tyler and the rest of the executives have their huge luxurious offices. Tyler's cousins Nick and Jason have offices up here too, as well as Mack, whose office seems to be the biggest.

I look around as excitement surges through my veins. *I wonder which office will be mine someday. Someday real soon.*

Susan straightens her top as she stares at Tyler's closed door. "Should we go in and say hi?"

"I better go in alone," I say, trying to get rid of her. I don't need someone as gossipy as her snooping around my fake marriage. "I'll see you later."

"Right," she says as her smile turns into a frown. "I'll just see you around."

She looks upset as she walks back to the elevators with her shoulders slumped down now that I took away her face-to-face with the sexy boss.

My stomach starts fluttering as I walk over to his office. This floor is absolutely spectacular, with dark wood beams running across the high ceilings, studded leather couches, and beautiful artwork hanging on the walls that should be in a museum. It looks like men in fancy suits are going to walk out any minute for cigars and brandy. It's much different than our offices in Hospitech. The fanciest part of our office is the little cactus in the break room named Spike.

I take a deep breath as I stand in front of the door, listening in. Tyler is having a heated conversation with someone on the phone. "I don't know who you people are or why the hell you keep calling me..."

His voice has a deep sexy growl to it that is making the flapping butterflies in my stomach move that much faster. For some reason I can't explain, I undo the top button of my shirt before pushing the door open.

"Tell you a prophecy?" he says to the person on the phone. I quietly walk in and look around. Tyler is at his desk, but his chair is turned and he's facing the huge wall of windows behind him with the breathtaking view of the Vegas strip in the background. He doesn't see me as I walk in, so I take the opportunity to look around.

It's a beautiful office with a nice Persian rug on the floor, healthy plants, a monstrous desk in the middle of the room, shelves of books along the walls, and of course, a hot guy in a tailored suit screaming into the phone.

"Here's a fucking prophecy, you weirdo!" he shouts. "You'll never get laid. You're going to die a virgin... Why are you thanking me? You're an even bigger nutjob than I thought. Now stop calling me!"

He shakes his head as he turns around with a frown on his face that instantly disappears when he sees me standing in front of his desk.

"Good morning," he says, smiling as he quickly hangs up the phone and stands up. "Welcome to McMillan World-wide Inc."

I run my hand over the smooth leather of the chair in front of me. "Very nice, Mr. McMillan," I say, nodding as I look around his office. "You've done well for yourself, it seems."

He looks me up and down slowly with a smoldering

heat in his eyes. "Yes, I did *very* well for myself, *Mrs. McMillan.*"

Warm shivers spread through me, and I hold onto the back of the chair as my legs go a little weak. He's wearing a light gray suit with a white shirt and thin black tie; a suit whose main purpose in life is to make my knees stop functioning.

"Nice office," I say, avoiding the compliment. "However, I was hoping for more N'Sync posters on the walls."

He smiles. "I tried, but my father made me take them down after I lost too many clients because of them."

I shrug. "They must have been fans of the Backstreet Boys."

He laughs and then points at the chair. "Sit, please."

"So, are you going to be moving out and giving me this office for the week?" I ask, grinning as we both sit down. "I think I saw an open seat beside Susan."

He shivers. "Susan the gossiper? I'd rather work in the cafeteria."

"I'll get you a hairnet."

"So," he says, smiling as he opens a drawer of his desk. "You forgot a few things at my hotel room during our one-night honeymoon."

"And why exactly did you have a hotel room if you live in Vegas?" I ask. It's something I've been wondering for days.

"I have no idea," he says with a shrug of his broad shoulders. "I don't remember anything from that night. We probably went back to your hotel room and I rented another one when you couldn't remember what room number you were in."

That sounds about right.

"What did I forget?" *Besides my dignity and self-respect.*

He gives me a sexy smirk as he pulls out the whip and tosses it on the desk between us.

"That's not mine," I say, rolling my eyes.

"But this is," he says, grinning as he pulls out my panties from the inside pocket of his suit jacket—the pair I left on the lamp.

My heart starts pounding as he drags them across the bottom of his nose, inhaling deep as he stares at me. "They're mine now."

My nerve endings start tingling as I watch him, holding them like an enemy holding a conquered flag.

"Is this how you treat all of your new hires?" I ask, glaring at him.

"Just the ones I fucked."

"And how many is that?" Actually, I don't want to know. I'm not going to like any answer more than zero. "Glad to know my husband is sexually harassing all of his coworkers."

"Not all of my coworkers," he says, sniffing my underwear again. My nipples harden inside of my bra as I watch him. "Just my hot new wife."

He's getting me breathless as dirty thoughts creep into my mind. I take a deep breath, trying to swallow them down as I try to take the focus off me. It's the first morning of my first day at McMillan Worldwide Inc., and I want to make a good impression. I want to be focused and alert, not wet and horny.

"Do you have *your* underwear from that night in your drawer?" I ask, grinning back at him. "Who the hell wears red underwear anyway? It's so impractical."

"Girls love it."

I laugh as I shake my head. "No, we don't. We *really* don't."

Maybe just a little bit.

He smirks as he plays with my panties in his big hands. My *unwashed* panties.

"You still remember the color," he says, "so they definitely were memorable. You can still picture them covering my big cock, can't you?"

Yes.

"No."

He gives a frustrating smirk that I can't stop staring at. "I bet you can't stop thinking about it."

I cross my arms and let out a huff of air. "Oh, really?"

"Yes, really," he says as he slowly gets up. My breathing stops as he walks around the desk still holding my panties in his hands. My back is rigid, and I'm staring forward as he comes up beside me and sits on his desk. His delicious cologne hits my nose, and I nearly let out a moan.

"I think you liked my red underwear," he whispers in a low raspy voice.

I gulp as I try to get him out from under my skin. He's trying to get to me, and I hate that it's working.

He's playing with me. That's all this is. He's the boss here, and he's trying to use his position and sexy suit to throw me off my game.

I take a deep breath as I look up at him with an angry glare. "You're frustrating, and arrogant, and full of yourself, and you're a bigger prick than what you have hiding in your ridiculously unpractical *red* underwear."

My body tenses as he leans in close, stopping his lips only an inch from mine. The heat from his breath is tickling my lips, but I hold my ground and don't move. "At least I don't have this arrogant prick's name tattooed on my ass," he whispers with a grin.

If I had a hot coffee in my hand, he'd be screaming in pain right now. And deservedly so.

I grit my teeth as he leans back with a smug look on his frustratingly handsome face.

"I wanted to keep my asshole company with another one," I say, glaring at him.

He chuckles. "You can never have too many assholes back there."

I grab his soft tie and yank him down until his face is back to being only an inch away from mine. "That's not funny!" I snap. I release my Kung Fu grip on his tie and try to regain some of my composure. I try but my composure seems to have taken a one-way trip to Madagascar.

"And why the hell did you not get a tattoo of my name?" I ask, furious that I'm the only one stuck with an unwanted tattoo.

He smooths out his tie as he smiles. "Probably because I know that getting a tattoo of the name of someone you just met is a *ridiculously* horrible idea."

I spring to my feet and grab his tie again with one hand. My other hand is squeezed into a fist. He's a dead man.

Luckily for him, Mack walks into the office at that exact moment. He frowns when he sees Tyler sitting on his desk and me holding his ties like I'm about to knock his head off, which I am.

I swallow my anger and quickly drop the tie. I give the billionaire my back as I redo my top button before turning to him with a smile on my face. Tyler tosses a folder over the whip that's still lying on the desk as he hops off it.

Mack doesn't look amused. He may be a nice guy who is all hugs and smiles at home, but he's all business here. He's like a different person when he has his billionaire face on.

"Good morning, sir," I say, pissed at myself for letting Tyler make me look so unprofessional.

Mack nods sharply at me before turning to his son. "The auto parts factory in Wellington," he says with a sharpness to his tone. "What were the total liabilities for that division last year?"

"Let me check that for you," Tyler says, hurrying around his desk to his computer.

I swallow my smile as I stand up straight. "Eleven million, three hundred thousand, six hundred, and seven dollars," I say confidently.

They both turn to me slowly, staring at me with their jaws hanging open in shock.

I hide my grin. *I'm just getting started, boys.*

Tyler searches for it on his computer and looks up at me with an incredulous look when he finds it. "She's right!"

I have Mack's attention now, and I'm not about to waste it. "And you can save seventeen percent in annual costs if you combine the auto parts legal office with your electrical components legal office in Alabama. They pretty much use the same laws, and the time saved could be used to set up the legal department for your new acquisition in Seattle. The motor factory is going to need a legal department now that they're under the McMillan Worldwide Inc. umbrella. But I would suggest moving everything to Alabama because there are fewer taxes on an operating litigation company."

Mack looks impressed. Tyler looks like I just took his king in a surprise checkmate.

"Well done, young lady," Mack says, nodding. "I'll be keeping my eye on you."

"I'll be keeping my eye on you too," Tyler says, looking me up and down with a smirk.

"Tyler," Mack says, letting out a frustrated breath as he turns to his son. "What are you doing?"

Tyler raises his eyes, looking confused.

"What is wrong with you?" he asks, pointing from Tyler to me and back again. "What is this?"

Tyler tilts his head to the side. "Lingering effects from your marijuana usage yesterday?"

Mack frowns. "I know what you're doing."

Tyler shrugs. "I'm just keeping it groovy, Dad."

I give him my 'I hate you' face.

Mack sighs. "How about you keep it a little less groovy and a little more *professional*? This flirting and sexual tension in the office—there is no place for that. I don't want any hanky panky in my building."

My new boss and father-in-law just said hanky panky. I want to die.

"If you want to be the head of this company someday," Mack says, looking exasperated, "you better start acting like it. Getting married was a huge step in the right direction, but don't let your marital relationship get in the way of your *work* relationship. When you two are in this building, you are coworkers above anything else. Got that?"

My back is as straight as a marine addressing his commanding officer. "Sir, you can count on me," I say firmly. "I'll whip your son into shape."

Mack frowns as he walks over to Tyler's desk. He grabs the folder that's covering the whip, tosses it off, and holds up the leather whip with two fingers. "That's what I'm afraid of, young lady."

He releases it like a mic drop and it lands with a slap on the table.

"I don't want any more foolishness," he says.

"Foolishness like getting stoned before breakfast?" Tyler asks with a raised eyebrow.

Mack frowns, grunts, and then leaves. Tyler laughs as I break out into nervous giggles.

I grab the whip and toss it at him. "Put that away. We don't know where it's been or how we got it."

"Or how we *used* it," Tyler says with his eyebrow back up.

I cringe. *Good thing we'll never know that...*

15

Linda

THE NIGHT...

I'M ALREADY HANDLING three cocks when a fourth guy comes over and starts rubbing his dick on my tit. I haven't seen him around here, but the way he's slapping his half-hardened cock on my nipple, it doesn't seem like he's going to add much to this dull orgy.

I sigh as I turn from one cock to the other, sucking it as I bounce up and down on the cock that's sliding in and out of my bored pussy.

It's always the same orgy, always the same twenty or thirty boring old cocks.

We need some new orgy friends.

Some different cocks would be nice for a change.

My mind starts drifting as the new guy grabs my head

and shoves his soft cock into my mouth. *Come on, dude. Get hard and then come over. I don't have time for soft dicks.*

I give him a few lazy sucks and then turn back to one of the other three dicks that are pointing at my face like arrows. I stroke the shaft and suck on the head as the guy lets out deep groans like he's about to come. He yanks his cock away from me and jerks himself off, howling like a madman as he dribbles half a teaspoon of cum on my unimpressed tits.

I sigh as he shuffles away.

My mind drifts to what I have to do tomorrow. It's a Saturday, and we have to go to the Hardware store to pick out the tiles for the bathroom renovations. *I should start pricing lawn mowers because ours is almost dead.*

A guy comes walking over and grabs my arm. "I'm going to take her for a turn, guys," he says, brushing the other dicks away from me.

I hold back a yawn as he guides me to the couch, turns me, and shoves me onto it. I land with my knees on the cushions and my arms on the top. This guy is big and muscular, but he's got a small cock.

He positions himself behind me, gripping my ass as he slides in and starts fucking me doggystyle.

I rest my chin on my arms, looking around the room as he gives my uninterested pussy a go.

There are naked people everywhere, in all sorts of sexual positions. Steven and Mandy host an orgy every Friday night in their apartment. I've been coming here for years, but I haven't cum in a while. Not with these same old boring dicks every week.

I think I have to get kinkier. These vanilla orgies aren't doing it for me anymore.

I'll go to that yoga class at nine tomorrow, and then we can head over to the Hardware store. Ah, shit! I think Lucas has a soccer practice at ten. That will screw up my yoga plans.

"Yeah," the small-dicked guy behind me grunts as he starts thrusting in harder. "You love my fucking cock!"

I like doggystyle because the guys can't see me rolling my eyes.

My husband Todd is standing by the fish tank, getting a blowjob from the girl who works at the car wash.

"Hey, Todd!" I call out across the ocean of moaning and writhing bodies.

He adjusts his glasses as he turns and looks at me over his shoulder. "Yeah?"

"Does Lucas have soccer practice tomorrow?"

The guy behind me starts really ramping up the pace, swinging me back and forth as he fucks me. I want to turn and tell him to slow it down because I'm trying to have a conversation over here, but I just let it go. He's close to coming anyway, and then he'll leave me alone.

"Yeah," Todd says with a nod. "At ten o'clock."

Shit. That means I won't be able to go to my yoga class.

I sigh as Todd turns back around. *That sucks. I really wanted to go to that yoga class. I hate soccer.*

I'm getting more bored with each short thrust when the door swings open and a new couple explodes into the room.

Here we go. I perk up with interest as I see the hot young girl burst in, looking smoking hot despite the condition of her outfit, which is wet and all scuffed up. My mouth drops when I see who's following her. He's thick with muscle, a gorgeous face, big hands, and I'd bet he's hiding a huge cock under those tailored pants.

I lick my lips as they look around with wide bulging eyes. *Finally, some new action.*

I'm definitely going to try him out. And her.

But they don't look like they're here for sex. The guy's eyes widen to the size of Magnum condoms when he spots the fish tank in the corner. He runs over, bumping into a guy getting a blowjob, and dunks his head into the water.

"What the fuck?" I mutter as I watch him. His head is submerged in the water, drinking sloppily like a British Bulldog who just crossed the desert in the middle of the summer.

His pretty little girlfriend starts walking around the room, staring at everyone with pure amazement in her eyes.

What the hell are they on?

Steven and Mandy have a strict no drug policy, so it's only a matter of time before they're kicked out. I just hope I get a taste of that cock before they do.

Mr. Five Inches behind me starts grunting heavily. In all of the excitement, I forgot he was even back there.

"Come on my dick," he grunts as he squeezes my ass.

I have to hold back a laugh. *It's going to take more than five inches to make me cum. You'd have a better chance with your fist.*

I turn my attention back to the new girl who is staring in wonder at a guy who's jerking off on a pair of tits.

"Wow," she mutters as she leans over closely and stares. The guy throws his head back and grunts, coming on the big tits in front of him.

The new girl looks like a crackhead scientist observing an experiment as she holds her chin in her hand and nods with a furrowed brow while she watches. When he's done, she reaches out and pokes his cock with her index finger then starts giggling.

Meanwhile, her boyfriend is still chugging water from the fish tank, splashing it everywhere. I wouldn't be surprised if he swallowed a couple of fish with the way he's going at it. He looks like he hasn't drunk anything for weeks.

Some naked guy walks up to the new girl, holding his hard cock in his hand. "Hello," he says, looking her up and down.

"Hello," she says in return, giving him a friendly wave. She looks down at his hard cock and points to it. "Sir, you have a blue eggplant growing out of your body."

The guy looks down at his cock with a frown, and she skips away, moving through the room. She stops at every couple, honking the girls' breasts and poking the guys' asses with her finger.

The new guy finally yanks his head out of the fish tank and turns around, taking deep gulps of air. His face, hair, and suit are drenched as he looks around with wide confused eyes.

"Why are these mannequins having sex?" he asks with water pouring off his chin.

I'd still fuck him.

The new girl circles back to him and he grabs her arm, looking panicked. He backs up until he's flattened against the wall like a drugged-up Spider-man, and then quickly slides along the wall toward the door.

The girl walks over to the coffee table and gasps as she picks up my leather whip. She tucks it under her arm and then grabs my favorite ball gag and an open box of Magnum condoms.

Her friend yanks the door open and leaps through it, disappearing into the hallway.

"Wait!" she says, running after him with my stuff in her arms.

I perk up on the couch, about to call them back so I can get my stuff when the guy behind me squeezes my ass and yells that he's coming.

"I'm coming!" he screeches.

Good for you.

I sigh as I slump back down, watching as Mandy closes the door. The guy and girl are both gone with my toys. *Oh, well. Those don't do anything for me anymore anyway. I need a lot more than a whip and a ball gag to get my motor going these days.*

Mr. Five Inches finally pulls out of me and walks away without saying a word. Before I can take a second to stretch out my legs, Steven takes his place, sliding his dick inside of me.

"Hey, Steven," I say, looking at him over my shoulder.

"Hi, Linda," he answers as he thrusts in and out of me. "Did you guys file your taxes yet?"

Shit! I wonder if Todd sent them in.

"Hey, Todd! Did you send in the taxes?"

16

Tyler

"So, as you can see," my cousin Nick says as he finishes up his proposal, "there is no other option than to close down the steel plant in Phoenix and move it to Honduras. I highly recommend that we start the process immediately."

Every person in the room looks to the head of the table where my father is sitting. He's watching Nick while he twirls his pen in his hand. He always does that when he's thinking.

"Sounds good," he finally says, nodding. "You can be in charge of handling it, Nick."

Nick flashes me a triumphant look before gathering his notes with a smirk on his face.

"If I may, sir," Dahlia says, straightening up in her seat. "I have an alternative option."

My ears perk up as I turn to my beautiful wife who is now a constant fixture in McMillan Worldwide Inc.'s top meetings. It's only been a week since she's been working here, but my father has already taken a liking to her. And it's not because she's his new daughter-in-law. It's because she's a killer business woman who knows her shit and who has an unlimited number of intelligent ideas.

My father turns to her with a smile on his face. "You have the floor, Dahlia."

She clears her throat and then spits out a whole speech on how we can not only save the factory in Phoenix but also cut costs while increasing profits by adding a gold refinery to the existing steel plant. I don't know how she comes up with these ideas.

"McMillan Worldwide Inc. just absorbed the Klineton Mining Corporation last month, correct?" she says, glancing down at her notepad. It's covered in notes. Even the margins have notes scribbled on them. I swallow hard as I glance down at my notepad. All mine has on it is a doodle of a penguin who looks more like a rocket ship than a bird.

My father nods. "We did."

"As you may know," she continues with a proud smile on her face. "The Klineton Mining Corporation has a small department that specializes in gold. Well, they just discovered a huge vein of gold in one of the mountains they were digging in, and those dole bars have to be processed. If we set that up in the steel factory in Phoenix, we could save a ton of money over the next five years."

My skin tingles as I watch her do what she does best. She could hold her own against any of these business sharks, and I can tell that she knows it *and* loves it.

"That's not going to work," Nick scoffs, waving a dismissive hand at her.

She ignores him, turning to my dad. "It's going to work."

My father is liking the idea. I can tell.

"Arizona has a lower tax on gold," I add, helping to drive the idea home. "If we refine the gold in Honduras and import it back, we're going to get slaughtered with importation taxes."

Nick is breathing heavily as he watches us trounce his presentation.

My father turns to my cousin Jason. "What do you think?" he asks him.

Jason is sitting at the end of the table, listening carefully. He nods, looking impressed at the idea. If Jason thinks it's a good idea, it's probably a good idea. That kid knows his stuff.

"I'd have to run the numbers but it sounds like it could work," he says.

"I already ran them," Dahlia answers quickly, grabbing some papers from her bag. She hands them around the table, grinning as she hands one to Nick.

My younger cousin Jason nods as he quickly looks over the numbers. He would make a better boss than Nick, but he knows that both his older brother Nick and I really want my father's position so he has pulled his name out of the running. I'm glad that he did because he'd be making it even harder for me to get the spot.

"It looks good," my father says, nodding in approval as he looks over the numbers. He takes a second to read the papers and then tosses them on the desk. "Good job, Dahlia. Create a full proposal for me and have it on my desk by tomorrow morning."

I've never seen her smile so wide. It's adorable.

My father turns to me. "Tyler, you can help her."

Wow, that smile vanished quickly.

"Anything else?" my father asks, looking around the

room. When no one speaks up, he dismisses us all and hurries out of the conference room.

Jason smiles at Dahlia as he passes her on his way out. "Great job, cuz," he says, giving her a fist bump.

Nick still looks furious. "She's not your cousin, Jason," he says, glaring at his brother.

Jason rolls his eyes and taps Dahlia's shoulder as he leans down close to her ear. "Yes, you are," he whispers.

She smiles shyly for a second before catching my eye and dropping it.

"I want a copy of that proposal as well," Nick says as he angrily shoves his notes into his bag.

"Why, so you can see what a real proposal looks like?" Dahlia asks, flashing him a dirty look.

"No, so I can find all of the mistakes that will inevitably be in there," he answers.

"The only mistake around here is letting you in through the door," I say, standing up. "That will be changed once I'm the boss."

I can't prove anything yet, but I have a strong suspicion that Nick is stealing from the company, and I'm not talking about sticky notes or highlighters. There seems to be seven figures mysteriously missing from the departments that he oversees.

I brought up my suspicions with my father a few months ago, and he got upset, claiming that I was trying to sabotage Nick's chances for the promotion. I've looked for proof, but I can't find any. He's covered his tracks well. He always has been a smart one.

"Maybe the factory in Phoenix won't go down," Nick says, smirking at Dahlia. "But the one in Summerland definitely will. I'll make damn sure of that."

"Not unless you go down first," Dahlia says as she

gathers her notes and stuffs them into her bag. "With my help, Tyler is definitely going to get the top spot."

"Your help?" he says with an amused grin. "You don't even work here. You work for the Hospitech division, which is now run by me. I want you back in Summerland tomorrow to help prepare for the layoffs."

"She's not going anywhere," I snap. Both of their heads whip around to me. "You don't tell her what to do. Ever."

"Actually, I do," he says, gritting his teeth. "She's *my* employee."

"She's my *wife*," I growl, staring him down. I didn't realize I was so possessive of her until this moment. "And she's staying here with me."

Nick drops his eyes to the table as his posture turns submissive. He knows better than to mess with me when I'm like this. We've gone at it a lot over the years, and I'm sure he hasn't forgotten all of those black eyes I've given him while growing up, so he backs off.

"She can stay tomorrow," he says, keeping his eyes on his bag, "just so Mack can see what a laughable mess her proposal is, but next week, she goes back to Summerland." He turns to her with a smile that I really want to slap off. "And you'll be the one in charge of handing out the layoffs."

Dahlia is breathing heavy with her nostrils flaring as Nick quickly exits the room. It's just the two of us left in the large conference room now.

"Was that guy dropped on his head as a baby or something?" she asks, shaking her head. "What an asshole."

"Now you see why I want to get the company so bad," I say, walking around the table to get closer to her. "The whole corporation will be in trouble if he's in charge."

"The whole *world* will be in trouble if he's in charge," she says, rubbing her forehead.

I walk up to her and sit on the table beside her. "Enough about him," I say, smiling down at her. "You did fucking great! You killed it!"

"I did," she says with a big excited smile on her sexy lips. My heart skips a beat as I stare at them.

Working with this girl for the week has been pure torture. Her outfits get sexier every day. They're all work-friendly and professional, but to a hungry lion like me, they're catnip. Tight skirts that show the tempting curve of her ass, white blouses with just the hint of cleavage; not too much to be unprofessional, but just enough to drive me crazy.

It's not just her beautiful face and stunning body that are torturing me, but her smell too. I've been working closely with her throughout the week, showing her the ropes of the company, and every time I get a whiff of her vanilla perfume, my dick throbs. She smells delicious, and it always leaves me wondering what she tastes like.

It kills me that I've already tasted her, and done a lot more than that, and I can't remember any of it. That's the worst thing about that drunken night. It's not the marriage, or all the lies, or the strange calls I keep getting from the Sunshine Happy Church. It's that I had this beautiful girl for a night and I can't remember a single thing.

I sigh as I watch her smiling, wondering if I'll ever get another chance. We're always bickering and are constantly at each other's throats, but strangely, I like it.

She doesn't annoy me half as much as I let on.

"Did you see your cousin's face when I handed him my notes?" she asks, biting her bottom lip as she smiles. "He looked furious! It was awesome!"

"He's probably having an angry cry in the janitor's office," I say with a chuckle. "And it's all because of you."

She looks thrilled.

"How do you come up with these ideas?" I ask, staring at her in wonder.

"It's easy," she says, perking up in her seat. She rambles on at a speed I can't even follow, telling me her in-depth research process, which is anything but easy. I just watch her lips moving as she talks, wondering what she would do if I leaned down and kissed her.

"So, you're going to help me?" she asks when she's finally finished talking.

"Of course," I say, holding my hand up. "We're a team, remember?"

She slaps her palm on mine for a high-five, but I hold onto her hand, letting the sexual tension build up between us.

Her cheeks flush an adorable pink as I finally let her go. She takes a deep breath and tucks a loose strand of hair behind her ear as she recovers.

"We should get started," she says, looking anywhere but at me as she gets up and heads to the door. "This is going to take all night."

My eyes are on her ass as she walks across the conference room, swinging those sexy hips.

This is going to take all night.

I grin as her words replay in my head.

This may turn out even better than I thought.

I POP open two beers as the clock strikes midnight. We're in my office surrounded by cold leftover pizza, mountains of spreadsheets, and a few empty bottles of beer.

Dahlia is sitting at my desk, hard at work. She's typing

furiously on her laptop as I walk over to her and hand her a beer. "Let's take a break."

Her fingertips dance across the keyboard for a few more seconds before she leans back in her chair and looks up at me. "Breaks are for the weak."

"You've been staring at your computer screen for the past four hours without coming up for air," I say, forcing the beer into her hand. "Just five minutes."

She reluctantly takes the beer from me, takes a quick sip, and then makes a disgusted face as she places it on the desk, far away from her. "I don't know how you drink that stuff. It's horrible."

"I'm sorry," I say, sitting on the desk in front of her, "but I don't have any white wine spritzers in my office."

"You remembered," she says, smiling. "I guess we remember one thing from that night."

She has one eye on me and one eye on her laptop. She groans when I close it. I want her full attention.

We're the only two left on the entire floor, and I want to take advantage of it. We haven't been alone since that first morning together, and we are now. Even the nighttime cleaners left about an hour ago.

"I can't believe I have to go back to Summerland next week," she says, taking a deep breath as she stretches her neck. "It feels like a lifetime has passed since I've been there."

I want to tell her that I don't want her to leave, but I just stay quiet instead.

"My back is so sore," she says, stretching as she gets up from her chair. She arches her back, pressing her tits in the air as she stretches. If my dick could talk, he would be letting out a groan right now.

My eyes never leave her body as she walks to the

window and stares out at the colorful lights of the Strip in the distance.

"What a magnificent view," she says.

My eyes are on her ass. "I couldn't agree more."

She rubs the back of her neck as she watches the blinking lights from the top floor of our high-rise building.

"Let me," I say, hoping off my desk and walking over. She tenses up as I walk up close behind her and slide my hand on the back of her neck.

"You're so tense," I say as I start massaging her neck. Just touching her soft skin with the sweet smell of vanilla swirling in my head has my heart pounding and my dick raging.

"I want to get this proposal right," she says, finally starting to relax as my hands take away her stress. She melts under my touch, placing her palms on the window for support.

I slide my hands down to her shoulders and begin massaging them, drawing little moans and groans from her sweet lips. I feel her bra straps under my fingers, which makes me imagine taking it off, which makes me start breathing heavier.

I can see her reflection in the glass. Her eyes are closed, her lips parted. She's enjoying the feeling of my hands, which are slowly moving down her back. I can tell she likes it, even if she'd never stoop so low as to admit it.

When I reach her waist, I don't stop. I slide my palms over the curve of her ass, and it makes my cock rock fucking hard. It also makes her turn around with a nasty look on her face.

"What are you doing?"

"Trying to consummate our vows," I say with my hands still down there.

"Our *drunken* vows?"

"Drunk or not," I say, moving my hands back up to her back to release some of the tension that has suddenly filled the office, "you said the words."

"Are you sure?" she asks, starting to relax again as I massage her back. She turns back to the window, and I can see in her reflection that she closes her eyes. "I haven't seen any video proof of me saying anything."

"The missing videos," I say, inhaling her sweet scent. "I'm still looking for those, but in the meantime, we can start our honeymoon. Tonight is as good a night as any."

Dahlia looks around the office and lets out a laugh. "Cold pizza. Warm beer. Pretty lame honeymoon, if you ask me."

I slide my hands back down to her ass as I lean in close to her ear. "Let me take off this skirt, and it will get really good, really fast," I whisper as her soft hair tickles my face. "You'll be in paradise in no time."

She licks her lips and then swallows hard, her body stiffening under my touch. She's considering it. I can tell.

"We should get back to work," she says, pressing her forehead against the window and squeezing her eyes shut.

"Don't run from this," I say, squeezing her waist with my hands to hold her in front of me. "There's something between us for real. I know that you feel it too."

She lets out a little moan as I press my hard erection against the top of her ass. I know she felt *that*.

Her beautiful skin becomes flushed as she holds her breath. She could move away from my cock, but she lets me press it against her.

"I don't know what you're talking about," she says as her body starts to tremble. Her words are saying one thing, but her body is saying another. And her body is saying it loud and clear as she presses her ass back into my hard dick.

I lean in next to her ear as I slide my hands up and down her trembling body. "I'm talking about pulling out my hard cock and bending this beautiful ass over." She shivers as I slide my hands down on it, gripping her ass cheeks with a firm grip. "This sexy ass that has my name written on it."

She looks over her shoulder at me with a frown on her face. "Don't remind me. You're not allowed to mention that again until you get the matching tattoo on *your* ass."

"You want to be on my ass?" I ask with a grin.

"I want you to get a tattoo of *my* name," she says. "We probably had a deal and you chickened out. Are you afraid of needles or something?"

I roll up my sleeve and show her my tatted-up forearm. "Do I look like I'm afraid of needles?"

Her eyes linger on my thick forearm as her breathing becomes quick and ragged once again. "You don't look like you're afraid of anything," she whispers.

I spin her around and press her up against the window, holding my body close against hers. I can feel her heart pounding as hard as mine as she looks at me with lust-filled eyes.

"I'm afraid I'll never get back the memory of our night together," I whisper in her ear. "It kills me that I can't remember the first time I slid inside of you."

Another shiver jerks through her body at my heated words. "*First* time?" she asks with her eyes closed. "You mean our *only* time. *Ever.*"

"That won't be our only time," I whisper into her ear. I give her soft kisses on the side of her neck, and she starts to moan. Her back is arched, her tits pressed against my chest as she moves her leg to find my hard-on. She presses her thigh against it when she finds it, and I let out a deep throaty groan.

"It's going to happen again," I say between kisses. I move my lips down her neck and kiss a trail over the top of her chest and back up to the other side. When my lips reach her neck, she's practically panting. "I know you want it too. I know you want to fuck your husband."

Our lips are so close. They're hovering over each other. I can practically taste her tongue, and it's making me crazy.

I slide my palm over her lower back and pull her into me until our bodies are pressed so tight against each other that a thin piece of paper couldn't slide through.

"I know you want to fuck me," I whisper on her lips.

Her body is saying everything that she refuses to say, so I let our bodies do the talking. I crush my lips onto hers and wrap my arms possessively around her as I deepen the kiss.

Her body melts in my arms as she kisses me back with equal urgency, holding me as tightly as I hold her.

After a knee-weakening, heart pounding, toe-curling kiss, she pulls away and looks at me with the sexiest, lust-filled eyes I've ever seen.

It's in that moment I know I'm fucking Dahlia tonight.

17

Tyler

Dahlia rips open my shirt, sending buttons flying through the air as we fumble around the office with our lips locked, and our hands frantically trying to rip off any articles of clothing within reach.

We're kissing hard and rough, all of the pent-up emotions and sexual tension finally boiling over, and it couldn't be more perfect.

This was inevitable. Us. We were destined to do this again.

I slide my hand into her hair, grab hold of her bun, and yank it down until her thick gorgeous hair spills out in a wild mess of brown curls.

She rips her lips away from mine and gives me a fierce look before lunging forward and crushing her lips onto mine once again. She moans into my mouth as our tongues collide against each other in a ferocious kiss.

I yank her shirt down, tearing the fabric, but neither of us seems to care. My lips are on the top of her tits, kissing, sucking, nipping, as she reaches back to undo the clasp.

We're stumbling around the office until her ass crashes into my desk, and we're finally stopped. She unhooks her bra, and slides it down one arm as I lunge on her tits, coating her hard nipples with my tongue.

Her curves are beautiful, her soft tits perfect. She feels so good it hurts.

"Shit, Tyler," she moans as she grabs a fistful of my hair and holds me against her chest like she never wants me to go.

I grab the back of her knees and she lets out a whimper as I lift her into a sitting position on my desk. Her skirt is tight so she can't spread her legs as far as I want them. I want them in the fucking splits so I can see every inch of her wet pussy.

Her hands are all over me, clawing my chest and abs as she breathes heavily and stares with her glazed-over eyes.

Both of our shirts are ripped open, but they're still hanging onto our arms. Neither of us takes a second to shake out of them, we're too busy trying to get to the rest of the good parts.

Dahlia grabs my belt buckle and yanks me forward, desperately trying to get my aching cock out. She curses as her fingers frantically fumble with my belt, trying to pull it open.

I'd help, but I'm too busy with her skirt. My whole body is stirring with a reckless passion as I shove her skirt up her thighs, bunching it around her waist.

My eyes are on her naked tits as I grab the sides of her panties in a hard grip and yank them down her legs. She lets out a whimper as they slide past her knees and down her calves.

I step out of her reach as I guide her heels out of her soaking wet panties. She moans as her hands fall away from me and to her sides.

I hold my breath as I stand back and take a second to admire the view. Dahlia is sitting on my desk with her big tits out and a look of pure lust on her face. Her black skirt is bunched up around her waist, and her legs are spread open, showing me her hot little pussy.

The beautiful sight nearly knocks me off my feet. It's like a peek into heaven. I stand there unmoving like a statue, staring at her sweet pussy lips that are glistening with arousal.

"Fuck," I whisper, never taking my eyes off her as she reaches for me. She grabs hold of my tie and yanks me forward.

I take her mouth once again, grabbing her voluptuous tits as I swallow her whimpers. I love the little noises she's making. Each one makes my hard cock jump.

"No," she gasps when I pull my lips away, but she won't be complaining for long. She's going to like where I'm going.

I drop to a knee and grab her soft thighs, spreading her legs even further apart in front of me. Her pussy is so close, filling my nose with its intoxicating scent.

Her body goes tight and rigid as I move in, grazing my stubbled cheek against her inner thigh. One delicious lick, and all of that tightness in her body just melts away.

She drops her head back and moans as I touch my tongue to the bottom of her pussy and slowly drag it up to her hard clit. I flick it with my tongue and her body shivers.

"Oh, Tyler," she moans as I eat her out. "I've wanted this so bad. I've wanted you so bad."

"I know," I say, grinning as I drag the tip of my tongue around her wet opening.

"Fuck you," she says in a raspy voice. Her head is dropped back, her eyes closed, and she's laughing softly. "Arrogant prick."

"I'm trying to concentrate," I say between licks. "You're distracting me with all of this vicious name calling."

"Aren't we sensitive all of a sudden?" she says, gasping as I flick her clit once again with my tongue.

"Speaking of sensitive," I say, wrapping my lips around it. Her back arches, and her legs start trembling as I suck on her clit.

She drops to the desk as I suck on it relentlessly, never easing up on the pressure even when she begs me to.

"Goddamn," she screams, grabbing her tits and tweaking her nipples. I slide a second finger inside her tight little hole as I flick the tip of my tongue across her throbbing clit.

I'm glad that no one is coming into the office until six tomorrow morning because I could do this all night. But the desperate cries coming from her mouth that are getting louder and harder by the second tells me that my time eating her pussy is just about up. She's on the verge of coming.

"Fuck, Tyler," she screams as she thrashes around on my desk. Her legs are trembling as I suck on her clit, pulling her orgasm from her body.

Her legs are resting on my shoulders, her ankles hooked behind my head. She squeezes my ears with her thighs as I ramp up the pace, flicking her clit relentlessly with my tongue.

"Gaawwwdd," she screams as her back arches off of the desk and she comes on my lips. Her sticky pussy juices coat my lips and chin, making me overflow with lust and need.

I can't hold back any longer. I can't take it anymore.

She's still writhing in her orgasm as I stand up and unbuckle my pants. I yank them down and pull out my cock as she moves her head from side to side, trying to catch her breath.

She doesn't see me coming, but she feels it.

"Oh, *fuck!*" she screams as I press the tip of my dick to her tight hole and slowly slide in.

A flood of warmth surges through me as I thrust all the way in, buried to the hilt inside of her. She's so tight. She's so soft. She's so perfect.

Once I feel her tightness engulfing me, I never want to leave. I hold my hard cock inside of her, loving how she squeezes me with warmth.

"See how hard you make me?" I ask, squeezing her knees as I slowly slide back out of her. "I've been this hard since the moment I met you."

She responds with cute little whimpers that get longer and deeper as I fuck her harder and faster. This isn't a slow and soft expression of love, it's a hard and reckless fuck. I've been waiting for this for so long, and I'm not capable of taking it slow right now.

Dahlia is going crazy on the desk in front of me, crying out and thrashing around as I thrust in and out of her at a ferocious pace. My eyes are locked on her big tits as they bounce up and down on her chest, looking fucking spectacular.

It doesn't take long until we're both on the verge of coming. I can feel it building up deep inside of me, about to surge forward at any second.

Our breathing is both ragged and fast, our cries both

desperate and intense. Our bodies are so in tune, like we've done this before, because we have. Even if our minds don't remember a thing, our bodies sure as hell do.

"Uh," Dahlia grunts, with pure agony on her face. "I'm going to come again."

My whole upper body flexes, and I grit my teeth as the tightness builds within me, demanding to be released.

I lean over her until my lips are a breath away from hers. "Come with me," I whisper, locking my eyes on hers. "Come with me *now*."

Her sweet lips part, and a loud cry rips from her mouth as another orgasm consumes her. Mine hits at the exact same moment and I hold onto her as it tears through my body, leaving pure bliss in its wake. She moans as I fill her with my seed, holding my hard cock deep inside of her clenching pussy.

I drop my cheek down on her breasts, holding her tight as I enjoy the amazing feeling coursing through my body.

It's like a taste of heaven. She feels so fucking good, and I can barely handle it. I know if we do this one more time, I'll be hooked forever.

I might already be there.

It's not just about the sex. It's more. A lot more.

I just can't quite figure out what it is yet, and right now I just want to enjoy this beautiful moment.

After a few minutes, I get up and fall out of her. She gasps at as I slip out, holding her legs shut as I pull up my pants.

"What the fuck?" she groans as she sits up on the desk and closes her shirt.

A small part of me dies as she hides her gorgeous breasts from me. I really hope I get to see them again, or the rest of me might die along with it.

She looks stiff and sore as she climbs off the desk and gathers her bra and panties, which are on the other side of the office.

"That was unexpected," she says, taking a deep breath as she rubs her forehead. Her big curly hair looks chaotic around her. I love it. "And probably a bad idea."

My heart nearly stops when her words hit me. *A bad idea?*

"What got into me?" she asks, shaking her head as she quickly steps into her underwear and pulls them up her legs. "This is so unprofessional."

"It's okay," I say softly, watching her as she hurries to the desk. "Nobody is here, and I won't tell."

She yanks her bag off of the desk and starts ramming her papers into it. "I worked so hard to get to this position, and I could have thrown it all away over a quick screw."

A quick screw? Was that all it was to her?

"Dahlia," I say, opening my arms as she finishes stuffing her notes into the bag. "Come on. That was more than just a quick screw."

She shakes her head as she storms across the office to the door. She grabs the handle without looking at me once.

"I'm going to finish the proposal in my hotel room," she says. She looks so pissed—at herself or at me, I can't tell.

"It's after midnight," I say, quickly doing the buttons up on my shirt. "Let me give you a ride back at least."

"I'll grab a cab."

What is going on?

And just like that, she leaves.

18

Dahlia

"How could you have done that? How could you have done that?" I mutter to myself over and over again as I walk to the office in the morning.

I had a deal with myself to treat this as a business arrangement—no feelings and *definitely* no sex.

Well, I broke the no sex part of the deal, but I'm still unsure of where I stand with the whole feelings part.

This is too important to risk screwing up with sex. There's a whole factory, no, a whole town depending on me to do the right thing. I have to stay focused and stay sharp for my friends and neighbors in Summerland. It's the only way.

Mack already warned us about fooling around in his building, and a few hours later I had my panties off, my legs spread, and Tyler's big dick filling me completely.

A warm shiver cascades through me as I think about it.

Fuck, that dick. I can complain about having sex, but I can't complain about the sex. It was definitely the best sex I've ever had. The fucking best.

He made me come twice! Nobody has ever made me come even once before without some assistance from me.

I take a deep breath of the cool morning air and then take a long sip of my warm coffee, trying to get the dirty thoughts out of my mind. It's much too early to be thinking about sex, and I definitely don't want to spend the day walking around in wet panties, so I try to keep Tyler and his big dick out of my mind.

Think of the proposal instead. I close my eyes for a moment as I walk down the sidewalk and imagine Tyler down on one knee with a diamond ring in his hand and a smile on his face. *Not that kind of proposal!*

I shake my head, trying to clear the unwanted images invading my mind. This is a big day for me, and I can't be distracted. Tyler and I worked on the business proposal for the steel factory in Phoenix all night until we got... sidetracked. When I got home, after my cold shower, I finished writing it up, and I'm proud to say that it's damn good.

All of the numbers worked out perfectly, and I even managed to cut an extra four percent from the budget. I can't wait to show it to Mack, and I really can't wait to see Nick's face when Mack approves it.

I'm smiling to myself as I turn the corner on the way to work. There are five cult members standing on a blanket up ahead who are handing out flyers to the businessmen and women walking past them. Well, they're *trying* to hand out flyers, but nobody seems to be taking them.

I can't blame them. The cult members look like freaks with their long yellow robes and bare feet. They're all completely hairless, including the women. They have no eyebrows, no eyelashes, and their heads are shaved down to the skin. They're looking around with big scary smiles plastered on their slightly crazed faces as they try to find someone to take their flyer.

I think of crossing the street to avoid them, but something catches my eye. They are all wearing flower necklaces that look strangely familiar.

Oh, no. I cringe when I recognize it as the same flower necklace that I woke up with after my drunken night with Tyler. It was stuffed in my purse next to the almost empty box of Magnum condoms and the Sunshine Happy Church flyer.

I get chills as I approach them. I have a really bad feeling about this. Tyler and I seemed to have done a lot of wild stuff that night, but even getting a tattoo on my ass won't hold a candle in the wind to joining a crazy cult.

I keep my eyes locked down on the sidewalk as I hurry past them. My stomach is rolling as one of them shoves a flyer in my face.

"Sunshine Happy Church," she says, following me for a few steps. "It all begun with the sun. Come learn about the holy healing power of the Sunshine Happy Church."

"No thanks," I mutter, keeping my eyes on my feet.

She gasps in recognition as she stares at me.

Shit!

"Blessed Prophet?" she says, still following me even after I pick up the pace. "Is that you?"

"Nope," I say, cursing that Lucky 7 drink that started all of this. Someone has to change the name of that drink. It's anything but lucky.

The cult member leaps in front of me and holds out her hands, making me skid to a stop in my heels.

"Blessed Prophet," she says, staring at me in complete

shock. Her eyes are popped out and her mouth is hanging open as she openly stares at me in wonder. "It is you!"

She drops to the ground like a bullet is headed for her head, grabs my ankles, and starts singing softly to them with her head lowered.

"Excuse me," I say, trying to get my legs free but she has an iron grip on them. "I have to get to work."

She raises her head and looks back at her friends. "Blessed Prophet!" she shouts. "It's the blessed Prophet!"

"No blessed Prophet," I say, shaking my head as the other four turn to me. "I'm like the opposite of a blessed Prophet."

Shit. Their eyes pop as wide as the girl at my feet's eyes as they rush over.

I'm going to kill Tyler for this. I don't know how it could be his fault, but it probably is.

"Blessed Prophet! Blessed Prophet!" they all shout as they gather around me, staring at me like I'm some sort of God. *Wait. Do they actually think I'm a God?*

"Uhm," I say with an ache in the back of my throat as several hands begin touching my arms, back, and legs. "I think you have the wrong person."

"Tell us a prophecy," the tallest one asks. "Tell us the future."

The one who is kissing my Kate Spade heels looks up at me. "Tell us we will make it into the center of the sun on our rebirth day?"

"Uhm, sure," I say, wanting to get the hell out of here. These freaks are sending a constant flow of cold chills running down my spine.

The girl smiles like she just won the lottery and returns to shining my shoes with her lips.

"All right," I say, shaking away from them. I slap away a

hand that's clinging onto my skirt and run across the street to the safety of the other side.

Luckily, they don't follow me, but when I turn back all five of them are kneeling on the ground and waving their hands up and down in the air, chanting.

"Freaks," I mutter, rushing down the sidewalk. I don't stop until I'm safely inside McMillan Worldwide Inc.'s corporate office.

I head to the elevators, rehearsing what I'm going to say to Mack when it's time to hand him the proposal when I stop next to a familiar face.

"Dahlia!" Emily says, hugging me. "I was hoping I'd see you here!"

"What are you doing here?" I ask. "I didn't know anyone else from Hospitech was going to be working here."

The elevator bings open, and a bunch of suits fill it up. Emily grabs my arm and pulls me to the side where we can talk in private. I have a few minutes to spare so I go to catch up.

"What's this I hear about you and Mr. McMillan being married?" she asks, staring at me in shock. "Is that true?"

"It is," I say, nodding. I swallow hard before spitting out the next few lies. "We fell in love quickly and decided to get married. We're so happy."

She laughs in my face as she listens, not buying any of it. "But by *fell in love* you mean get really drunk, and by *decided to get married* you mean, you woke up hungover and married. Right?"

I sigh. "Right."

She knows me too well. I forgot that she was in the office with me that morning when I discovered the engagement ring.

"You're staying married?" she asks. "I don't get it."

There's no point in hiding it from her. She's just going to wear me down until I tell her, which she always does, so it would just be easier on both of us to get it out now.

I explain to her about the plans to shut down the Hospitech factory in Summerland and the importance of Tyler getting Mack's position. There's a lot more that I can say—particularly about last night's office shenanigans—but I don't. She doesn't have to know everything.

"So, all of Tyler's family think you two are married?" she asks, giggling to herself. She loves gossip. I have to remember to keep her away from Susan.

"We are married," I say, shaking my head. I still can't believe that part, and saying it out loud always comes with a touch of anxiety.

She just giggles as she watches me. "You two are married like Britney Spears was married to that guy for a day. Oh, my God, are you going to shave your head?"

I cringe as I think back to the woman with the shaved head who was tasting my shoes a few minutes ago. *I really hope not.*

"As far as you're concerned, we are married and we love each other. Okay?"

Emily is trying to hold back her laugh as she nods her head. "Did you two... you know?"

"No," I say quickly but my cheeks are heating up, trying to expose my lie.

She laughs. Like I said, Emily knows me too well.

"So, do you like him?" she asks, leaning against the wall as she stares at me.

I take a deep breath, not knowing how to answer. I don't even know how I feel. Anytime I start to think about Tyler like that, I curse myself and change the subject, focusing on how important it is to the town of Summerland to keep feelings out of this.

"He's okay," I say with a shrug. "But I don't like him like *that*."

So what if my heart seems to swell up in my chest whenever I see him, and so what if I constantly look around for him whenever I'm in the office? And so what if I leave the diamond ring around my neck when I go to bed at night and hold it in my fist as I fall asleep, and so what if I catch myself daydreaming of him living in Summerland with me? None of that means I like him.

Oh, crap. I like him.

"You liar," Emily says, seeing straight through my bullshit. "You're in love with him!"

Now it's my turn to laugh. "No, I'm not," I fire back. "This is just a mutual arrangement so we can both get what we want. We're working together so his father will give him the top spot in the company when he retires. The factory in Summerland is going to be closed if anyone but Tyler gets the position. That's all this is. There's no feelings involved."

"Sure," she says, giggling.

I grit my teeth, wanting to slap the chai mocha cappuccino out of her hands. She knows me better than anyone.

"You know you can do all of that and still be in love with each other," she says, giving me that look. "Love is all you need."

I shake my head and sigh. "My parents had love, and look where it got them. No. A career, stability, that's all you need."

She reaches out and takes a strand of my curly hair, twirling it in her fingers. "Oh, Dahlia," she says sadly. "If only you'd open yourself up to love. The result would surprise you."

"The result would be the factory in Summerland getting shut down," I say with a little more aggressiveness than necessary. Why can't anyone but me see that?

"And what brings you to McMillan Worldwide Inc?" I ask, trying to get the subject off of me and onto her. Luckily for me, Emily loves to talk about herself. It's her favorite subject.

"Mr. McMillan asked me to come," she says, standing proudly. "We met at the Hospitech East Coast office, and he wants to show me around."

"My Mr. McMillan?" I ask, furrowing my brow. "Tyler?"

She grins. "No, not *your* Mr. McMillan. His cousin, Nick. He's so hot!"

"Oh, that guy," I say, gritting my teeth as I think about how nice it would feel to punch him in the nose. "Just be careful with him. He's the one who wants to shut down our factory."

She smiles as we head back to the elevators to get up to work. "When I get my hooks in his hot little ass, he's going to do whatever I want."

I hold my tongue as we squeeze into a crowded elevator.

"Just be careful," I whisper.

She turns to me with a grin. "What fun is that?"

TWO HOURS LATER, and I still haven't seen Tyler. I'm twirling the ring around my neck anxiously as I peek out of the staff break room, hoping to catch a glimpse of him.

I left in such a hurry last night, and we haven't talked since. I hope he's not mad.

I'm still not sure why I left so abruptly. I just kind of freaked out.

A McMillan walks into the break room, but it's not the one I want to see. It's the one I want to watch drown.

"That's what I said," Nick shouts into the Bluetooth clinging to his ear. "The whole department."

I grab an empty coffee cup from the cupboard and rinse it out as I listen, keeping my eyes off of him.

"Nope," he says, shaking his head as he walks over to the fridge beside me. He opens it, pulls out a brown paper lunch bag, looks inside of it, and then shoves it back in. "No. *No* benefits... I don't care what that means."

He pulls out another brown paper bag that has Susan written on it and looks through it. "Then legal will deal with it," he says, looking annoyed as he pulls out a sandwich and throws the bag back into the fridge. He slams it shut and walks over to the coffee pot. "Just get it done!" he shouts before hanging up.

He grabs the coffee pot as he curses under his breath about how all his employees are incompetent and overpaid.

"What department are you closing down now?" I ask, glaring at him.

He turns to me, acting like this is the first time he's noticed me in the small empty kitchenette of the break room.

He looks me up and down and laughs. "You're on a need to know basis," he says, moving his arms as he talks. What little remains of the coffee is sloshing around the bottom of the pot.

I grin as I turn and stare him down. "I need to know because I'm going to be running the company soon."

He bursts out laughing.

"What's so funny?" I ask, crossing my arms as I stare him down with my no-fucking-around face on. "I wouldn't be laughing at my future boss. Especially with a stolen sandwich in my hand."

He looks down at Susan's sandwich in his hand and grins. "Everything in this office is mine," he says, smirking at me. "Even your friend's tight little ass."

As if on cue, Emily comes skipping into the room. "I'm ready for you," she says, shooting me a quick smile before focusing all of her flirty attention on Nick. "I did everything like you asked."

Her hands are folded in front of her as she looks at him with sparkling eyes. She has her chest thrust out, and she's biting her bottom lip. She's interested. *Shit.*

I want to puke as he smiles back at her. "Perfect. Go get comfortable in my office, and I'll show you what I really want you to do when I get back."

Her eyes dart up and down his body as she grins. "I can't wait."

She flicks her hair as she spins around, skipping back out of the office. His eyes are on her ass, blatantly staring until she disappears out the door.

"Nice to see you're making *fuck* friends around the office," I say, rolling my eyes.

Nick laughs. "*You* should talk."

My cheeks heat up as I turn to him, but it's not out of embarrassment. It's out of anger.

"What?" I ask, giving him a stare that would send the Grim Reaper fleeing in terror.

He laughs, clearly proud of himself that he got under my skin.

"We all know the only reason you're here is because you make a nice dick warmer for my cousin. Something for him to fuck in between his massive office screw-ups. Otherwise, why the hell would my uncle let a *glorified* assistant like you into our executive meetings?"

My body tenses as heat flushes through my body. I've worked way too hard in my career to get accused of favoritism and unfair family treatment, especially from a sandwich-stealing asshole like Nick.

I raise my chin as I glare at him with my nostrils flaring. "The only thing this *glorified* assistant fucked was your shitty proposal in the meeting yesterday."

He grins in amusement as he watches me. "I can see why my cousin likes you," he says with a laugh. "You two are perfect for each other. But just remember, I am the master of this place and have eyes and ears all—"

"Wait, what?" I say, interrupting him.

His shoulders slump down in disappointment as he sighs. "You ruined my evil speech."

"Why do you think we're perfect for each other?" I ask. Normally I wouldn't care what he thinks, but I have to know. Nick has known Tyler his whole life and maybe he's seeing something that I'm not.

He rolls his eyes. "Because you're both idiots who are horrible at business. So just remember, I am the master of this place and have eyes and—"

"That's not what you were thinking," I say, interrupting his evil speech once again. "Why do you think we're perfect for each other?"

He huffs out a frustrated breath. "I can see it by the way he looks at you."

My breath catches in my throat as I stare at him with my heart pounding. "How does he look at me?"

He rolls his eyes. "Like he's happy he finally found you."

Awwwww. I wonder if he can see my heart swelling up in my chest.

His eyes harden once again as he glares at me. "But just remember, I am the master of this place, and have eyes and ears all over the—"

This time it's Susan who interrupts him as she walks in and heads to the fridge. His face looks panicked as he watches her with her stolen sandwich hidden behind his back.

"Again!" she shouts when she looks into her lunch bag. "Who the hell keeps stealing my sandwiches?"

She throws her bag back into the fridge and slams the door closed, breathing heavily as she stares at us with an angry tightness in her eyes.

"Not sure," I say, grinning at Nick as I head for the door. "Maybe Nick has some answers hiding behind his back."

Susan rolls up her sleeves as she charges at him, trying to look behind his back. He turns and spins, trying to keep her from seeing it, but she looks relentless, pissed off, hungry, and determined to see what he's hiding behind his back.

I laugh to myself as I sneak out of the break room and into the hall.

Nick's words replay in my head as I head straight for Tyler's office. *Tyler likes me. We're perfect for each other. He looks at me like he's happy he finally found me.*

Those dangerous words leave me lightheaded and dizzy with a big stupid grin on my face.

But that all fades when I think back to what's on the line. I have to stay focused. I have to stay professional.

Tyler and I can be friends and that's it. No more flirting. No more sex.

And that's exactly what I'm going to tell him now.

I just hope he's not looking as hot as he was yesterday.

19

Dahlia

I EXPECT it to be awkward when I see Tyler for the first time since we've had sex, but surprisingly it's not.

"Good morning, Mrs. McMillan," he says as I walk into his office.

My heart jumps in my chest as it always does when I see Tyler in a new outfit. It seems impossible, but every outfit he wears makes him look hotter than the last. Today he's wearing a light gray suit with a fitted white shirt and a bright green tie. His jacket is folded and draped over one of the chairs in front of his desk, and my eyes are thankful that it is. He looks absolutely gorgeous sitting behind his monstrous desk with his tight sleeves rolled up his thick tattooed forearms. The bottom of his pen is pressed to his lips, looking seductive as he fucks me with his eyes while I close the door.

I immediately flash back to last night when I was lying

on that very desk with my legs in the air as he slid his big cock inside me. Arousal swirls through me, settling in my now wet panties.

Ugh. This is not the time or place to be aroused—although my body never listens. To my frustrating body, any place with Tyler is a place to be aroused.

"Good morning," I say, feeling shy as I look at him. I don't want to talk about sex at work, but last night needs to be addressed. It's better to treat it like a band-aid and rip it right off. "About last night..."

"Last night?" he says, tilting his head as he looks at me with confused eyes. He's not going to make this easy on me.

"Yes. *Last night*," I say with my eyebrows raised.

"Oh," he says, feigning like he finally understands what I'm talking about. "You mean the hot sex on the desk."

I narrow my eyes on him. "Did I say the sex was hot? It was mediocre at best."

"You did come twice," he says, smirking at me. "So, I assumed..."

"You know what happens when you *assume*," I say, ignoring the comment about my double orgasm. "You make an *ass* of *you* and *me*."

He smirks. "Or in your case. *You* have *me* tattooed on your *ass*."

"Don't remind me," I say, rolling my eyes, "or we're going to have lunch at the tattoo shop so you can get my name tattooed on your ass."

"I'd like something of yours on my ass, but it's not your name," he says, giving me that sexy smile. The frustrating one that usually makes my neck and cheeks turn red.

"Why did you run off last night?" he asks as I sit down with butterflies in my stomach. "I'm usually the one who is running out the door after. That's twice you've done that to me, and I have to say, it doesn't feel very good."

"The player got played," I say, giving him a smug, satisfied smile. "I hope you learned your lesson."

"The player is married and has hung up his jersey," he answers, leaning back in his chair. "I thought you of all people would have known that, Mrs. McMillan."

I swallow hard as I glance over at his massive chest straining against his fitted shirt. He has a shiny green tie on that matches his beautiful eyes, making them pop even more than usual. His biceps look huge under his shirt, and for some reason, I just really want to wrap my hands around them.

I shake my head, trying to clear it and focus on anything other than his piercing eyes or chiseled body. "I gave the business proposal to your father," I say, staring at the plant behind him.

"And?"

"He said he was going to read it tonight."

Tyler rolls his chair in front of the plant so that he's back in my view. "Then it looks like you have nothing left to do for the rest of the day," he says, grinning. It's my last week in Las Vegas and my last day in the office. I'm headed back to Summerland on the first flight out of here tomorrow morning. I still don't know how I feel about that.

Originally, we had planned to pretend that we're married by choice this week until I head back home. We were going to keep up the charade from a distance until Tyler got the company, and then we would announce that we decided to split up. He would go his way, and I would go mine.

That makes this our last day of being together in person. I should be happy and relieved, but I'm sad and dreading it.

I kind of like having him around, even though he's as frustrating as trying to open a tiny milk carton with greasy fingers.

"I'll have to think of something to keep you busy *all* afternoon," he says, looking up as he taps his sexy lips with his pen. He looks under his desk and grins. "Do you think you can fit under here?"

My pulse starts racing as I picture dropping to my knees under his desk and pulling out that big thick cock. That's definitely how I would like to spend my last afternoon, but thoughts like this are definitely not helpful.

"That's the best you can come up with?" I ask, crossing my arms and pretending like I'm not interested.

He smiles as he reaches down and pulls open his bottom drawer. "If you want to get kinky," he says, pulling out the whip and ball gag, and dropping them on the desk in between us, "we can still try these out before you go."

"Why are those still here?" I say, shaking my head as I stare down at them. "Can you please throw them out?"

"No way. They're mementos from our wedding night."

I narrow my eyes as I glare at him. "I didn't peg you for the sentimental type."

"And I didn't peg you for someone who would run out after sex," he says, staring back at me.

His words linger in the air between us as we stare each other down.

He takes a deep breath and smiles. "I like you, Dahlia."

I jerk my head back in surprise. "What?"

His smile nearly makes me melt. "Why do you look so surprised? We did have sex a few hours ago."

"I know," I say, narrowing my eyes at him once again.

"Right here."

"I know!"

"On this desk," he says, grinning as he taps it.

"*Tyler*," I warn. I no longer want to talk about this.

He leans back in his chair, looking at me with a cocky smile on his lips. "And I think you like me too."

I laugh. "Just because I have your name tattooed on my ass, doesn't mean I like you. In fact, it means the opposite. This way you can kiss my ass for all eternity."

He stands up slowly and grins at me as he walks around his desk. I gulp as I stare at his swiveling chair, hoping I'll be able to control myself. My heart speeds up as he sits on the desk in front of me, looking down with his impossibly bright green eyes.

I close my eyes and start thinking of unsexy things. *Used Q-Tips. Maggots. My parent's dirty laundry. Old men eating chocolate pudding.*

Nothing seems to be working. His delicious cologne is hitting my nose and overriding my thoughts like a computer virus.

"I'm going to miss you," he says softly.

I try to force my eyes to stay on the empty chair, but they're not taking orders from me anymore. They belong to my sexy boss who's sitting on the desk in front of me.

"I'm sorry," I say, staring up at him in disbelief. "I thought you said that you're going to miss me."

He chuckles before hopping off the desk and kneeling in front of me so that our eyes are level. Warm shivers rip through me with his intense eyes on me like this. "If you tell me you regret last night, I'll never bother you again, but I want you to think very carefully before you answer."

I swallow hard as I squirm in my chair. *Oh, no. He's going to make me talk about my feelings.*

"I had a great time with you last night," he says, placing

his hand on mine. "I want to see you again. I want to do *that* again. Do you?"

I take a deep breath before raising my chin as I answer. "Sure. We can work on business proposals together whenever you want."

"Sounds great," he says with a sexy smile. Before I can react, he moves in and gives me a soft kiss on the lips. I moan as his silky tongue slides past my tingling lips and into my mouth. It feels so good that all I can think about is staying in this kiss forever.

But unfortunately, before I'm ready to let go, he pulls away.

He leans back and looks at my dazed face with a smile. "I thought so."

"You thought nothing," I say, catching myself as he stands up and walks to the door. He clicks the lock closed and walks back over with heat in his eyes.

"Why are you locking the door?" I ask. My brain is hoping that I'm reading his body language wrong, but my pussy is more excited than ever, getting as slick as a water slide in a rainstorm.

"I want to continue what we started last night," he says, loosening his tie as he sits on the desk in front of me.

I stand up, and when I do I'm in between his legs, inches from his face. "Great," I say with my skin tingling. "I'll continue where we finished last night. With me walking out the door."

His hand darts out and grabs my wrist, holding me in place.

"If you leave now," he warns. "That's it. We'll stick to the plan, and you'll never see my big cock again."

I stand my ground, glaring at him as my head fills with betraying thoughts. I want to see him again, and I definitely want to see his big cock again, but it's too much to risk. It's too selfish to consider.

"But if you stay," he whispers, slowly looking me up and down. My nipples harden as his eyes roam over my breasts. "You and my big cock can get reacquainted."

The ball gag is lying on the desk, just waiting to be used. If he wants to try it out, then I'm happy to oblige.

"You talk too much," I say, grabbing it and stuffing the ball into his mouth. His eyes are smiling with laughter as I tie it around his head and secure it in place.

I grin as I lean back and look at him. *Damn it.* He still looks sexy with it on.

"That's much better," I say with a smirk. "You were saying?"

"Roo rawnt muy beag kawk," he answers, only able to speak in vowels with the ball gag in his mouth.

"Thank you for the compliment," I say, nodding at him. "I agree. I am much better at business than you are."

His eyes are locked on mine, and the air between us is thick with tension and electricity. My mind wants to leave, but my body is on the same horny page as him. My chest is fluttering, my fingers tingling with the need to touch him, and my pussy is getting wetter by the second.

I take a deep breath, trying to calm my excitement as I step back from him.

His hand darts out once again and grabs my wrist. Every tiny hair on my arm stands up in response to his touch. Each strand is standing straight up and leaning toward his hand like they are all trying to get as close to him as possible.

My eyes close, and my breathing stops as he gently pulls my hand to his cock. I let out an involuntary gasp as he presses my palm against his hard erection. It feels so big as my palm drags up and down his thick shaft. I'm not sure if it's Tyler or me who's moving my hand up and down his impressive length, but I don't really care anymore. It feels too good to stop.

He releases my wrist, but my hand doesn't stop moving. I'm breathing heavily as I focus on his rich masculine scent and the big cock that's getting harder and thicker with every stroke.

Tyler unbuckles his pants and pulls them down, and before I can call him a pig or a pervert, I'm dropping to my knees and opening up wide.

A deep moan escapes my lips when he pulls his big cock out in front of my face. Long. Hard. Gorgeous. I've tried to ignore it, but I've been thinking about his dick ever since I saw it that first morning together.

My hands are shaking as I reach up and grab it. It feels even thicker in my hands, and my pussy clenches as I wrap my fingers around it.

"Fraccck," he groans, still unable to talk properly with the ball gag in his mouth.

I laugh to myself as I lick my palm and then run my hand up and down his length with slow and steady strokes. His grip tightens on the desk until his knuckles are white and he's breathing heavily.

"If you tell anyone about this, I'll kill you," I say before opening wide and taking him in my mouth.

We both moan as I wrap my lips around him, tasting the delicious drop of pre-cum on my tongue. It's salty and sweet, and I want more of it, so I get to work.

I swirl my tongue around his shaft, as I take him in deeper, sucking his cock with an eagerness that surprises me. His strong hands sink into my hair and guide my head up and down his length. I'm forced to open wider the deeper he goes, but I'm loving every second of this.

I didn't realize how much I've been wanting this until now, and I'm still not sure what it all means.

I'm in heaven as I reach up under his shirt and feel his warm hard abs under my fingertips. His moans and groans are coming out deeper and stronger as I coat every inch of him with my tongue.

His hands find my breasts and begin unbuttoning my shirt as my nipples become painfully hard behind my bra.

It's only when he frees my breasts that I snap out of my trance and remember where we are. I whip my head around to the door and take a breath of relief when I see the lock firmly in place. We're at work. Mack McMillan is down the hall.

There are people all around us, and I have Tyler's dick in my mouth. Have I lost my mind?

I shake my head, trying to clear the dangerously dirty thoughts that have taken it over, and lean back. His hands fall away from my breasts, and he looks down at me in shock, looking ridiculous with the ball gag still in his mouth.

"Tyler this is crazy," I say as I tuck my breasts back into my bra, and quickly start buttoning up my shirt. "We're at work!"

He shakes his head as he wraps his hand around my arm and pulls me into him. He's so strong, pulling me easily—not that I'm fighting to pull away or anything.

My hand falls back onto his cock and I start stroking it as we're eye-to-eye. "We shouldn't be doing this," I say, leaning into him. I want to be strong. I want to back away and go hide in my office, but I can't stop touching his dick. I can't stop wanting it inside of me.

He moans softly as he reaches down and slides his hand up under my skirt. I swallow hard as his fingers graze over my aching pussy, and it's then that I realize I'm not going anywhere until I get fucked.

He peels my wet underwear to the side and glides his fingers through my soaking wet folds, making my legs tremble. My mouth drops open, but no sound comes out as he slides a finger inside my hole while pressing the heel of his palm against my throbbing clit.

"Fuck, Tyler," I whisper as I dig my fingernails into his muscular arm. "This is a bad idea."

But everything about it feels so good as he adds a second finger inside of me, making me moan.

I place a hand on his hard chest and try to push away but he's not letting me go. His fingers are rooted deep inside of me, and they're not going anywhere.

"We should stop," I moan, hoping more than anything that he doesn't stop. This feels too fucking good.

My body trembles with each curl of his fingers, and it melts with every press of his palm against my clit. It doesn't take long until my body is leaning on his as my focus switches entirely to his fingers inside me.

His hot breath tickles my neck as I struggle to stand up on shaky legs. I grind my hips to the rhythm of his fingers until I'm riding his hand with his deep skillful strokes pushing me closer to orgasm.

I open my mouth to tell him to stop but I can't talk. I can't breathe. I can't focus on anything but his hand.

I close my eyes, feeling an orgasm coming, feeling it burning through me. I grip his forearm, digging my fingernails into his tattooed skin as I wait for the release.

But it never comes.

Tyler slides his hand out from between my legs, leaving my pussy burning.

"Wha—" I whine, looking up at him in confusion.

His eyes are smiling as he stands up and takes my wrist. He brings me to the other side of his desk and points to it. "Brend rover," he says, gripping his cock.

I immediately do as he says, hiking my skirt up to my waist as I bend over the desk, anxiously waiting for him to slide inside me.

My cheek is pressed against the cold wood as I thrust my ass in the air, desperately waiting for him.

He drags the tip of his cock through my folds and I let out a deep moan as warm shivers rip through me. "Stick it in," I beg. "*Please.*"

He chuckles as he reaches past me and grabs the whip. I gasp as he lightly touches it to the bare skin of my ass, making me even wetter.

My heart is pounding, my mouth wet with anticipation as he brings the whip back and gently smacks it against my ass. I let out a small whimper as I feel the light sting, which only heightens my want. It only amplifies my need.

"Roo rwont it huardar?" he asks, tickling my skin with the leather tassels.

I nod as I close my eyes. I'm breathless. Completely consumed in the moment.

He smacks me harder, and I let out a loud whimper.

This is crazy. I'm at work.

I don't do these things. I don't play these games.

Tyler whips me a few more times until my ass is stinging but for some unknown reason, it just makes me wetter.

"Fuck me, Tyler," I beg, thrusting my ass up for him. I want him to take me. I need him to fuck me.

"Wron moar," he grunts, bringing the whip back.

Out of nowhere, the lock on the door clicks and my eyes whip up to it just in time to see it open. *No!* My heart nearly stops as the door handle turns, and the door swings open.

There's no time to react. There's no time to move.

All we can do is stand there helplessly as Mack and Nick barge into the office. They both skid to a stop when they see Tyler with the ball gag in his mouth, whipping his almost naked wife who's bent over his desk with her bare ass in the air.

Nick is grinning. Mack is standing there in shock.

I hear Tyler swallow hard behind me. "Roops."

Roops is fucking right.

Brother Solarion

THE NIGHT...

"BREATHE IN SLOWLY," I say softly as I look at all of the peaceful faces looking back at me. "One, two, three. Three, two, one."

Every one of my beautiful brothers and sisters follows my words as I guide them through our nightly chants. All twenty-six members of the Sunshine Happy Church are giving over to the bliss, giving their souls over to the Sun Gods whom we worship.

The soft instrumental music is playing in the background as we all focus on our breathing, letting the lingering light from the sun fill up our souls in the most beautiful way. The sun gives life. It is our savior, but it is the

Gods of fire who live inside the bright star who we are letting into our hearts.

"Open your minds," I sing softly, swaying as I sit on the floor with my legs crossed. "Open your hearts and let the Gods of light enter your bodies to purify your souls."

My twenty-six brothers and sisters are sitting crossed-legged in front of me, swaying from side to side as they let my holy words penetrate them.

We are the true believers, the only ones on the planet who know the truth. The Gods of fire, Franesca and Lukania, live in the center of the sun and are waiting to take the true believers back to an eternity of bliss and pleasure where we belong.

When the day of reckoning comes, the non-believers will perish in horrible ice as we will be warming our feet with the eternal flames alongside the only true Gods.

"One day the Prophets will come," I whisper as we breathe slowly, in and out, in and out. "The Gods of fire, Franesca and Lukania will send them with a message. They will tell us how to reach the center of the flaming star. And when we follow their holy instructions, the day will come when we will ascend from this planet of cold and hate into the warmth of the center of the sun."

"We bask in the light of Solaris," they all chant as one.

"We must do what we can to save others," I whisper, looking around the rooms. My brothers and sisters are devoted and hardworking. They have donated all of their money and worldly possessions to the Sunshine Happy Church, and they have recited the vows. They have shaved their bodies of every last hair, which is necessary to enter the heavenly ball of fire. But we must do more. When the Prophets come, and they will, all of the non-believers will perish. We must save as many of them as we can. Every soul who enters Solaris will please Franesca and Lukania, the only true Gods.

"There are boxes of flyers by the door," I whisper to my family. "We must reach more people. We must try to save their souls, because that is what Franesca and Lukania demand."

"We bask in the light of Solaris," they all chant as one.

"Sunshine Happy Church is our new family," I whisper. "Our old families laugh and criticize the Church, saying we believe in false Gods, but if they only kne—"

The door explodes open, upsetting the peacefulness of the room. All calm eyes open abruptly and dart to the two non-believers who are bursting into the room, making a mockery of our Holy Church.

"Aliens!" the female non-believer says, pointing at my brothers and sisters.

"I know this place!" the male says as he looks around. "You rub their bald heads for good luck."

The male and female rush around the room, rubbing the heads of each of the true believers.

"Excuse me!" I shout, but they do not listen. They do not stop until they've touched every shaved holy head.

Their clothes are wet and torn, their eyes are wide open like bugs. Their arms are shaking, and they can't seem to hold their attention on anything for longer than three seconds.

"Look!" the girl says, pointing to our large statue of the sun in the corner of the room. "It's an Easter egg!"

My brothers and sisters are all looking to me for guidance as the two non-believers rush over to our Holy relic, pawing it with their sinister hands.

"Break it open!" the girl says, pointing to it. "I want chocolate!"

"Do *not* break it!" I shout as I stand up.

They turn and look at me, seeing me for the first time. "I know you," the female says, staring at me. "You're one of the guys in the Blue Man Group, but you peeled your blue skin off."

Her words pass through me as I'm seized with awe. The shock of seeing them hits me like a solar flare. *It can't be!*

But it is.

A gasp tears from my throat as I fall to my knees in front of them, staring up at the two Prophets with a heavy feeling in my stomach but with a floating feeling in my heart.

They are the true Prophets.

I'm surprised they have hair, but who am I to question the Gods?

They have the other sign of the Prophets: wet clothes.

I stare up at them in shock as my heart races. Their clothes are wet from the waters of Franesca and Lukania. They doused them with water so they could pass through the surface of the sun without getting burned to deliver the Holy message to us.

This is the moment we've all been waiting for. This is the moment we've given up everything for. And it is more beautiful than I can imagine.

"Is there chocolate in here, Mr. Blue Man Group?" the female Prophet asks me.

The warmth of the sun radiates through my trembling body as she speaks to me. *The Prophet is speaking directly to me!*

It's too much to handle. I drop to the floor and bow, raising my hands up and down in a show of worship. My twenty-six brothers and sisters drop to the floor as well, chanting together now that they've recognized the male and female as the true Prophets.

They will tell us how to reach heavenly Solaris so we can spend all eternity with Franesca and Lukania in the center of the sun. They will tell us the steps we have to take to get there.

The male punches his powerful fist through the statue of the sun, and every last one of us cheers in excitement.

"Yes!" I shout as he pulls his hand out of the hollow statue. "That is where we want to go. Into the sun like your fist. Please, blessed Prophets, please tell us how to get to Solaris."

"Do they have chocolate there?" the female asks.

My sister Solarip stands up and takes a flyer from the box. She slowly walks up to the female Prophet with her eyes on the floor.

"Praise Franesca and Lukania," Solarip says, handing the Prophet a flyer. When the Prophet takes it and shoves it in her purse, Solarip takes off her flower necklace and places it over the Prophet's head.

"We bask in the light of Solaris," my brother and sister believers all chant as one.

We all cheer and cry, hugging each other in pure happiness as the blessed moment has finally come.

The male Prophet breaks off a piece of the statue, puts it in his mouth, and then spits it out. "This is not chocolate," he says.

It is better than chocolate. This is the moment. It's pure bliss.

I turn and hug a sister and then a brother as happiness fills every cell in my body. I am going to the promised land. I am going to Solaris!

After hugging each member of the Sunshine Happy Church, I turn back to the Prophets so they can tell us the path to eternal life. The path to Solaris.

I gasp when I don't see them. "Where did they go?"

The door is wide open, and they are gone. A thousand questions fill my head as everyone looks to me for guidance.

Are they coming back? Why would the fire Gods Franesca and Lukania send the Prophets only to take them away before telling us the true path?

I swallow hard as I stare at the open door.

We have to find them. It is our only way into the center of the sun where we can bask in Solaris for all of eternity with the two true Gods, Franesca and Lukania.

They are the path to get there. They are the path to endless bliss.

And we won't stop until we find them.

21

Dahlia

EVERYTHING LOOKS THE SAME, but it feels different.

"Hi, Dahlia!" Martha says, waving as I bike past her bakery. "How was Vegas?"

"Interesting," I say, cringing as I pedal past her.

"Come back on your lunch break. I want to hear all about it," she says, tapping the ashes from her cigarette as I hurry down the street. "The coffee is on me!"

I wave to her as I keep biking through the town of Summerland, breathing in the cool morning air on my way to work.

What part does she want to hear? The part where I got married to a stranger, or the part where I got caught by my boss and father-in-law having sex with that same stranger at work?

She probably wants to hear it all, but I definitely don't need that story getting out around town. I'm taking that one to my grave.

I close my eyes and shake my head as I pass the small diner where Audrey is writing down the daily specials in chalk on a blackboard.

"Hi, Dahlia," she says, smiling at me.

I say hi back to her, but I don't stop. I don't feel like talking to anyone this morning.

It's my first day back at work in Summerland, and I should be happy and relieved to be home, but I'm not. The familiar town that I love feels different.

Maybe it feels different because I'm different now.

Or maybe I'm just upset.

I turn onto Blueberry Lane, waving to John who's walking down the sidewalk as I head to work.

There's a heaviness in my chest as I pedal down the beautiful streets, ducking my head as I roll under the huge maple tree on Lou and Cynthia's front lawn.

He never came to say goodbye.

It still hurts.

Yes, it was humiliating to get caught by his cousin and his father, and yes, we weren't married by choice, but we had still been through a lot together, and he should have come to say goodbye.

But he didn't.

I usually look around, enjoying the beautiful view as I bike to work, but today I'm just looking forward with an empty stare. I didn't realize how much I liked having Tyler around until now. And now it's too late.

He's not going to want me around after what happened.

I still cringe every time I think about it. Tyler and I sitting in front of Mack's desk with our eyes in our laps while he tore us a new one. I'll never forget sitting there with no panties on, my inner thighs sticky wet, the taste of Tyler's come still coating my mouth, all while the head of the company I work for blasted us for being immature, sexual freaks.

I can't imagine what he must have been thinking when he walked in and saw his son with a ball gag strapped to his mouth, whipping his half naked wife with a whip in the office that he built from the ground up.

My knuckles turn white as I squeeze my handlebars, thinking of Nick and the satisfied smirk on his face as he watched us trying to explain what we were doing while we got dressed in a panic.

He had a key to Tyler's office. He was the one who opened the door hoping to find us in a compromising situation, and he hit the fucking jackpot.

After chewing us out for half an hour, Mack told us both that we would be fired if it ever happened again. He then turned to Tyler and told him that he just used up his last chance. If Tyler did one more thing to displease him at work, he'd be out of the running for the top position at McMillan Worldwide Inc.

I left the office shortly after that and just hung around in my hotel room feeling sorry for myself, waiting for the phone to ring. It was my last night in Vegas, and I was hoping Tyler would come over for some support. Some comfort.

Some anything.

But the phone never rang. The door was silent.

He never came.

I got on my plane the next morning, and here I am, back in the town that I love, which now feels strangely empty and distant.

The factory comes into view as I turn down Foresthill street on my old bike. I returned the Ferrari to the dealership before I left and had the money refunded to Tyler's account.

It was impractical anyway, and I just couldn't keep it after what happened.

And what can I say? I love my bike.

"Hey, boss!" the security guard, Michael, says, coming out of the booth as I approach. He has a big smile on his face as I skid to a stop in front of him. "How was Sin City?" he asks with a grin as I step off my bike. "I know, I know. What happens in Vegas stays in Vegas."

I wish that was true, but unfortunately the tattoo on my ass refused to stay on the West Coast.

"That's right," I say, forcing out a smile as he takes my bike and places it on the bike rack for me. "Anything happen while I was gone?"

Michael shrugs. "Nothing but a pesky raccoon who keeps trying to get into the garbage cans."

I smile. Nothing ever happens in Summerland. Just the way I like it.

We wish each other a good day, and I join the line of workers who are walking into the factory. The huge Hospitech sign has been taken down over the entrance and has been replaced with a shiny new sign that says McMillan Worldwide Inc.

I keep my head low and my shoulders up as I take the stairs up to my office. I'm still upset at how the Vegas trip ended, and I don't really feel like having fifteen hundred and ninety-two people asking me how it went. I just want to sneak into my office, lock the door, and get back to work while I still have a job to get back to work on.

With Tyler likely out of the running for Mack's promotion, this factory will probably get closed down, and I'll probably be let go along with it.

I take a deep breath as I arrive at my office and pull out my key. I stick it in the lock, but the door is already open. *That's weird.*

"Good morning, Mrs. McMillan," a familiar voice says as I swing the door open.

I jump back, swallowing a scream as I see Tyler sitting in my chair with his feet on my desk. It takes a second for my confusion to dissipate, but when it does I'm smiling like a crazy person.

"What are you doing here?" I ask, staring at him in shock.

He smiles as he takes his feet off my desk and stands up. "I came to see my beautiful wife," he says, looking ravishing in a dark fitted suit.

I tilt my head and raise an eyebrow as I narrow my eyes on him. "Great. And what's the real reason?"

"You kept raving about Summerland, so I decided to come have a little visit."

"And?"

He nods as he walks to the window and looks out. "It's cute. I can see why you like it."

My heart starts pounding as I slowly walk over to him and look out the window as well. The workers are still pouring into the factory, holding their coffee thermoses and lunch boxes.

"So, are you here on vacation?" I ask, watching him from the corner of my eye. He's wearing a black suit with a gray tie, looking gorgeous as usual. He's beautiful by Vegas standards, but in Summerland, he's a full-blown God.

"Business," he says, turning to me with a smile. "And of course, to see you. You really came through for me last week, and I appreciate it, even though it didn't work out quite as we had planned."

"Is your father still mad?"

He laughs. "Furious."

I close my eyes, wanting to die of embarrassment.

But Tyler just laughs. "It's not the first time he's caught me having sex. The first time was in grade ten with Rebecca Forrester. He got over that time, he'll get over this time too."

"But the promotion?"

"We'll see what happens," he says with a sigh. "But it's not looking good."

"I'm sorry," I say, feeling awful.

He shrugs. "It was my idea," he says, looking back out the window. "We should have stayed professional like you wanted to."

I decide not to remind him that it was me who put the ball gag in his mouth and strapped it to his head.

"So, what are you doing here?" I ask, feeling my stomach harden. "Closing the factory?"

He shakes his head. "Not exactly. I'm here to live up to my side of the deal. You went along with everything back in Vegas, so now I'm here to help you find a way to save the factory. Plus, it seemed like a really good idea to lay low and stay away from my father for a few days."

"A few days?" I ask, feeling my pulse start to race. Tyler is going to be here for *a few days?*

"What ten-star hotel are you staying at in Summerland?" I ask with a laugh. There are zero hotels within an hour's drive from here.

He smiles as he looks down at me. "Aunt Wilma's Inn."

"Oh," I say, laughing at him. "Fancy. She makes delicious crumpets, but I've heard there's no hot water past seven a.m."

"Good to know," he says with a nod. "Thanks."

The thought of Tyler staying at a place like Aunt Wilma's

Inn keeps making me giggle. I keep wondering how he likes the dusty flowered curtains and the small bathrooms with the separate faucets, one for hot and one for cold. If I was out of my element in Vegas, he is definitely out of his element here in Summerland.

"Come," I say, hooking my arm around his. "I'll show you around."

"Please do," he says, following me with a grin. "I want to see where my wife is from."

"You expect me to ride on that?" Tyler asks, staring at my bike.

"What's the problem?" I ask with a laugh as I ring the bell on the handlebars. After spending the day touring the factory, introducing Tyler to the workers, and unsuccessfully trying to find a financial solution that would allow the factory to stay open, I'm taking him back to Aunt Wilma's Inn. And we're taking my bike.

"The problem is I buy you a half-million-dollar car and you expect me to ride on a rusty old bike," he says, crossing his arms as he stares at my beloved bike with an unamused look on his face.

"You mean Lightning over here?" I ask, slapping the seat. "She's reliable *and* sturdy."

"So is a Ferrari."

My cheeks turn a guilty red as I look away.

"I got a call from the dealership," he says, tilting his head as he stares at me. "Why did you return it?"

I sigh. "It was too much, Tyler. And I couldn't replace poor Lightning like that? She would have been devastated."

He rolls his eyes and laughs. "Rainbow and Lightning," he whispers to himself, clearly amused. "She's a tad rusty."

I shrug my shoulders as I get up on her. "Perhaps she could use an upgrade, but I like to ride around town on a bike. I'm not a Ferrari kind of gal."

"All right," he says, dropping his arms to his sides. "I have to try out this bike that rides better than a half-million-dollar Ferrari."

I grin as I scooch forward. "Then hop on."

He's looking at me in shock. "I don't get to drive it?"

I shake my head. "Nobody drives Lightning but me. You couldn't handle her."

He smiles as he climbs on the back, sitting on the long seat as I stand up. "She's not the only one I can't handle," he whispers as I start pedaling.

I take him on a tour of the town and he seems to love it. We ride through the huge park in town, riding around the lake where the kids are feeding the swans and past the volleyball courts where the factory's janitors are taking on the factory's marketing department in a competitive game of beach volleyball.

"This is the opposite of Vegas," Tyler says as we head down the main street past the mom-and-pop Hardware store and the old firehouse, which is now a cute little library.

"I know," I say, smiling at the complete lack of obnoxious blinking lights. "Isn't it great?"

Tyler doesn't answer, but I can tell he likes it. He keeps looking around and pointing at the old Victorian architecture, the kids playing street hockey, and the neighbors who are out on their lawns actually talking to each other.

"I can see why you like it so much," he says when we pull into town and take a break. My legs are killing from pedaling for so long with his huge body on the back.

"It's worth trying to save," I say as I rest my bike on a large maple tree. "And you haven't even experienced the best part of Summerland."

He looks right at me and smiles. "I think I'm experiencing it right now."

I grab his hand and pull him down the cobblestone sidewalk. "I'm talking about Lou's submarines. They're absolutely phenomenal."

"What about your bike?" Tyler says, looking back over his shoulder. "Don't you have to lock it up?"

I chuckle. "Not in Summerland."

We walk over to Lou's submarine shop, and I order two large subs with everything on them and two root beers to go.

Tyler insists on paying since I did all of the pedaling, and I'm not about to argue about that. We walk to a nice bench under a beautiful weeping willow tree and sit down to eat our sloppy but delicious dinners.

"Wow," he says, staring at me with wide eyes after he takes the first bite. "Incredible."

"I know, right?" I say through a mouthful of chewed-up food. This is my favorite dinner in the world, and it tastes even better with Tyler by my side.

We sit in a comfortable silence as we eat and watch the people casually walking around with a relaxed vibe that only a small town like Summerland can provide. I'm surprised how nice and natural it feels to have Tyler sitting here with me in my town. It feels even more homey than usual.

"What happened to your parents?" he asks as he crumples up the wrapping after he's finished his sub.

"They probably took off to God knows where again without saying goodbye," I say, taking a deep breath. "If you're looking for your six-hundred-dollar investment, I'm afraid it's blown up in smoke."

He laughs. "That's what I was expecting."

"I'm sorry again about them," I say, feeling embarrassed like I always do when I think of my parents.

Tyler shakes his head. "Sorry for what? They're super cute together. After all this time, all they need is each other. You can tell how absolutely in love they are."

I take my last bite as I watch an elderly couple in the distance, shuffling through the park. My parents never needed careers or a fancy house or expensive cars. All they needed was each other. All they needed was love.

I crunch up the brown paper bag and toss it in the garbage. *And they left me to do everything else.*

"All right," I say, pushing the thoughts of my parents out of my head. "Your tour is almost finished. My legs are starting to get tired."

"I can drive."

"No way," I say, shaking my head. "Nobody rides Lightning but me."

Tyler gets up and we walk back to my bike, enjoying the gorgeous evening, and enjoying each other's company.

"Back to Aunt Wilma's Inn?" he asks when I climb onto my bike. "Want to come hang out with me? The flowered curtains are sick. You won't regret it."

I'm sure I wouldn't. But if we end up hanging out in private, we're definitely going to end up having sex.

"I don't think so," I say with a laugh. "I don't want all five rooms and poor Auntie Wilma herself to hear us having sex through the thin paper walls."

Oh, shit. That just slipped out.

Tyler's face lights up like the Vegas strip at midnight. "I

didn't say anything about sex," he says with a grin, "but now that it's out there, let's figure out where we want to do it."

"Forget it," I say, looking forward. "I changed my mind."

"Too late," he says with a grin. "It's out there. We're doing this."

"We just had dinner, we went on a walk, so technically this is our first date," I say. "And I *never* put out on a first date."

He sighs. "That's fair," he says, looking understanding but also a bit disappointed. "But now that I have you on a first date, what would you like to do?"

"Let's rent a movie," I say, climbing off my bike. I grab his hand and pull him across the street. "There's a video store a block away from here."

"I didn't think they still had these," he says, looking awed as we walk into the video store. "I thought they were extinct."

"They are," I say, smiling at the guy who's reading a comic book behind the counter, "but Summerland is one of a kind. It's frozen in time."

"I can see that," Tyler says, picking up a cheesy action movie and looking at the back.

"It's part of its charm," I say, taking the action movie from his hands and putting it back on the shelf. "Let's watch something good."

We walk through the aisles of the small shop, browsing the movies and arguing over which movies are good and which are bad. I'm shocked when we reach the romance section and he hasn't seen any of them.

"Even *The Notebook*?" I ask, holding up the DVD with a disbelieving look on my face.

"Haven't seen it," he says, crinkling his nose up when he

takes the DVD from my hands. "I wouldn't take you as the type who likes romantic movies."

I've heard that before. You can't have romance *and* a career, but just because I've chosen the latter doesn't mean I don't need a fix of romance once in a while. I can't have it in real life, so I watch the movies instead.

"We're getting it," I say, ripping the DVD from his hands and heading to the cash.

"Hey!" Tyler says, opening his arms in protest. "Don't I get a say? It's my hotel room. I should get a say."

I shake my head as I plop *The Notebook* on the counter and pull out my wallet. "Then we'll watch it at my house. Now you get zero says."

I pay for the movie and we head back to my place. This time I let Tyler bike and I sit on the back, wrapping my arms around his hard stomach. With abs like these, I'll let him pedal more often.

This is starting out as a really good first date.

22

Dahlia

"*I WROTE you every day for a year,*" the hunky Ryan Gosling says. I whisper the words as Tyler sleeps softly behind me. We're spooning on the couch watching *The Notebook*, and my favorite movie has never been as good as it is right now. It's probably the thick muscular arm wrapped around me that's bringing it to the next level.

"*You wrote me?*" a soaking wet Rachel McAdams asks.

"*Yes. It wasn't over. It still isn't over.*"

My heart swells as they kiss in the rain, but I'm not sure if the lightness in my chest is from the movie or from the beautiful moment around me.

I grab the remote and turn off the TV, just enjoying the relaxing sound of Tyler breathing softly behind me, his warm breath tickling my neck, and the crackling and popping of the fire in my stone fireplace.

The toasty fire is casting a warm orange glow in the room, and I smile as I watch it eating my decorative logs.

It's the first fire I've ever had in the fireplace. I never knew how to start one, so I never did, but Tyler insisted on making one.

"You've never used this fireplace?" he had asked, staring at me like I'm crazy. "Look at the stone. It's so beautiful. You should be using it every day."

"I don't know how," I said as I knelt down in front of the DVD player, getting it ready.

"Then what's this?" he asked, pointing at the pile of logs beside it. "Why do you have logs if you don't make fires?"

I cringed, suddenly feeling very foolish. "They're decorative."

He laughed as he grabbed a few logs and opened the glass doors. "Well, I'm burning your decorations."

And I'm glad that he did. My house has never felt so warm and inviting, so cozy and full of love.

The warmth seems to radiate out from the fire and into my body, making me feel weightless in Tyler's arms. He mumbles something in his sleep and shifts on the couch, squeezing me tighter with his thick arm.

I smile to myself as I look down at his tattooed arm wrapped tightly around me like he never wants to let me go.

This feels so natural and safe and perfect. When we take away all of the complications around us, all of the evil cousins, angry parents, factories, businesses, drunken nights, and cult members who are strangely fascinated with us, and it's just us—it feels nice.

It feels like I could do this every day. It feels like I could fall in love with this man.

A feeling of breathlessness hits me when I look down at his forearm that's holding me tight and see something hidden in one of his tattoos. On the tattoo of a rose, in one of the pink petals, my name is written in cursive.

It's simple. Six small letters, but it changes everything.

Dahlia.

He did get my name tattooed on his arm during that drunken night, and it's absolutely perfect. I'm marked on his body, like he's marked on mine.

Tyler lets out a soft moan as I trace my fingertip over my name as love fills every inch of my body. I slowly turn around, spinning in his arms until we're face to face.

His eyes are closed, and he has a faint smile on his face as he dreams about what? Me? I hope it's me.

I want to give us a chance. I want to see what my life could be like with Tyler in it for real, but I'm afraid all that I've worked for will go down the drain if I try.

Will I turn out like my parents? They found love, but it took them over, ruining everything else in their lives. They could never hold down a job or stay in a town for more than a few months. I don't want to go back to that. I'm afraid to return to that kind of life.

But a life with Tyler holds so much promise. If I can be held in his arms every night like this, wouldn't it be worth giving up everything else?

I guess I can try it for one night.

I take a deep breath and give him a soft kiss on the lips. His eyes slowly open when I pull away, and he moans contently as he licks my taste off of his lips.

"Are you kissing *me* or are you pretending that I'm Ryan Gosling?" he asks with a groggy voice. He smiles as I kiss him again.

"We should watch *The Notebook* every night," he says with a satisfied smile on his delicious lips.

"Sounds good to me," I answer, running my fingers

through his hair. "But one of these days, you're going to have to stay awake through it."

He smiles. "You have yourself a deal."

I take his arm and run my finger over his rose tattoo. My body tingles as I see my name on him once again.

"Did you know you had this?" I ask, showing him.

His brow furrows as he raises his arm and looks at it. "So, that's where it is," he says with a warm smile. "I love it. Now you'll always have a place on my arm *and* a place in my heart."

I kiss him once again, long and passionate until I'm ready to break my first date rule. "I'm glad you're here with me," I whisper to him once we pull away from the kiss.

"I'm glad I'm here too."

We kiss for a few heavenly minutes until arousal begins coursing through our veins and our bodies start demanding more. Our hands begin to wander, touching skin, sliding under clothes, and it's all making me lightheaded. My heart starts thumping when his hand slides under my shirt and over my breast.

He hardens against my leg and the feeling makes me even wetter than I already am.

Our bodies shift until I'm on top of him, straddling his sexy body as the fire roars beside us.

"You're so sexy," he says as I sit up and pull off my shirt. His hungry eyes are focused on my breasts as I lean down and kiss him once again.

Our kiss is deep but soft, passionate but romantic.

Tyler reaches behind me and unclasps my bra.

"Fuck," he moans when he pulls it off and my breasts spill free on his hard chest. He caresses them softly in his strong hands as our lips connect with another deep kiss.

I've done this with Tyler before, but it's never been like

this. It's more than just pent-up sexual frustration this time. It's more than just lust. There are feelings here, perhaps even a hint of love. This euphoria can only be the beginning stages of love. It has to be.

In the next few moments, we undress each other between kisses until we're both lying on the couch naked, me on top of him.

"I thought you don't put out on the first date," he says with a smirk as I reach down and stroke his hard cock.

"We're already married," I whisper on his lips as I squeeze his thick shaft, making him groan. "It's a little late for first dates."

"Lucky me," he says, sliding his hand behind my head and pulling my lips down onto his.

I shift my hips forward until my throbbing pussy comes down on his hard shaft. We both moan into each other's mouths as I press my aching clit onto his hardness.

I'm so wet. He's so hard. I haven't been able to stop thinking of the sex we had and how good he felt rooted deep inside me. It was quick and hurried in his office, but now we have time to take it slow. We have time to properly enjoy each other's bodies.

He runs his hands down my sides, grips my hips, and starts rocking my body back and forth along his length as he takes my nipples into his hungry mouth and sucks on them, making me moan.

I place my hands on the side of the sofa to stabilize myself as I enjoy the feeling of Tyler's masculine hands on me, his warm tongue coating my tingling nipples, and his long cock sliding through my folds, teasing my clit.

With one last soft kiss, he releases my breasts and pulls me down until we're face to face. His green eyes look mesmerizing in the light of the fire as he looks at me with all the emotion that I'm feeling for him. "I want to make love to you," he whispers, making my chest swell.

I run my hand through his messy hair and kiss him softly on the lips.

This isn't just about sex. It's more. We're sharing a deep human connection on a level I didn't know was possible. I can't quite wrap my head around it.

I think it may be love.

"So, what are you waiting for?" I ask him with a smile on my wet lips.

I arch my hips up as he reaches down and grips his cock. He slides it through my folds until his thick head is pressed up against my opening, making me moan with anticipation.

"Oh, Tyler," I moan as I sink my hips down on him, taking in every heavenly inch of his cock. My body shudders as he stretches and fills me, making me hyper-aware of every tingling cell in my body.

My pussy is soaking wet, dripping for him, but his huge size still makes me cry out with every slow inch that I take in.

My body molds against his as my burning clit reaches his hard pelvis. I wonder how long it will take to get used to his size. He feels so fucking big.

His strong hands slide down to my ass and he grips me hard as he guides me back up the length of his cock. My hands are on his sculpted abs as I slide up and down, my pussy easing into it with every stroke.

He's so beautiful. I can't get over it. His chiseled abs, his wide muscular chest, round tattooed arms, and gorgeous face. It all helps to build up the pressure inside me.

I slide down on him, rocking my hips and just enjoying the feeling of him deep in my pussy. I want to hold him here forever. I never want to let go. I've never felt so happy and at home in my whole life than I do in this moment, and I never want it to stop.

I want Tyler with me forever.

He groans as I move my hips back up, shivering as his beautiful cock hits every spot in me. My body is on fire. It's a heavenly burn that roars through my veins, and I can't get enough of it.

His intense green eyes are locked on mine, and something tender passes between us as I ride him up and down, taking him deeper and deeper with every plunge of my hips.

We grip each other tightly as the slow pressure speeds up. He thrusts his hips up as I come down, making us both cry out as he slams into me, burying himself completely inside me.

My breath quickens; so does his. Heat begins flooding my body as I feel an orgasm coming on.

He squeezes my ass, making me moan and cry out for more as my muscles tighten and my body prepares for the sweet release that's building up deep within my core.

"*Fuck*," he groans, his gorgeous face twisted in pleasured agony. "Oh, Dahlia."

I can tell he's close to filling me with his hot come, and it only spurs me closer to the edge. I tremble in tight anticipation, wanting to feel him coat my insides with his seed.

This is all so perfect. My body was made for him. That's how this feels. Like we were designed by fate to be here together in this moment.

His hand slides to my clit as I ride his hard length, and he begins to rub me with hard circles, and it's too much to take. I throw my head back and cry out as the tight ball unravels and a fierce orgasm consumes me.

"Oh, shit," I scream through clenched teeth as a rush of heat and pleasure runs wild through my body like a whirlwind. It hits me hard, and Tyler's hands on me are the only thing keeping me upright. I squeeze my eyes shut and my mouth falls open as I give myself over to the intense bliss ripping through my veins.

Tyler's grip on me tightens, and I open my eyes just in time to see his back arch and his muscles clench as he fills my pussy with his hot sticky seed.

It feels so fucking good and just brings me higher as I ride the intense rush of my orgasm.

When the heat in my body subsides, I'm totally spent. I fall into Tyler's open arms, and he wraps them around me, holding me tight. His skin is hot against mine. His heartbeat feels so soothing as I feel it beating hard against my naked breasts.

This moment is more perfect than I ever thought it could be.

My hand finds his and we thread our fingers together, enjoying the closeness of the moment. Enjoying the feel of each other's bodies.

His erection begins to fade inside of me, but I keep my legs squeezed against his, not ready to let him go. I want this moment to last because I'm not sure if I'll get another.

Tyler will be back in Vegas soon, and I'll be looking for another job if the factory gets closed.

The thirty-day deadline to get our annulment is coming up on the horizon, and as soon as the decision of who gets the promotion is made there will no longer be a reason for us to stay married.

We have a connection, but I'm worried it may not be enough to keep us together. Once we get that annulment, I might not ever see him again.

I hold him tight as I lay my head beside his, enjoying his

smell and the sound of the fire crackling softly in the fireplace.

It feels like my house is finally a home.

But that scares me.

What's it going to feel like when I'm all alone again? What are my priorities going to look like then?

Will I still be focused on my career at the expense of a love life? Or will I choose love over work?

Love always seemed so terrifying to me, but lying here, falling asleep in Tyler's arms, it doesn't feel scary.

It feels perfect.

23

Dahlia

MY STOMACH TURNS as I park my bike and take the soggy Chinese food out of the rusty basket that's screwed to my handlebars. The town of Summerland has a lot going for it, from the warm and inviting people to the charming small-town scenery, but it does have some faults. Mainly one in particular.

The Chinese food sucks.

I was so hungry on my way home from work that I didn't care that the sweet and sour pork tastes less like pig and more like something that was caught in the alley behind the restaurant. I just wanted to stuff my face with anything, even if it is laced with MSG and has a questionable origin.

"Tyler," I call out as I open my front door. "Get the Pepto-Bismol ready because I have dinner." I walk in and slip off my shoes as I hold the greasy bag. "If you can call it that," I whisper to myself.

It's been three days since Tyler arrived in town, and he's been staying at my place ever since. To say it's been going amazingly is a massive understatement. It's been absolutely perfect.

It's like once we both gave in, we can't get enough of each other. We've had sex about fifty times in the past three days, and even the heartburn and upset stomach that this Chinese food will surely bring probably won't be enough to slow us down.

He'll be leaving soon, so we have to take full advantage now. We haven't talked about what's going to happen with us when he leaves, and I can't bring myself to think about it. I just love having him here in my home, and I don't want to ruin it with anything.

We usually ride home together on my old bike, but Tyler grabbed a cab and left early today, saying he needed to work in solitude for a bit. The ride home was lonely and wasn't the same without him, but at least my legs aren't aching now from having his weight on my bike.

I smile when I look down and see his shiny shoes next to mine. I reach up to my neck for the wedding ring that he gave me, which is usually hanging from my gold chain, but my hand hits nothing but air.

Right. I couldn't find it this morning, and since we were already late from having sex in the shower and on the bed after, I didn't have time to look for it.

"Tyler," I call out as I walk through the family room and into the kitchen. I hear sizzling on the oven and when I pass the couch, the mouthwatering smell hits me and makes my stomach groan.

"What are you doing?" I ask with a big smile as I walk into my tiny kitchen. Tyler looks huge in it as he moves around gracefully, throwing some spices into the sizzling pan. He's wearing his ripped-up jeans, the ones that force my hands to gravitate to his sexy ass whenever he wears them, and a black polo shirt that shows off his big arms and round shoulders.

He turns to me with a happy smile on his face and a platter of barbecued shrimp in his hands. "I'm making dinner," he says, placing the shrimps in front of me.

My mouth waters as I stare down at them.

"What's that?" he asks, motioning to the oily bag in my hands with his eyes.

"Garbage," I say, handing it over.

He takes it and walks to the garbage as I sit down at the table that's set with a brand-new tablecloth, wine glasses, candles, and fresh flowers. But it's too hard to focus on any of that with my starving eyes on the plump juicy shrimps.

"Eat up," he says, smiling as he returns with a bottle of red wine. He pours me a glass as I devour three shrimps, tails and all.

"Delicious," I say, but my mouth is full so it comes out as "Rarishous."

I wash it down with the smooth red wine as he walks behind me and slides his rugged hands on my shoulders. "Mmmm," I moan as he begins massaging me, filling me with more hunger, but this time it's not for food.

"I didn't know you could cook," I say, feeling like I'm in heaven with his skilled hands taking all of the stress from my back. "What are you making?"

"Salmon Wellington, rice, and veggies."

I groan in anticipation. It sounds so good and it smells fantastic.

"Where did you learn to cook like this?" I ask. His family is extremely wealthy, so he was probably trained by some famous French chefs that his father helicoptered in or something equally fancy.

He pulls his phone out of his pocket and shows it to me. "I'm following along to a YouTube video."

I laugh as he finishes massaging me with his skilled hands. Every now and then, he takes a four-second break so I can take a sip of my wine without spilling it on my shirt. If I wasn't ready for him to move in before, I definitely am now.

"So, when is this amazing Salmon Wellington going to be finished?" I ask once all of the shrimps are gone. If the main course tastes as good as the appetizers, I'm in for a real treat.

"Shortly," he says, releasing my shoulders and stepping in front of me. He looks nervous with his fidgeting hands and eyes that keep darting to the door that leads to the garage. "But first, I have a surprise."

"Is it another Ferrari?" I ask with my eyebrow raised. "Because I'm really enjoying biking to work with you. My ass has never been so toned."

"I know the Ferrari wasn't exactly your style," he says, taking my hand. He pulls me up and smiles as he guides me to the garage. "This is more you."

I close my eyes as he opens the door even though he never asked me too. I just love getting surprise presents.

"Can I open my eyes now?" I ask with my heart pounding in excitement.

"I never said you had to close them," he says with a chuckle.

I open them and gasp when I see a brand-new bike in the middle of the garage with a red bow on the matching red handlebars.

"A new bike?" I squeal, staring at in shock as I step into

the garage. It's an old retro bike, but it looks brand-new with shiny parts and a coat of bright red paint that really makes it pop. The large wheels are nice and firm with new treads, unlike the flat slippery wheels on Lightning. There's not a spot of rust on it, and even the basket is in perfect condition, unlike the tattered and frayed basket on my old bike.

My pulse is racing as I walk around it, inspecting every beautiful inch.

"What do you think?" Tyler asks, watching me as he leans on the door frame.

"I love it," I say, not taking my eyes off it. The seat looks so comfy, and the chain isn't all stiff and tangled like the one on Lightning. "Where did you find it?"

"It took some digging," he says with a laugh. "There's a guy who restores old bicycles like this down in Nashville. He's really popular, but I managed to get him to bump me up to the front of the line. I had it flown in this morning."

"I love it," I say, still staring at it in shock. It's the nicest thing anyone has ever done for me.

"Better than a Ferrari?"

"*Way* better."

I sit on it and moan. The seat seems to be massaging my ass as I grab the handlebars. *Wow.*

"There's even footholds in the back for me," he says, smiling as he points to them.

I love it, but guilt starts creeping in. "Can I still keep Lightning?" I ask. "For sentimental reasons?"

Tyler laughs. "Of course. What are you going to name this one?"

"Vegas," I say, smiling. "Can we take her out for a ride?"

"Definitely," he says with a grin. It's such a nice summer evening, and the annual fireworks are in the center of town tonight. Every year the town celebrates the founding of

Summerland with a firework show, so we decide to pack up the lovely dinner that Tyler made and eat it in the park. The whole town will be there, so it should be a lot of fun.

It's a gorgeous night as I pedal down the quiet streets, enjoying the summer breeze on my face as Tyler waves at some kids who are drawing on the sidewalk.

"That's the security guard Michael's boy," I say as they wave back at Tyler. "And those two girls are Nancy in HR and Phil in shipping's twins."

Tyler exhales long and hard as we ride away. It's only been three days, but he's already getting attached to the workers and the town. At the factory, we all work together like a big family, pitching in and helping each other out. There's a huge sense of community which Tyler doesn't get on the isolated top floor of McMillan Worldwide Inc.'s huge skyscraper. He keeps telling me how much he loves it here.

He keeps saying how he loves what Hospitech has accomplished and all of the good work that we've done.

"You save lives here," he said this morning when we were looking over a shipment of incubators that were about to be sent out to a prenatal hospital in Virginia. "What you do matters."

He finally saw that we are making the world better by saving lives and keeping families together. We develop and build specialized high-quality hospital equipment here in Summerland, and if the factory gets shut down, the quality will suffer. They just don't have the same kind of skilled workers in any of the third world countries that the factory will reopen in. The quality won't be nearly as good when McMillan Worldwide Inc. tries to save money by cutting corners, and the patients will be the ones who have to ultimately pay the bill—with their lives.

Tyler is more committed than ever to saving the factory

after seeing the good we do, but it may not be enough. We've tried hard, but we haven't even come close to finding a solution that will save it. And even if we do, his cousin Nick might close it anyway out of spite. I wouldn't put that past him.

"So, you want to save the factory?" I had asked this morning after the incubators shipped out.

He nodded. "The factory, the people, the town. I want to build it up even more to save even more lives, not tear it down. It's the right thing to do."

We both stood uncomfortably as we watched the truck get smaller as it drove down the street. We didn't say it, but I could tell we were thinking the same thing: unless he gets the job, which he probably won't after what we did, the factory is shutting down.

I turn the corner, riding away from the kids drawing on the sidewalk, hoping that this won't all be gone in a few months. Everything will still be here rotting away, but without jobs, the people won't be.

The park is full of people as the sun starts making its slow descent down to the horizon. There's an excited energy in the crowd as people chat and mingle before the fireworks start.

Groups of kids are playing in the playgrounds and on the soccer field as their parents talk and laugh, not worried about their children's safety in this cozy family town.

"Dahlia! Tyler!" Emily says, waving us over to where she's sitting on her picnic blanket.

"I didn't know you were back," I say, smiling to her when I arrive. Tyler says hello but then leaves to go say hi to some of the guys he's made friends with at the factory.

I have one eye on him as I catch up with Emily. He's so natural and friendly around them as they hang on his every word. He has all of the authority and power of a boss at work, but he can act like one of the guys after five o'clock, and they accept him as one of their own.

"I totally fucked Nick," Emily says, making me whip my head around to look at her.

"What?" I ask, jerking my head back in surprise, or maybe it's in disgust. "Why?"

"He's rich, and he's hot!" she says, grinning at me. "Well, besides his big thick eyebrows, he's hot."

"Emily," I say, glaring at her. "He's trying to put us out of a job." I lower my voice so none of my smiling neighbors can hear. "He's trying to shut down the factory."

"He's sweet," she says, playing with a strand of her hair. "I can convince him to keep it open."

A horrible thought springs into my head. "Please don't tell him the truth about me and Tyler. Mack can't know that we got married by accident."

"I won't," Emily says, reaching into her bag for her makeup case.

"Emily," I say in a warning tone. "This is important."

She rolls her eyes into the tiny mirror in her hand as she fixes her mascara. "What do you take me for?"

A gossiper.

I don't say it, but that doesn't mean it's not true. Emily has stayed quiet from what she's told me, but if Nick starts digging for incriminating information about us, it won't take long for her to open her big mouth about that night.

"So, you two seem to be hitting it off," she says, smiling as she sees me watching Tyler. "You like him, don't you?"

"He's my boss," I say with a huff.

"So?"

"We've agreed to keep it professional," I say, smiling as he high fives a six-year-old boy who runs by him. "We're staying friends so that we can focus on trying to keep the factory open."

"Right," she says with a laugh. "The only thing you're focused on keeping open is your legs."

"Shut up!" I say, turning to her with a shocked look.

"Oh, please," she says, laughing as she rolls her eyes. "You look more relaxed and less uptight than I've ever seen you before. You're getting some dick."

I slap her arm playfully as my cheeks get red. "Am I that obvious?"

"You're basically fucking him with your eyes right now."

"I am not," I say, staring at his ass.

"Summerland isn't the only one with fireworks around here," she says. "He likes you too. I can tell."

"Really?" I ask. "How can you tell?"

"He's here, isn't he?" Emily asks with a shrug of her shoulders. "He didn't fly all the way out here for a shitty three-minute firework show."

My pulse races as Tyler says goodbye to the guys and comes back with a big smile on his face. He fits in here. He fits with me.

"Those guys are great," he says as he sits behind me like it's the most natural thing in the world and wraps his arms around my body.

I glance over at Emily who is giving me a knowing smirk. I stick my tongue out at her.

We break out our dinner, sharing it with the nice people around us, and have a great time eating and talking as a group.

When the sun is gone for the night and the bright stars are popping up in the sky, the mayor announces that the fireworks are about to start.

The children race over from the playground and soccer

field to snuggle up to their parents as they start to get excited for the show.

There are people all around us, but it feels like it's only Tyler and me. I'm always completely absorbed in his presence when he's around.

The crowd cheers as the first firework whizzes through the air and pops over our heads, exploding into a chandelier of blue sparks. Tyler holds me tight as we watch the show, and I realize how happy I am with him. It's nice to have a man to share these kinds of nights with.

I let out a contented moan as three fireworks explode in the sky. There's nowhere I would rather be in this moment than wrapped in Tyler's muscular arms in my cute little town.

Everyone claps when the show is over, and before long they've all returned home and it's only Tyler and me still left in the park. We're sitting on the blanket that Emily left us, facing each other as we look up at the stars.

"You can't see any of these from Vegas," Tyler says, staring up at the cosmos in fascination. The stars are looking spectacular tonight, but I'm staring at his face instead. Nothing is as spectacular to me as Tyler's gorgeous face.

We spend hours talking, only taking breaks to make out, and before long the evening has flown past us and we're deep into the night.

"You forgot this," he says as he digs his hand into his pocket. He pulls out my wedding ring, but there's no chain attached to it.

"Where's the chain?"

"At home," he says with a grin. "I guess you'll have to wear it on your finger."

I hold my breath as he takes my hand and slides it on my

ring finger. This time it doesn't slide off. It's no longer too big.

"What happened to it?"

He smiles as he holds my hand, looking at the diamond ring on my finger. "I may have had it fitted."

My stomach flutters as my heart starts hammering in my chest. I should take this off. It's not real.

But it feels real, and the look in Tyler's eyes looks real.

So, I keep it on.

Tyler will be gone in two days, and I might not see him again. Plus, I love the way it feels.

And I love that it came from him.

I'm staring at the diamond on my finger when he lightly touches my chin and guides my head up until I'm looking into his deep green eyes. "I love you, Dahlia," he whispers, staring at me with his cheeks glowing.

"What did you say?" I heard what he said, but I just want to hear him say it again.

He smiles as he repeats those three perfect words. "I love you."

"That's what I thought you said," I answer, smiling as I melt into his arms.

He holds me tight as I enjoy the best moment of my life.

"Do you have something to say to me?" he asks after a few moments of silence.

"Yes," I say, taking a deep breath. "Thank you."

I feel it, but I'm not ready to say it yet.

It's too dangerous. There's too much on the line. I gave into my feelings in his office in Vegas and look where it got us. I messed up the whole plan because I gave in.

I won't give in until he is assigned Mack's position and the future of the factory is secure. It's too risky to do otherwise. We can fall out of love or just end up throwing everything else away like my parents did. It's safer to stay friends, act professionally and stick to the plan.

I have to remember that I can't have love and a career.

And it's even more important to remember that if I pick the wrong one, the whole town is going to suffer.

24

Tyler

"Prophet! Prophet!" the crazy bald guy with the flowers around his neck shouts as the two security guards hold him back. He's wearing a long yellow robe with no shoes on, and he's struggling like crazy to break free from the security guards.

He's staring right at me as he hollers through the lobby with a panicked look in his eyes. "Tell us the divine words of Franesca and Lukania, blessed Prophet!" he shouts, looking right at me. "Please!"

I'm back at McMillan Worldwide Inc. in the lobby by the elevators with no one around me, but I still look behind my back to see if he's talking to someone else.

I don't know this guy, and I'm definitely no prophet, but there's nothing behind me but the marble walls, which means he's talking to me.

It's then that I remember the strange phone call a week or two ago. *The nutjob on the phone called me a prophet as well.*

I'm about to go over to talk to him when I catch myself and turn back around to the elevators. This is exactly the kind of thing I don't need. I'm trying to lay low and get back in the good graces of my father before he retires and hands the company over to Nick. Catching me with Dahlia bent over my desk was my last chance. If I was a cat, I'd would have already lost eight of my nine lives, and I'd be walking on a wobbly tightrope in a hurricane, about to lose my ninth.

I have to stay professional, and engaging with a crazy Shaolin monk wannabe in a dress isn't the way to impress my father.

"Prophet!" he screams as the larger security guard drags him out the door. The smaller guard comes rushing over as his coworker launches the whack-job into the street.

"Mr. McMillan," he says, trying to catch his breath as he jogs over. "A second of your time please."

The elevator doors bing open, and I sigh as I lean against them, preventing them from opening back up. "What's up?"

"There was a break-in last night," he says, wincing as he stares up at me. "In your office."

"In my office?" I say, jerking my head back. "Only my office?"

"It appears so," the guard says, rubbing the back of his neck. He looks uncomfortable. It's never fun to be the one to give the boss bad news. "It was *them.*"

"*Them?*" I repeat, pointing at the crazy hairless fuck who is trying to look in through the mirrored windows from the sidewalk. "Did they steal anything?"

"Nothing that we noticed," he says, biting his bottom lip.

"But perhaps you can check when you get in. I have a police report ready to be filed."

"No police report," I say, waving my hand at him. I don't want this to become a big deal. I still have no idea why they're so interested in me, but it's bound to go away if I just ignore them. I have a bad feeling that it has something to do with the night I met Dahlia and we went tearing through Las Vegas. If my father finds out about any of that, my last chance will be over.

"Just keep them out of the building," I say, giving the weirdo one more look before I slip into the elevator. "And make sure my father doesn't find out about any of this."

"Yes, sir," he says, nodding as the door closes in front of his face.

I take a deep breath, trying to put all of that weirdness out of my mind as the elevator shoots up the floors to the top.

It feels weird to be back home without Dahlia here. Summerland was amazing. I got a glimpse of what my life could be like with Dahlia, and it was pretty incredible.

Being with her for three days was enough to fall madly in love. I can't stop thinking about her, and I already miss her like crazy.

It still hurts a little that she didn't say I love you back, but I just have to realize she's not the type to rush into things like love. It's going to take her some extra time to come to terms with her feelings, and that's fine. I felt the connection. I read the signs. I know she loves me back, even if she doesn't realize it yet.

I look at my blurry reflection in the stainless-steel doors of the elevator and grin. *What's not to love?*

The doors bing open on the top floor, and I take a deep breath before walking out. It's the first time I'm seeing my father since the day of the incident, and I'm still not sure if he's cooled off yet. He hadn't been that pissed at me since I threw a house party in grade ten with three hundred and fifty of my closest friends.

"Hi, Mr. McMillan," the receptionist, Ruth, says as I walk past her desk. "Your father would like to see you as soon as possible."

"Sure," I say, flashing her a smile. "I'm just going to check out my office first." *And make sure those wackos didn't steal anything or sacrifice a baby lamb on my desk.*

"He said immediately," Ruth says, cringing. "'As soon as he steps off that fucking elevator,' were his exact words."

I gulp as I turn around and head for my father's office. Checking my office can wait.

The door is open a crack, so I let myself in. "Hey, Pops!"

He sighs when he looks up and sees me. "Sit," he says, motioning to the chair in front of his desk. He returns to the paperwork he's going through as I walk over, feeling like I'm a teenager again and took the car without asking.

I have an empty feeling in the pit of my stomach as I sit down and wait for another earful. He scribbles his signature on the bottom of the paper, puts it to the side, and finally turns to me with his hands clasped on the desk in front of him and a stern look on his face.

"Where have you been?"

"Hiding out."

"That was a good move," he says, narrowing his eyes on me. "I should have fired you both."

"Probably," I say, shifting in my seat. "Thanks for keeping us around."

"How could you do something so stupid?" he asks, staring at me in disbelief.

"I love her, Dad," I say, trying to play the romantic card.

"Don't you remember what it was like when you first met mom and you couldn't take your hands off her?" *Gross.*

His eyes tighten as he leans back in his chair. "I don't recall being so in love that I felt the need to whip her. At work."

"Well, then you couldn't have been that much in love," I joke. He's not in the mood for jokes. "I'm kidding," I say quickly, showing him my palms.

"This is serious, Tyler," he says, deepening his tone. "Do you really think I'm going to put the company in the hands of someone who thinks pulling a stunt like that is a good idea? What if you had my position and something like that came out in the media? How do you think that would make the company look? Do you think it would be easy to raise money from investors or the banks with a sexual perversion like that hanging over your head? Do you think the employees would respect you if they knew you were getting freaky in your office? How would you be able to discipline them when you got caught doing something even worse? This *is* serious."

I swallow hard as my eyes drift down to my lap.

"It won't happen again, Dad." I mean it this time. It won't.

He takes a deep breath as he watches me with his eyes full of disappointment. Maybe I'm not cut out for the top position. Maybe it would be better to hand it off to someone else—as long as it's anyone but Nick.

"I've given you too many chances already," he says, looking exasperated. "This is your last straw, end of the road, rock bottom, very fucking last chance. You got that? You're on thin ice."

"I won't blow it, Dad," I say, really hoping that I don't blow it.

"I mean it," he says, glaring at me. "You're on thin ice and carrying cinder blocks in your hands. Got that? If I walk in and see you drinking coffee at your desk without a coaster, you're done. Understand?"

"I do."

"One more screw up and I'm giving the company to your cousin Nick."

My body tenses at the sound of his name. This has gone on long enough. Why can't my father see that my cousin is no good? He's always quick to point out how I'm no good, but he's oblivious when it comes to Nick.

"Dad," I say, feeling my pulse speed up. "He's stealing money from the company."

My father drops his head and sighs. "Do you have any proof of this?" he asks, looking up at me with hard cold eyes.

"I've gone over the numbers, and there are large amounts of money disappearing from his departments," I say, trying to make him see.

"Do you have *conclusive* proof?" my father asks in a firm not-fucking-around voice.

I sigh. "No."

He stands up, looking furious. "This is exactly what I'm talking about," he shouts, throwing his pen onto the desk. "Wild accusations. Slander. You're always trying to bring down your cousin instead of lifting yourself up."

"Dad. Just take a look at the numb—"

"Enough!" he shouts, shaking his head as he walks to the window. "I don't want to hear about this anymore. Your cousin is a good man and an even better businessman. He would make a fine leader of this company. I just wish I could say the same about you."

My chest stings like I was just punched in the heart.

"One more chance, Tyler," he says, looking old and tired

as he stares out the window. "I want to retire, and I want my son to have the company. It's the American dream."

He turns and looks at me with exhaustion in his eyes. The old man worked hard all of his life and deserves to retire. He deserves to have someone responsible to leave the company to, so he can spend his golden years relaxing without a care or worry.

"I want you to have it, son," he says, his voice softening. "Really I do. But this company is bigger than you and me. We have to look out for our employees and make sure they're taken care of in the years to come." He sighs as he turns back to the window. "I just need you to prove to me that you won't screw up."

I leave the office hoping I won't let him down but I seem to be screwing up a lot lately. I'm walking back to my office, wishing that Dahlia was here with me, when I bump into my cousin Jason.

"Tyler," he says, looking up at me with a smile. "I looked over the proposal that you and Dahlia wrote up for the legal office in Alabama. Very impressive. You married a smart cookie."

I smile for the first time this morning as he shuffles through the files in his hands and pulls out our proposal. A compliment like that from an intelligent hardworking and professional guy like my cousin Jason means a lot and makes me feel great.

"I made a few minor corrections that I would like to go over with Dahlia," he says, looking at the papers in his hands. He has some notes carefully written in the margins.

"I'll fly her over on the next flight," I say, feeling my pulse start to race in excitement. I've been looking for an excuse to bring her back here as soon as possible, and now that I have one, I'm thrilled.

"She doesn't have to fly all the way over here," he says, shaking his head. "I'll just call her about it."

"But in person is so much better," I answer quickly. "We can bounce ideas off her." *And after work, she can bounce up and down on my dick.*

He grins as he looks up at me. "Are you missing your new wife?"

"I don't know what you're talking about," I say with a grin. "This is purely business."

"Sure," he says, rolling his eyes. "But I do have some other ideas to discuss with her if she does come."

"She'll be here sometime tomorrow," I say confidently. *Even if I have to send my father's private jet to fetch her.*

"All right," he says, chuckling as he walks away. "You picked a good one, cuz. Don't forget that."

I won't.

My head is swimming with thoughts of my sexy wife as I head into my office. I look around quickly, but nothing seems to be out of place or missing. *I wonder what those weirdos were doing in here.*

I get a tingling feeling as I sit down at my desk and reach for the phone. It's been a few hours since I last spoke to Dahlia, and I'm already missing her like crazy. I dial her office number and wait with my pulse racing as the phone rings.

She hasn't picked up the phone yet, but I hear breathing on the line. *That's strange.*

"Hello," I say between rings. The breathing stops immediately but no one answers.

Weird.

"Dahlia speaking," my hot wife says when she picks up the phone. Her voice makes me forget about the strange breathing, and all of a sudden, I'm back in Summerland

with my arms wrapped around her, breathing in her delicious vanilla perfume.

"Great news," I say, grinning as I hold the phone to my ear.

"You got the company?"

"Not that great. You get to come back to Vegas."

"I thought you said great news. I hated Vegas."

"Jason said he absolutely needs you here first thing tomorrow. He has to go over your proposal for the legal office in Alabama and positively needs you here."

"Can't we do it over the phone?" she asks. *"You know how much I love Summerland. I want to enjoy it while I still can."*

"Sorry," I say with an evil grin that she can't see. "You definitely have to come here. Jason's words, not mine."

"Okay," she says reluctantly. *"Am I staying at the same hotel?"*

"This time you'll be staying with me."

"This trip is looking better and better."

"Don't forget to pack that sexy nightie I like. You know... for business."

I can hear her smiling on the other end of the line. *"Right,"* she says. *"For business. I hope you're ready to work... hard."*

My father's recent warning is still ringing in my ears, so I change the subject, trying to keep it professional. "You can take this opportunity to impress my father with the proposal."

"I'm not sure if I can face your father yet," she says, sounding down. *"That was the most humiliating moment of my life."*

"He's over it already," I lie. "I just spoke with him, and he's already forgotten all about it."

"Yeah, right," she answers. *"He's never going to forget that image. It's probably seared into his brain forever."*

Unfortunately, I think she's right.

"Do you hear breathing?" Dahlia asks.

I hold my breath to listen, but all I hear is a click like someone just hung up. *Did someone tap my phones?*

"I'll have HR send you a plane ticket," I say, ignoring it for now. "Don't forget the nightie."

"I won't," she says as my door swings open.

Shit. Nick walks in with a smug look on his very punchable face.

"I'll see you tomorrow," I tell my wife before hanging up.

"You'll see who tomorrow?" Nick asks, taking a seat in front of my desk even though I hadn't offered him one.

"That's none of your business."

"This company will be mine very soon," he says with a smirk, "so it is my business."

"Well, if you must know," I say, leaning back in my chair. "Dahlia is coming over to get approval to set up the Alabama legal office. Remember? That's the proposal that you totally fucked up and she nailed."

"The only thing she nailed was the last nail in your coffin when we walked in on you while you were doing your Fifty Shades of Grey impression. Do you really think that Mack is going to give you the company after that embarrassing spectacle?"

"I'm sure he'd rather give it to me than to someone who's stealing from the company."

"This thing again?" he asks, rolling his eyes as he slides his sleeve over the new Rolex watch on his wrist. "You have no proof."

"Not yet."

"And what are you hiding?" he asks, eying me with a

suspicious look. "Mr. Playboy for life shows up with a wife out of the blue that he's been dating for two years? I don't buy it. Something is up."

"I'm in love." *That's the truth now.*

"The timing is convenient," he says, staring me down with interrogating eyes. "Mack wanted you to settle down before you got the company, and you just show up with a ready-made wife? Sounds like you picked her out of a catalog or something."

"Sounds like you've lost your mind. A fake wife? Who would stoop so low as to do something like that?" I say confidently, but I'm cringing on the inside.

"Somebody has to know something," he says, eying me coldly as he gets up. "And I'm going to find out what it is."

My heart starts pounding as he walks to the door. *Isn't he dating that girl from Hospitech? Emily? I wonder if she knows anything.*

"Are you tapping my phone lines?" I ask.

He turns with a raised eyebrow. "Tapping your phone lines?" he repeats with a laugh. "Now who sounds like they've lost their mind?"

I lean back in my chair and take a deep breath after he's gone. Tapped phone lines, constant competition, angry fathers. I close my eyes and dream that I'm back in Summerland with Dahlia where life is nice and simple.

I could get used to nice and simple.

25

Dahlia

"Fuck," I cry out as Tyler thrusts into me. We only made it two steps into his condo, and I'm already on the floor lying on my back as he slides his hard cock deep into me.

"I've been dreaming of this tight little pussy every second since I left," he whispers into my ear as his thick shaft stretches me wide. He groans as he buries his cock in all the way to the hilt.

This was definitely worth the plane ride over. I jumped on the first plane leaving for Vegas after his phone call this morning, and now I'm really glad I did.

I wrap my arms around him as he starts to fuck me hard and deep. Our clothes are still on. We were in too much of a hurry to take them off, just taking enough time to fumble with our belt buckles and slide our pants down to only get the necessities out.

I cry out loud as he starts to fuck me hard and deep.

There will be time for slow, romantic sex later tonight when we can take our time and properly enjoy each other's bodies. But right now, I just need to feel him inside me.

It's not long before our groans become louder and our cries more incoherent. He ramps up the pace, and before long my body gives in and I'm crying out as my pussy pulses in orgasm around him. His body tightens as he gives me one last hard thrust, holds himself deep within me, and comes.

"Welcome back," he says when we're both lying on our backs after, looking up at the ridiculously high ceiling while trying to catch our breaths.

"Thanks," I say with a laugh. "If the foyer is this good, I can't wait to see the rest of your place."

"You'll see it all," he says, reaching for my hand. He threads his fingers through mine, making me even happier that I made the trip back here. "And don't worry, we'll have sex in every room before you leave."

I'm not thrilled to face my angry boss after what happened, but it's still worth it to see Tyler. Especially if I get fucked in every room of his beautiful penthouse condo.

After a few minutes, we get up, get dressed, and he gives me a tour of his sick condo. He has almost no outer walls, mainly just windows from the floor to the ceiling, and since it's a top floor of a high-rise building overlooking the Las Vegas strip, to say the view is spectacular is a massive understatement.

"Wow," I gasp as I marvel at all of the bright shiny lights down below. It's beautiful.

"It's a fun city," he says, walking up behind me and taking me in his arms. We melt into each other as we watch all of the action down below. "But it gets old after a while. I think I'd like a small town like Summerland better."

I turn in his arms until we're face to face, both smiling at each other. I can't tell if he's being serious or if he's teasing me.

"Sure, you might have some of the best chefs in the world here," I say, grinning at him, "but can you get a submarine as good as Lou's?"

He shakes his head.

"And sure, you can watch Cirque du Soleil or listen to Celine Dion live, but can you rent *The Notebook* on DVD? Can you leave your bike on the street without a lock or get food poisoning from the only Chinese takeout place?"

Tyler smiles as he holds me tight. "That's why Summerland wins, but you haven't even mentioned the best part."

"Which is?"

"You," he says, giving me a soft kiss on the lips. "Any place with you in it is the best place in the world."

We finish the tour of his condo, and I'm stunned at how nice it is—a huge flat-screen TV over the fireplace, a kitchen that would make Gordon Ramsay weep in envy, and walk-in closets that you can park a car in.

I'm admiring the nineteen jet shower when my phone rings. It's Emily.

It's really late at night back home and it could be an emergency, so I answer it even though I just want to let it go to voicemail.

"Hey, Em," I say, sitting on the ledge of the bathtub as I answer it. "Everything okay?"

She's crying.

"What happened?" I ask, straightening up as a worried feeling digs deep in my stomach. "Are you okay?"

"I'm sorry, Dahlia," she says between sniffs. *"I didn't mean to get you into trouble. You've been such a good friend to me."*

I can feel the color draining from my face. "What happened?"

"*Nick,*" she says as a new wave of sobs hits her. "*He broke up with me.*"

I take a breath of relief. *Thank God.*

"It's probably for the best," I say in a soft tone. "You can do a lot better than him."

"*I don't deserve better,*" she says in a shaky voice. "*I fucked up.*"

I swallow hard, waiting for it.

"*He tricked me into telling him what happened.*"

"What happened with what?" I ask, but I already know the answer.

"*Between you and Tyler. How you guys got drunk and got married by accident.*"

I drop my head as the air is knocked out of my lungs.

"Oh, Emily," I say, shaking my head in disbelief. "You didn't?"

"*I'm so sorry, Dahlia. I thought he liked me, and I was just telling him a funny story. I didn't think he would do anything bad with the information. He's Tyler's cousin.*"

My stomach flutters as I think it over. He doesn't have any proof, and we can just deny it. It might not be as bad as it seems.

But with everything that has happened lately, Mack is probably going to believe Nick.

"If Mack asks you what happened, please deny everything," I say, suddenly feeling nauseous. She says she will. "Just try to get some sleep, Emily. I'll call you tomorrow."

She apologizes a dozen more times before I hang up the phone with shaking hands.

"Tyler," I call out as I walk into the bedroom. "Something happened."

He looks even worse than I feel. He's on the phone with someone, looking anxious as he paces around the room.

"Of course we're in love, Mom," he says as he runs his hand through his hair. I cringe as he nearly yanks out a fistful of his hair. "What was on the video?"

The video? My legs weaken as I listen. It must be our wedding video.

"Yes, the marriage is real," he says, looking panicked as he walks in circles. "It's okay, Mom. Stop crying. You're going to get your gra—"

Tyler lowers the phone and stares at me in shock.

"She hung up on me."

I gulp. "What video was she talking about?"

He drops onto the bed and puts his hands on his head. "Our wedding video. They got it in the mail."

"Oh, shit," I say, dropping onto the bed beside him. All of a sudden my legs can't support my weight anymore. "I can't imagine what's on there."

"Wait a second," he says, going through his phone. "I should have checked my email about this before." After a tense minute, he perks up and then quickly slumps down onto the bed. "I found a receipt from the Pineapple Chapel in my email."

"And?"

"And it looks like we ordered five wedding videos and sent them to our family and friends."

I close my eyes and pretend that this is not happening. "That can't be good," I whisper to nobody in particular.

Tyler is looking shell-shocked, like he just walked in on his parents having sex.

"There goes the company."

I want to cry. "There goes the factory."

I look at Tyler and wonder if something this big is going to break us. I sigh.

There goes my marriage. It was fun while it lasted.

Dahlia

A DEEP FLUSH creeps across my cheeks as Tyler pops our wedding video into the DVD player.

Kirsten and Mack are sitting on the couch to my left watching the TV with bitter faces. They've already seen what's about to play, and they don't look very excited about witnessing it again.

"Should we make popcorn?" Tyler asks, trying to lighten up the mood.

His parents stare forward, not even cracking a smile. If the mood got any heavier in here, we'd collapse through the floor.

"I didn't want to believe your cousin Nick when he told me that your marriage was a sham," Mack says, staring forward with his arms crossed over his chest. "I didn't believe it until I saw this video." He shakes his head, refusing to even look at us.

My chin dips down and my stomach hardens as Tyler sits beside me. "We can explain everything," he says as the DVD starts.

Oh, no. I cover my face with my hands to escape the humiliating version of me on the screen. There's no explaining that.

The video starts with Tyler and me in The Pineapple Chapel, swaying on our feet as Drunken Asian Elvis chugs scotch straight from the bottle. My hair is a hot mess like I styled it by sticking my finger into an electrical socket, and my face looks like I took makeup lessons from a raccoon. I'm wearing a white plastic dress with the pineapple bra, only it's not doing its job because I have a tit hanging out in plain view.

Tyler doesn't look any better. His suit is a ripped-up mess as he stands there, scratching his balls while Drunken Asian Elvis takes another long chug from his bottle. Tyler seems to have an attention span of a nano-second because he gets bored and wanders over to the pineapple-shaped podium and begins humping it.

My neck, face, and ears feel impossibly hot as I glance over at my in-laws who are watching with clenched jaws and flared nostrils.

"Oh, my God," Tyler groans beside me. "This is so humiliating." And this is coming from a guy who has an N'Sync poster on his wall. I mean, what's more humiliating than that?

Drunken Asian Elvis tries to sing Suspicious Minds but forgets most of the words, which would normally be bad, but of course, Tyler and I top him, forgetting each other's names later on in the short ceremony.

"I, Tyler, take... what's your name again?" he asks, slurring every single word as he stares at me with half closed eyes.

I curl my hands around my middle as I watch with nausea creeping up my throat. This is the most unromantic wedding I have ever seen.

"Rainbow Solstice the First," I answer. At least I can remember my own name. "But you can call me your Cum Dumpster from now on."

"Classy," Tyler whispers beside me. I slap his thigh. He shouldn't talk.

We watch the rest of the painful marriage ceremony, and I'm exhausted and more embarrassed than I've ever been in my life when it finally shuts off.

"So, that's our wedding video," Tyler says, turning off the TV when it's done. "We wanted something classy yet simple."

"How could you?" Kirsten asks, turning to her son with hurt and disappointment written all over her face. "You lied about all of this? Are you two even dating?"

We look at each other, but neither of us answer. *Are we dating?*

"Great," Kirsten says, throwing her hands in the air. "I guess I have my answer."

"We're dating," Tyler says firmly. Despite the horrible circumstance I'm in, I let out a smile. It's the first time either of us said that we're a real couple.

"I just don't understand why you would lie about something like this?" Kirsten says, looking like she's on the verge of tears. "We threw you that lovely party and you made us look like fools in return. Your Aunt Margaret called me and was deeply disturbed by your video."

"Aunt Margaret got a copy?" Tyler asks with a wince.

Mack sits up. "I'll tell you why he would lie about something like this. So that I would give him the company. Isn't that right?" he asks Tyler, turning to my husband with an accusing look on his face.

Tyler's eyes fall to his lap.

"Actually," Mack says as he stands up. "I don't want to hear any more of your lies. You are officially out of the running for the top position at McMillan Worldwide Inc." He takes a deep breath as he stands up straight with his chest puffed out. "Nicholas will be getting the company. My decision is final."

"Dad!" Tyler says, leaping to his feet. "You can't be serious. Over this? I've worked my ass off every day at that company for the past six years. This is my birthright!"

"It was," Mack says softly. He looks crushed as he turns to his only son with old, tired eyes. "And I really wanted to give it to you, but I can't. Not after this."

"Dad!" Tyler calls out as Mack leaves the room with his head down. "We can talk about this. We were just having a little bit of fun."

"A little bit of fun?" Kirsten repeats, looking heartbroken. "What is fun about deceiving your entire family with a sham of a marriage? I thought I was going to get grandkids," she says with her chin trembling. She covers her mouth with her hand and runs out of the room so we can't see her cry.

"Fuck," Tyler says, collapsing back down on the couch. He runs his hand through his hair as he stares at the floor, shaking his head in disbelief.

I feel like I'm going to be sick as I collapse down beside him. Nick is getting the company, which means that the factory in Summerland will surely be closed. Everyone in town will lose their job, and Tyler and I will be right there with them, getting pink slips of our very own.

I was right all along. You can't have a career *and* love. I should have stuck to my gut instead of following my heart. If I did, none of this would be happening.

"What now?" I whisper to the crushed man beside me.

He takes a deep breath, staring at the floor as he answers. "What does it matter? We've lost everything."

"Maybe we should get that annulment," I say, wanting to take back the words the second they pass through my lips.

I'm hoping he'll say no. I'm hoping he'll tell me he loves me and that he's willing to fight for us. I'm hoping he does the right thing and takes me in his arms and shows me how much he loves me with a passionate kiss.

But he just slumps down in the couch and sighs. "Maybe."

It's one word, but it's enough to break me. "Okay," I say, feeling my heartbeat slow to a stop. I have to get out of here before I start crying.

We shuffle back to the car, not saying a word as we get in. Tyler is the first to speak when we're on the highway back to his place.

"The thirty-day deadline for the annulment is next week," he says, gripping the steering wheel hard as he coasts down the dark highway.

"I'll take a flight in for it," I say, feeling like I'm going to throw up. "The whole getting married thing was a mistake. It's the right thing to do."

He nods and doesn't say a word for the rest of the drive back to his place.

I sit there trying to convince myself that it is the right thing to do, but more than anything, I keep wondering why it feels so wrong.

27

Tyler

I STAND in the corner of the conference room, eating the cardboard-tasting cake as everyone congratulates my father and congratulates Nick.

After fifty-two years of hard work, my father has finally announced his retirement. And he named Nick as his successor.

It shouldn't come as a surprise after last week when Dahlia and I were forced to watch our wedding video in front of my parents. It was the final straw that broke my father's back, and he decided that the future of the company will not be with me at the head of it, but instead, it will be in Nick's cold corrupt hands.

Everyone turns their attention to him as he begins to make a speech, thanking my father for his trust in him and saying that he's going to try his best to live up to the wonderful legacy that my father started all those years ago with McMillan Worldwide Inc.

The dry crappy cake is threatening to come back up, so I sneak out of the room, tossing it into the garbage as I leave. I loosen my tie as I walk through the empty floor to my office.

Everything got all fucked up.

My future, my job, my dreams—but what hurts the most more than anything is losing Dahlia. I still can't believe that she suggested we go through with the annulment. Yes, the video was embarrassing, but was it bad enough to throw away everything between us? Apparently, it was.

I lock the door when I'm back in my office and slump down in the chair behind my desk. My chest aches as I open my bottom drawer and pull out the cheap plastic mug from our wedding night. My heart is broken, but I still manage to smile when I look at the ridiculous picture of me and Dahlia.

After a minute of regrets, I reach for my phone with a heaviness in my heart. I want to call her. I want to talk to her and tell her that the past few weeks with her have been the best of my life. I want to tell her that I love her, and I've never felt this way about anyone, ever. I want to tell her I miss her, and I don't care about having the company as long as I have her.

I dial nine numbers before I hang up the phone and sigh. She always wanted to get the annulment, and after this humiliating experience, she probably wants it more than ever.

I'm slumped over in my chair, staring down at my empty hands when the door of my office unlocks and the door swings open.

"You left my party so early," Nick says, walking in with a

triumphant smile on his face. "It's almost as if you're not happy for me."

"Why do you have the key to *my* office?" I ask, glaring at him.

"Your office?" he says with a chuckle. "That's cute. Didn't you hear your father back there? This whole building and every office in it is mine now. You're only here because I'm allowing you to be here. That is, until the papers are signed and the company is officially mine. Then you and your paid wife will be out on the streets."

"You're going to fire us?" I ask, feeling my body tense up.

Nick laughs as he walks over and sits in the chair in front of my desk. "I'm going to do more than that," he says, grinning as he puts his feet on my desk. "I'm going to ban you two from the building, tell every CEO, manager, and HR department in the country that you two are toxic, and then I'm going to take that factory that your wife loves so much and turn it into an abandoned building."

Heat flushes through my body as I listen to him. I don't care about what he plans for me—I can take care of myself —but it kills me to know that he plans to close the Hospitech factory. I spent five amazing days there making friends with the wholesome employees and their families, seeing the good work they accomplish by manufacturing hospital equipment that saves lives, and living the small-town life, which felt more like home than Las Vegas ever did.

"Nick," I say, trying to keep my voice steady despite the anger surging through my veins. "Don't punish an entire town over our childhood grudge. They never did anything to you."

"But you did," he says, glaring at me. "All my life I tried to live up to you. Do you know what it was like living in your shadow? The girls would only talk to me to get to you."

"You had a thick unibrow, Nick," I say, trying not to laugh when I remember how crazy his eyebrows were. "I told you to pluck it."

"You were the good looking, athletic, charming one," he says, ignoring me, "and I was nothing."

"Oh, get over it," I say, rolling my eyes. "You get girls now, your eyebrows only look slightly ridiculous, and you're rich. I know because you've been stealing money from the company."

"I've been taking what's rightfully mine," he says, crossing his arms over his chest as his eyes harden.

"Stolen money from the company is rightfully yours?" I ask with a disbelieving laugh.

"Yes," he says firmly. "I deserve it. This company would be nothing without me."

"How much did you take?" I ask, leaning forward.

He grins. "Millions," he says, clearly proud of himself. "And I deserve every last penny of it."

"You don't deserve any of it," I say, shaking my head. "And you don't deserve this promotion. You deserve to go to jail."

"I'm not the one who's going to be going to jail," he says. His face turns dark as his mouth twists up in an evil smirk. "The money I stole was deposited into an account that is registered to you. And when I show your father what I've found, you'll be off to jail, and I'll be left alone to run the company the way I want to."

"You're sick," I say, staring at him in disgust. He's even worse than I thought. I seriously underestimated him, and I'll probably be going to jail because of it.

"No," he says as he gets up with a proud look on his face.

"I'm in charge. Of everything. Now if you'll excuse me, I'm a very busy man. I have a factory to close and a town to devastate."

A coldness grips my core as he struts to the door and leaves. This is worse than I thought.

Not only is my job and the town of Summerland on the line, but now my very freedom is on the line too. There is no way my father will believe me over Nick, especially with all of the lies I got caught telling lately.

The factory will close, Dahlia will lose her job and the town she loves, and I'll probably be headed to jail for stealing millions from my father.

"Shit," I mutter under my breath as I stare at the wall.

"I'm so fucked."

28

Dahlia

EMILY IS SITTING on my front stoop with a plastic bag in her hands when I get home from work. Her eyes are red and splotchy like mine have been way too often in the past few days.

"That's funny," I say as I hop off my bike and place it on my porch, "I don't remember ordering a sarcastic coworker off the Internet."

"How about a sad one?" she asks, looking up at me with puffy eyes.

I give her a smile as I sit down beside her. "If you're sad, then you came to the right place. What's in the bag?"

She grins as she opens it. "We both have broken hearts. So tonight is our wallowing night."

"Wallowing night?" I repeat.

"Wallowing night," she says, nodding her head firmly. "We're doing everything wallow."

I laugh as she starts pulling stuff out of the bag. "I rented *Willow*, I got walnut ice cream from Walmart, and we're drinking Walla Walla Wine. We're going balls to the walls wallowing."

"Are we allowed to sit on the couch, or do we have to lean against the *wall*?" I ask with a laugh.

Emily scrunches her face up. "I haven't thought about that."

"Let's do the couch," I say, grabbing the red wine from her hands. I unscrew the cap and take a big gulp, already feeling a bit better.

I've been so sad for the past few days since I got back home, and I could really use a night like this where I can just be sad and teary eyed with a close friend.

Emily feels really bad about telling Nick about our drunken wedding, so I've decided to forgive her since she's heartbroken too. And Tyler's parents would have gotten the video in the mail anyway so it didn't make that much of a difference in the long run. Plus, we're all going to have to go our separate ways once the factory is closed, so I've let it go, and I'm just trying to enjoy what little time we do have left together.

We head inside and curl up under blankets as we watch the movie. I haven't seen *Willow* in years, and it's not nearly as scary or mind blowing or good as when I watched it as a kid.

"Wow, Val Kilmer was so hot back then," Emily says as she shoves a heaping spoonful of walnut ice cream into her mouth. "I wonder what happened?"

"He probably ate too much walnut ice cream," I say with a smirk. She turns to me with a glare as ice cream drips from her chin onto her shirt.

"It's wallowing night," she says, frowning at me. "Anything goes on wallowing night."

I laugh as I turn back to the bad movie, trying to focus on it, but my mind keeps wandering back to Tyler. I wonder what he's doing, if he's happy or sad, if he's thinking of me.

"Stop it," Emily says, pointing her finger at me. "I can see the longing in your eyes. Tonight is a night of wallowing, not longing. Keep that shit tucked away until tomorrow."

She refills my glass of wine as someone turns onto my street. I turn and look through the window behind me to the headlights driving up the dark road. I hold my breath as the lights slow to a stop in front of my house.

"Who is that?" Emily asks, turning.

My heart is pounding and my mouth is dry despite all the wine I've been consuming. Could it be him?

"Ah," I say, dropping my shoulders in disappointment. I'd recognize that van anywhere. "It's my parents. What the heck are they doing here?"

I jump up to go find out while Emily searches for the remote control. "I'll pause it for you."

"Please don't," I say as I head outside.

"Rainbow!" my mother says as she steps out of the van. "I love your house. It's so cute!"

"Thanks," I say, turning around and taking a quick glance at the house I love. "What are you guys doing here?"

A thick cloud of smoke follows my father as he steps out of the driver's seat. "Hey, Rainbow," he says, smiling as he takes my mother's hand and they walk over.

I give them a quick hug, and then we're standing on my front lawn awkwardly. "So, what brings you two to Summerland?" I ask.

"We were passing through on our way to Hippiefest, and we decided to come say hi," my mom answers. "We had such a good time seeing you in Vegas, and we want to start doing it more often."

"Really?" I ask, jerking my head back in shock. "You guys want to see *me* more often?"

"Of course," my father answers. "You're our Rainbow. Didn't you have fun with us in Vegas?"

"Yeah," I say, biting my bottom lip. Besides the nude swimming, weed smoking, awkward comments, sex in the hammock, and just about every other time they were around other people, I had fun. Kind of.

"Is Tyler inside?" my father asks, looking at my house. "I want to apologize to him. I spent all of his t-shirt investment money on weed."

"That's okay," I say with a shrug. "I don't think he's going to mind."

"Can we say hi to him?" my mother asks.

I take a deep breath, wanting to crumple to the ground. "He's not here. We're no longer together."

They both looked crushed. "Why not?" my mother asks, touching my arm. "You two seemed so perfect together."

My body feels so heavy whenever I think about this. "I can't have it all," I say, feeling cold and tired as I tell them. "I can't have a career and love at the same time. I tried, and it didn't work out. If I wanted to succeed at a career, then I had to let him go. So, I did. It's better this way."

"No, it's not," my mother says with a frown. "If anyone can have both, it's you. You're the smartest, most capable person I've ever known. Why are you selling yourself short?"

My dad shakes his head, looking disappointed. "The Rainbow I know takes whatever she wants and doesn't let anything stop her."

"But how can I focus on my career when my head is in the clouds with love?" I ask, feeling a tightness in my chest.

"You two loved each other fiercely, but there was no energy left to devote to a career. I'm sorry, but I don't want to end up like that—constantly moving from campsite to campsite, no money to pay bills or buy food. I'd rather have security and a place to live."

"You have a place to live," my mother says, pointing to my house. "But it's not a home until you have someone you love inside."

My heart hurts as I remember how nice and warm my house felt when Tyler was staying with me. It felt like home. It felt better than anything else.

"There's a balance to everything in life," my father says, lifting up one hand then the other. "You have to find a way to have your love life and your work life at peace. It's the only way you'll be happy."

He's right. I won't be happy with only work in my life. Working overtime and weekends to get promotions and raises won't bring me the kind of happiness I felt when I was wrapped in Tyler's arms. And I won't be truly happy either if I just go for love like my parents did and stop striving for a successful career. That's not me either.

I never thought I'd say this, but my father actually said something profound that may change my life. I smile as I watch him, looking at him with a new-found respect.

"Does your house have a shitter?" he asks, starting to squirm. "Or should I go in the bushes?"

Well, that respect was nice while it lasted.

"You can go in," I say, pointing to the front door. "First door on your right."

He hurries in as I walk over to sit on the porch with my mom. For the first time in my life, I start to open up to my mother, telling her what happened between me and Tyler.

"I know we haven't been the best parents," she says with

a sigh. "But if we've taught you anything, I hope that we taught you that love is all you need. I love your father with every breath that I take, and I can see you had that with Tyler."

I drop my head as I listen.

"You don't need a fancy career or a big house or clothes from a store when you have someone to love. Love can fulfill you in ways that nothing else can." She taps my knee and smiles. "You should try it sometime."

We sit in silence for a bit and then go into the house to check on my dad. I laugh when I find him under the blanket next to Emily with a glass of wine and a bowl of ice cream in his hands while they watch the end of *Willow*.

My mother and I squeeze beside them on the couch, and we watch the rest of the horrible-but-amazing movie together.

"Do you guys want to stay the night?" I ask after Emily leaves and it's getting pretty late.

My father's hands are all over my mother, and he's looking pretty frisky.

"Are we allowed to make love in your house?" he asks.

"Absolutely not," I say with my hands on my hips.

My mother looks at her watch and then frowns. "Then we should really get going. We'll drive a bit and then sleep in the van."

"We're not going to be sleeping," my father says before slapping my mother's ass.

I smile even though it's something gross that I never want to see again. After all of these years, they're still so in love. I envy them.

That's why they never needed a permanent home. That's why they wandered around so much. Their home was each other, and *that* was permanent.

"I love you, Mom," I say, giving her a warm hug. I can't remember the last time I said those words to her. She looks thrilled when I pull away.

"I love you too, Dad," I say, giving him a hug next. They tell me they love me too, and I feel better than I've felt in a long time as I stand on my front lawn and wave to them as they drive away.

In that moment, I forgive them for everything, and it's like a weight has been lifted off my shoulders.

I finally get it. Love is all they needed. They had that and they didn't care about anything else.

I've spent my whole life trying to be the opposite of them when what I really needed was to be more like them.

I'm ready to try and have a balance in my life of love and career, but our annulment is scheduled in two days and I'm afraid that it's already too late.

29

Dahlia

MY STOMACH IS a mess of nerves as I walk into the court-house on the morning of the annulment. I flew into Vegas to get dumped.

I'm sure I'm not the first person to leave Vegas with a broken marriage, but the thought doesn't make me feel any better. I've had a tightness in my chest since I got on the plane, and it just gets worse as I walk up to the reception desk and ask where to go.

"Down the hall and to the right," the young woman says after pulling up my file. "You're with Judge Roth."

A heaviness settles over me as I shuffle down the hall, wishing the floor would open up and swallow me whole so I can escape all of this.

It gets even worse when I look up and see Tyler sitting on the bench outside of the door. His head is down, and he's fidgeting with the videotape in his hands. He's wearing a nice suit, but his tie is loose around his thick neck and his coat is a tad wrinkled. It doesn't look as crisp as normal.

I hope he's doing okay.

His eyes look blank as he stares at the tape in his hands. I can't help but wonder what he's thinking.

I take a deep breath as I walk up to him. "Hello."

He jerks his head up like I just yanked him out of a deep thought. "Hi," he says with his shoulders slumped. "Did you have a good flight?"

"Yeah," I answer. There's an empty seat beside him, but I sit on the bench across the hall instead. He gives me a tight smile as we glance awkwardly at each other.

It's the first time we've had an awkward moment since our first morning waking up together, and even that wasn't this awkward. I don't like it.

He stares back down at the tape in his hands, and I take the opportunity to study him. This may be the last time I ever see him, and that thought sends a sharp pain jolting through my chest. I don't want the last time I see the man I married to be like this—sitting awkwardly in a courthouse.

I take a deep breath, wanting to tell him that I do love him and that I think we're making a mistake, but I'm scared. I'm terrified of what that might mean.

"Tyler," I whisper, not knowing what I'm going to say next.

His head rises with a hopeful look on his face. "Yeah?"

"I..." My voice trails away as the door opens and Judge Roth steps out. He's a large man with light gray hair that matches his gray collared shirt.

"Mr. McMillan and Mrs. Winters," he says, waving us in. We both stand up, looking nervous as he disappears back into his office.

Tyler lets me walk in first. He raises his hand to put on

my lower back as I walk past him, but he thinks twice about it and lets his hand fall to his sides instead.

Judge Roth is sitting behind his desk, reading over our file with a furrowed brow. "So, you want an annulment," he says, dropping the paper on his desk as we take the two seats in front of him. "On what grounds? Impotence? Are you two cousins? Is one of you already married? I've heard them all."

Tyler clears his throat. "We were hammered."

"I've heard that one too," he answers. "What happened?"

"We're still trying to figure that out," Tyler says, swallowing hard.

Judge Roth leans back in his chair. "I'm going to need proof, and not just a pocket full of bottle caps. *Real* proof."

Tyler sighs and then hands him the videotape.

"Wait," I say before taking a deep breath. Both Judge Roth and Tyler turn to me with raised eyebrows. "Tyler, I don't want to get an annulment."

The words pass through my lips before I can process the ramifications of what they mean. My heart is doing the talking now. It's been silent for far too long.

"You don't?" Tyler whispers.

"No. I want to stay married."

Judge Roth clears his throat. "So, you weren't drunk? This is all a lie?"

"No, we were drunk," I say, turning to him. "And we did get married, and it was a mistake. At first."

I turn back to the wonderful man beside me, and he's staring at me with hopeful eyes. "It was a horrible mistake, but it turned into something more. Something real. Something beautiful. I do love you, Tyler. I love that you have an N'Sync poster hanging in your room, I love that you bought me a brand-new bike, I love that you made my house feel like a home for the first time since I got the keys. I love your sense of humor, your kindness, your passion, and your drive. And I love that you wear red underwear. I love everything about you."

He's staring at me in stunned silence. I wish he'd say something soon because it's getting pretty awkward in here.

"He has an N'Sync poster hanging on his wall?" Judge Roth asks with a crinkled-up nose. "That should qualify you two for an annulment right there."

"I want to stay married too," Tyler finally says, ignoring the judge. "I've loved you since the moment I saw you at the bar. I just didn't know it yet."

I leap forward and kiss him with every ounce of love that I'm feeling, nearly toppling his chair over with him in it.

"Excuse me!" Judge Roth shouts as he slaps his desk. "How would you two like to be arrested for contempt of court?"

I immediately pull away from him and sit back in my seat with my lips tingling.

"I'll spend life in jail for another kiss like that," Tyler says with a big goofy smile on his face.

Judge Roth doesn't look too upset. "So, are we getting annulled or what?" he asks.

We both shake our head. "No, thank you," I say with a wide smile.

He grabs the tape off the desk. "Can I still watch this?"

"Go ahead," Tyler says, grabbing my hand as he stands up. "It's the best moment of my life."

We say a quick goodbye and head outside, closing the door behind us. After a long kiss, Tyler holds me close and looks down at me with a warm smile.

"I really didn't want to go through with that," he says, exhaling long and deep.

"Neither did I."

"I don't know what the future holds for us," he says, holding me tightly, "but I can't wait to find out. We've had a few bad surprises in the past few weeks, but I think we're due for some good ones."

I couldn't agree more.

We kiss each other until we hear the muffled sound of our wedding playing behind the closed door, and hear Judge Roth laughing hysterically.

"Do you think he's going to put it on YouTube?" I ask, suddenly worried.

Tyler cringes. "Isn't your boob hanging out of your dress?"

My eyes widen as I remember the horrifying details of the video. Tyler goes back into the office and comes out two minutes later with the tape in his hands. "Let's get the hell out of here."

We hurry out of the courthouse, and we walk down the street together to his office building which is only a few blocks away.

"All right," I say, smiling up at him when we're almost there. "I admit it."

"What?"

"The Lucky 7 drink was indeed lucky."

He smiles, making me smile too. "Want to go have another one?"

"I don't think so," I say with a laugh. "I'm afraid of who I'll end up married to this time."

Tyler's smile fades to a scowl when he looks across the street. I turn to where he's looking and see three of those crazy cult members darting through oncoming traffic on their way over.

"These guys again?" I say, gasping as one almost gets hit by a car.

"You know them?" Tyler asks, looking at me in shock.

"They seem to like me for some strange reason."

He turns back to them and clenches his jaw. "They broke into my office."

"*What?!?*"

"Blessed Prophets!" one of them shouts as they leap onto the sidewalk and rush over in their bare feet.

Tyler grabs me with a strong hand and pulls me behind his big frame protectively as they come running over.

"Please tell us the mighty word of Franesca and Lukania," one of them says.

Another shoves a tape recorder into Tyler's face. "Tell us how to reach the center of the flaming star," he begs, recording everything.

Tyler shoves his hand away, but the weirdo puts the recorder right back in front of Tyler immediately.

"Why are you following us?" I ask, peeking out from behind Tyler.

The completely hairless guy moves the recorder from Tyler to me. "On what day will we ascend from this planet into the sun?"

"Into the sun?" I ask, staring at him in disbelief. They're even crazier than I thought.

"Yes, blessed Prophet," he says, dropping to his knees. "Please tell us your divine wisdom."

Tyler grabs one of the guys by his yellow robe, turns and slams him into the brick wall behind us. "Why did you break into my office?" he hisses in his face. "Why are you tapping my phones? Did Nick hire you?"

The guy is just staring at Tyler with a big happy grin on his face. Tyler jerks him forward and then slams him into the wall again.

"Thank you for honoring me by pushing me against the wall, blessed Prophet," he says, looking thrilled.

"Please slam me into the wall next, blessed Prophet," one of the other guys says, looking jealous.

Tyler releases the man and steps back, looking frustrated. "What the fuck are you guys talking about? Why do you keep calling us Prophets?"

The three of them drop to their knees and lower their foreheads to the sidewalk. "You two are the blessed Prophets sent with a message by the true Gods, Franesca and Lukania," one of them says. "The holy scriptures say that you will tell us how to reach the center of the flaming star, and the members of the Sunshine Happy Church will ascend from this planet of cold and hate, into the warmth of the center of the sun."

Tyler laughs. "And you guys believe this?"

"With all of our hearts."

I step on my toes and lean into Tyler's ear. "I think we may have joined their cult on our crazy night."

I tell him about the flowered necklace that I found in my purse, exactly like the ones around their necks, and about the pamphlet from the Sunshine Happy Church that was stuffed next to the big box of Magnum condoms.

"That's why you've been harassing us?" Tyler asks as they climb back up to their bare feet. "Because you're waiting to hear a prophecy?"

They nod.

Tyler curls his hand into a fist. "I'll break your noses. That's the fucking prophecy."

"Please do!" one of them shouts as all three of them stick their chins in the air. "It would be such an honor."

I grab Tyler's flexed arm and hold him back. "I am the

blessed Prophet," I say, stepping forward. "Sent by Franky and Lukey."

"Franesca and Lukania," one of them corrects.

"That's what I meant," I say, puffing my chest out. "I want you to tell us exactly what happened the night we arrived."

One of them tells us how we entered with wet clothes, which is the sign of the Prophets, and broke their holy statue of the sun, signaling the entrance to Solaris.

"This is too weird," Tyler whispers to me. "Let's get out of here before they brainwash us."

I agree.

"That's a wonderful story," I say, smiling at them as we slowly back away. "But we have to leave now."

Another one steps forward and bows. "May you bask in the light of Solaris," he says. "We will continue to monitor you until we hear the prophecy you were destined to bring."

We both stop and turn. "Monitor us?" Tyler asks. "So, it was you who tapped my phones."

"Yes," the cult member says, nodding proudly. "We also bugged your office with tape recorders. Franesca and Lukania would be proud."

Tyler grabs my arm as he turns to me with wide eyes. "Tape recorders?"

I'm about to ask him why he looks so excited when he hurries back over to them, leaving me alone on the sidewalk.

"Take me to these tape recorders," he says.

"THERE'S MORE OF THEM," Tyler whispers as we walk into the Sunshine Happy Church's headquarters, which is nothing more than a small apartment over a Vietnamese restaurant. The creeper vibe is off the charts but it sure does smell delicious.

The twenty or so members are all staring at us in awe as we walk in. I inch a little closer to Tyler as they surround us with wide eyes and gaping mouths.

"Tyler," I whisper, tugging on his shirt as I stare past the group of brainwashed cult members to the pictures on the far walls. "Look at that."

Tyler gasps when he sees what I'm looking at: a wall full of pictures of us. Walking to work, sitting in a restaurant, waiting in line at a coffee shop, even our wedding photo is hanging on the wall.

If I didn't have Tyler's large protective frame beside me, I'd be terrified.

I'm still a little terrified.

I gulp as I turn to the TV and see a video playing of me walking down the street. *What the fuck is this place?*

They are all staring at the two of us, waiting for something.

"Hello," I say. They all burst out into smiles and cheer. One lady starts crying.

"Where are the tapes?" Tyler asks in a firm voice. "The tapes from my office."

One of the three men who brought us here rushes into the bedroom and comes back out with a shoebox full of tapes.

"We listened to each one at least ten times," the man says, handing Tyler the box. "There is no mention of the prophecy. Do you speak in code?"

Tyler grabs the box and begins rifling through them. There are dozens of tapes. It's going to take us days, if not weeks, to go through them all.

"Yes," Tyler says with a grin. "The prophecy is stated in one of these tapes."

"Oooohhh," they all say, leaning forward with excitement in their wide eyes.

"Which one?" a bald woman asks.

"I'm having a conversation with a man," Tyler explains. "About stolen money, unibrows and a promotion."

"The Saint Nicholas," the man beside him says. He reaches into the box, rifles through the tapes, and pulls one out. Tyler grins at me as the man runs to the tape recorder and pops it in. He takes a few seconds to find the spot, but when he does, he plays it loud enough for everyone to hear.

Sure enough, Tyler and Nick's scratchy voices ring out in the room.

"You get girls now, your eyebrows only look slightly ridiculous, and you're rich. I know because you've been stealing money from the company."

"I've been taking what's rightfully mine."

"Stolen money from the company is rightfully yours?"

"Yes. I deserve it. This company would be nothing without me."

"How much did you take?"

"Millions. And I deserve every last penny."

"You don't deserve any of it. And you don't deserve this promotion. You deserve to go to jail."

Tyler hurries over, stops the tape player, and slips the tape into his pocket. He looks thrilled as he turns around and smiles at me.

"You crazy fucks don't know how happy you've made me," he says, grinning as he walks back to my side. "I was about to press charges against you, but now I just want to give you all a hug."

One of the men leaps onto Tyler and hugs his waist. "It was a figure of speech," Tyler says, pushing him to the floor.

"Can we go now?" I ask, stepping back toward the door. Those pictures of me on the wall are creeping me out. I don't want my head to be removed from my body and put on the fireplace mantel. I wouldn't put anything past these freaks.

"You can't leave without giving us the prophecy," a woman shrieks, looking terrified. "Please, blessed Prophets!"

"All right," I say, stepping forward. All eyes are on me as I puff out my chest and thrust my chin in the air. "Here is your prophecy from Fruity and Lupus."

"Franesca and Lukania," one of them corrects.

"Whatever."

Tyler laughs as he watches me. I stick my tongue out at him.

"Everything will be okay from now on," I say, looking them in the eyes one by one. "Leave this place. Go back to your families, your civilian clothes, for God's sake grow your hair out, and try to enjoy your lives with someone you love."

They look confused as they turn to one another, muttering something about the center of the sun.

"For only those who live a long, meaningful life full of laughter and love will enter the sun when they die," I say. "That is the message from Franesca and Lukania."

Tyler clears his throat. "And the Gods also told us to tell you to delete any tapes or videos with us on it. Burn the pictures, destroy the tapes, stop tapping our phones, and stop following us."

"That's right," I say, nodding. "We have to go back to our dimension now and will be leaving these mortal bodies that we inhabited."

They look confused at first but begin nodding one by one.

"Remember," I say, grabbing Tyler and pulling him as I step back toward the door. "If you see these mortal bodies again, they will have no recollection of this event. We are the Prophets about to return home to our dimension, and these human bodies cannot ever know about us."

"That's right," Tyler says, nodding. "If you ever come near us again, you will be denied entry into the center of the sun."

They all gasp, looking horrified as they watch us.

"Thank you, blessed Prophets!" one man says before throwing himself on the ground. They all quickly follow until every single cult member is lying on the ground with their foreheads pressed to the floor.

Tyler and I look at each other with raised eyebrows as we quietly sneak out the door.

"That was the weirdest moment of my life," he says as we race through the Vietnamese restaurant and out the door.

"Weirder than waking up married to a stranger?" I ask as we hurry down the sidewalk.

He nods. "Yeah. Much weirder than that."

I laugh. "Where are we going now?"

Tyler pulls the tape out of his pocket and grins at me. "We're going to go save your factory."

30

Tyler

MY FATHER IS HAVING a meeting with Nick and Jason when I burst into his office with the tape in my hand.

"I have something you have to listen to," I say, ignoring my father when he snaps at me for interrupting them.

He frowns as I walk up to the radio in his office. "I've seen enough of your tapes," he says sternly. "Your mother and I are still recovering from the last one. She's removed all of the pineapples from our house after seeing you try to make a baby with one."

"You'll want to hear this," I say, putting the tape in anyway.

"We're very busy," Nick says with a hint of panic in his voice. "We don't have time for more of your lies."

Dahlia is waiting in the lobby downstairs. She didn't want to be here to remind my father of our own tape. Probably a smart move.

Nick jumps up and rushes over as I slip the tape in. "If you don't leave, I'm going to have security escort you out," he says, grabbing my arm.

"Nick," Jason says, trying to calm the situation down. "Let him play the tape."

Nick reaches for the tape, but I shrug him off and hit play. He freezes as his voice fills the room.

"How much did you take?"

"Millions. And I deserve every last penny."

"You don't deserve any of it. And you don't dese—"

Nick hits stop and turns to my father with open arms. "Lies," he says, shaking his head. "More horrible lies like the one about his marriage. I'm afraid we can't trust Tyler at all anymore."

My father looks at me with hard eyes. "Play it again. From the beginning."

Nick lunges for the tape player, and I push him back, flashing him a warning with my eyes. He is my cousin and we are in my father's office, but I would still take any excuse I can get to knock him out cold. Jason seems to sense that and jumps between us, pushing his older brother away from me as Nick's voice fills the room once again from the beginning of our conversation.

My father listens attentively as we argue through his speakers.

"That's cute. Didn't you hear your father back there? This whole building and every office in it is mine now. You're only here because I'm allowing you to be here. That is, until the papers are signed and the company is officially mine. Then you and your paid wife will be out on the streets."

I keep my eyes on my father, watching as his stern face gets even sterner as the conversation goes on. When Nick admits to stealing millions, my father looks ready to put him through a wall.

His skin is turning an angry red as he glares at Nick, looking furious that he supported and trusted this man who is openly bragging on tape about stealing money from him.

"I've heard enough," he says when the tape is almost finished.

I turn the tape off as Jason stands like a bouncer by the door in case his brother tries to leave. Jason would never betray my father. He's proven his loyalty time and time again.

My father stands up from his desk and walks up to Nick with a high chin and a hard tightness in his eyes. "What do you have to say for yourself?"

"It's all lies," Nick says, trying to put the blame on me, but his body language is giving him away. His breathing is quicker, and he keeps shifting from foot to foot, darting his eyes around the room nervously. "He made that tape."

"Dad," I say, looking him dead in the eyes. "He's stealing from the company. Look closely at the financials in his departments and you'll see it too."

"That's not true!" Nick shouts defensively. "*He* had sex in his office. *He* shouldn't even be allowed in this building."

Jason steps forward. "I've seen the financials too, Mack. I think Tyler is right."

Nick shoots an accusing look at his brother. "You're going against your own family?" he spits out.

"Tyler and Uncle Mack are my family too," Jason says, "and I'm not going to sit around while someone steals from them."

"Even if it's your brother?"

"Especially if it's my brother," he answers.

My father grabs the phone off of his desk and dials security. He asks them to come, and a few seconds later they come rushing through the door.

"Am I getting arrested?" Nick asks indignantly. "You can't arrest me. I'm the head of this company!"

"Not anymore," my father says, shaking his head. "You'll never step foot in this building again."

Nick starts to look panicked as the three security guards start closing in on him. "Uncle Mack," he says, sounding desperate. "I'm sorry. I'll give the money back. I promise."

My father ignores him and turns to the security guards. "Put him in the holding room and call the police. I want to press charges."

"No!" Nick shouts as he shakes his head in denial. His eyes are bulging, and his body is tense. "Please, don't do this."

He makes a desperate run for the exit, but I put out my foot and trip him. Before he even slams into the ground, the security guards are on him, cuffing his hands behind his back.

The whole top floor of the building is gathered in the main area, watching as he's being dragged out.

"You should probably go with him, Jason," my father says to my younger cousin. "Make sure he gets a lawyer. He's going to need one."

Jason nods and then joins his brother and the security guards by the elevators.

My father steps out into the main area where everybody is gathered. "Get back to work!" he shouts, and they all scatter like frightened mice.

He sighs. "I'm really going to miss doing that when I'm retired." He turns to me with a tight expression on his face. "In my office. Now."

He storms back into his office, and I follow him in,

closing the door behind me. His eyes are locked on me like heat-seeking missiles as he sits behind his massive desk.

"I still can't give you the company," he says as I sit down in front of him. "Not after what you did."

"I know," I say, exhaling hard as I sink into the chair. "I don't want it anymore. From now on, I'm putting my heart first."

"With your fake wife?"

"With my *real* wife," I say, staring him down. "I love Dahlia. More than anything. She's the one for me, and we're going to stay married."

My father looks skeptical. "If this is another scam of yours to get me to sign over the compa—"

"It's not a scam," I say, interrupting him. "It's true we didn't know each other when we got married, but we know each other now, and she's the most amazing woman I've ever met. She's the one for me."

His face softens, looking like he finally believes me. "I thought you two were good together," he says, nodding. "I didn't believe Nick when he told me it was all a sham. You two looked genuinely in love. Dahlia's eyes always light up when she looks at you, and I've never seen you so focused on one girl before."

"Is Mom really mad?"

"She's upset," he says, making me sigh. I really didn't want to hurt her feelings or make her upset. "But she'll be happy to know that you two are in it for real now."

"I'll talk to her."

We sit in silence for a minute until my father exhales and leans back in his chair. "I really wanted to retire," he says, staring up at the ceiling.

"You still can."

"I can't give you the company," he says, looking sad as he looks at me.

"I told you, I don't want it," I say with a laugh. "I think you should put Jason in charge."

"Jason?" he says, jerking his head back. "He never showed the slightest interest in having the position before."

"He backed off because he knew that both Nick and I wanted it," I explain. "He's one of the smartest people in this building, and he's completely trustworthy. He'll make an excellent CEO. He has a level head, and he'll always do what's best for the company and the employees."

"Jason," my father whispers, nodding his head as he thinks about it. "He would make a fine choice."

"You'll be able to sit back and relax during your retirement with him at the helm of the ship. He'll do you proud."

My father seems to really like the idea, and I can tell that the wheels and cogs in his brain are turning.

"I think you're right," he says with a grin.

"I am right," I answer, driving the point home. "He's going to do great."

"And what about you?" he asks. "What do you see as your future role in McMillan Worldwide Inc?"

I don't see my future here at all anymore. I see it with Dahlia in the town that we both love.

"That's what I wanted to talk to you about," I say, wringing my hands nervously. "I have something I want to ask you."

31

Dahlia

"So?" Susan the gossiper says as she walks over with a big grin on her face. "What's this I hear about a video of something?"

Oh, God.

"What did you hear?" I ask with a sigh.

"Why don't you tell me what you know, and I'll tell you if that's what I heard?" she says, trying to fish for information. Well, she's not going to catch anything from me.

Just in time to save me from the company's official gossiper, the elevators open and three security guards walk out, escorting Nick. His brother Jason is walking behind them, looking disappointed.

"You want a video," I say, pointing at Nick. "There's your video."

Susan gasps when she sees him with his hands cuffed behind his back, being escorted through the lobby. She yanks out her phone and starts filming as she rushes over, leaving me in peace.

I can't help but grin as I watch him get escorted into an area that's reserved for security only. *I guess my husband's plan worked.*

A few tense minutes later, Tyler walks out of the elevators with a big beautiful smile on his face. I run up to him with my heart pounding. "Tell me everything."

I can't stop smiling as he tells me how he played the audio tape for his father and how Mack finally believed him about the missing money.

"What about the company?" I ask with a fluttering feeling in my stomach. "Did he reconsider you for the job?"

He shakes his head no but he has a smile on his face. "I'm not getting the company. Jason is."

It feels like I got punched in the stomach. My breath catches in my throat as I fight back tears. My beloved factory will be closed down, and the town that is the only home I've ever known will be ruined. My friends, coworkers and neighbors will all be jobless, just like me.

"Why are you smiling?" I ask with a trembling chin. My eyes are burning from fighting back tears. I can't believe this is happening.

"The factory is staying open."

"What?" It doesn't make sense. "Why would Jason agree to that? It can make more money overseas."

"It's not up to Jason anymore," he says with a widening grin. "It's ours."

"What?"

"I bought it. For us."

I'm speechless. Utterly shocked as I stand in front of him.

"You bought it?" I ask slowly. It's still not sinking in.

"Consider it a wedding present," he says with his jade green eyes sparkling. "A *real* wedding present."

My thoughts are so fuzzy. I wasn't expecting this at all and now I seem to have lost my ability to think. So I just stare at his gorgeous face with my jaw hanging open.

"Hospitech is no longer a part of McMillan Worldwide Inc.," he says. "It's a separate company, and it's all ours. Well, as soon as you come upstairs and sign the papers."

"But you live in Vegas."

"Not for long."

"You're moving? To Summerland?"

"If you'll have me."

My heart is racing in excitement.

"There are no mansions in Summerland," I say.

"Good."

"No Ferrari dealerships either."

He shrugs. "I have a free ride on a bike whenever I want."

"You're getting your own bike from now on," I say with a laugh. "I don't want my calves to be more muscular than yours."

"Deal."

A flush of adrenaline is tingling through my body as I try to process all of this. "Where are you going to live?"

He just stares at me with a grin.

"You want to move in with me?" I ask, staring up at him in disbelief.

"You are my wife."

"But you've seen my house," I say, suddenly feeling ashamed. I live in a cute but simple house. I don't have a five-car garage, an inground pool, or a penthouse condo overlooking the Vegas strip. My television is as thick as a microwave, my couch is the same one that I bought second-hand in my twenties, and my lawn mower doesn't start without hitting it with a hammer first. I don't live in the same level of luxury that he's accustomed to. It's not even close.

"I love your house," he says, stepping forward. He takes my hands in his and stares me in the eyes. "Most of all because you're in it."

"But your condo," I say with my pulse racing, "and your amazing kitchen. I can't compete with that."

He shakes his head. "No. They can't compete with you. The nice condo, the expensive toys, and cars are nice, but what I really want is a home. And when I'm with you, I feel like I'm at home."

I jump into his arms as tears of joy stream down my face. All I've ever wanted was a place to call home, and now I have it for real. I'm part owner of the best company in the world, in the town of my dreams, with the man that I love. It can't get any better than this.

"I love you, Tyler," I say, staring into his eyes.

He leans down and gives me a soft slow kiss on the lips.

I pull away with my cheeks flushing red. "We shouldn't. We're at work."

He pulls me in even tighter. "We don't work here anymore," he says before giving me another long romantic kiss on the lips. This time I let him.

When we finally pull away, I see Susan videotaping us from the other side of the lobby. Normally I would get upset at the lack of privacy, but I flash her a smile and then kiss my man again. Our video collection of the two of us needs some new additions that we can show our kids one day, and this is a great time to start.

"So," he says with a grin as he holds me in his arms. "Want to be part owner of Hospitech with me?"

My heart starts pounding in my chest. "I can't believe this," I say with a wide grin on my face. "I have so many ideas for growth and for expanding our distribution. We can add a new wing to the factory for diagnostic equipment and one for biomedical equipment." I keep rambling on, spitting out ideas and future plans until I'm blue in the face.

"Hold on, Pumpkin," Tyler says, putting a hand up. "First things first, you have to sign the papers."

I grab onto his thick forearm and squeal in excitement. "Let's go!"

He laughs as I practically drag him to the elevators and pull him inside.

As soon as the doors close, I jump back on him, kissing every inch of skin that I can find.

"Is your father still mad at us?" I ask when the doors open on the top floor. I hesitate, not wanting to leave the safety of the elevator and face Mack McMillan's wrath again.

Tyler takes my hand and pulls me out. "We're happy and in love," he says, looking like he doesn't have a care in the world. "What can he possibly be mad at?"

"The lying, the video, breaking your mom's heart."

He smiles as he pulls me down the hall to the big man's office. "As for the lying, we're in love and staying married, so we're not lying anymore. Our wedding video was horrific, but it will get funnier the more times he watches it. And as for breaking my mom's heart by not giving her grandkids, well, we'll just have to take care of that for her."

"Wha—" I mutter as I try to process his words. Children? With Tyler? It's two thoughts that shouldn't go together, but for some reason, it sounds perfectly natural. For the first time ever, I can see myself pregnant with his children, and it brings a smile on my face.

He pulls me into Mack's office and I straighten my back, staring at him as nerves ripple through me.

"Dad," Tyler says, presenting me. "I would like to introduce you to my wife, Dahlia. My *real* wife."

Mack lowers his reading glasses, looking over them and at me with skeptical eyes. "I believe we've already met."

"You met my *fake* wife," Tyler says with a firm voice. "This is my *real* wife. The woman I love. The woman I want to have children with. The woman I want to spend the rest of my life with."

Mack takes off his glasses and drops them on his desk. "I don't know what to believe anymore," he says, rubbing his eyes.

"Believe that I love your son," I say, stepping forward. "And believe that he loves me. Believe that against all odds, the universe found two soulmates on opposite sides of the country and brought us together. Believe that we started off rocky but finally found our groove. And believe that we'll be together forever. Or believe whatever you want, but know that all of that is true. I love your son with all of my heart, and I would love to be a part of your family, if you'll have me. For real this time."

Mack's eyes are narrowed on me as he listens with a blank face. I can't tell what he's thinking. It doesn't look good.

"I'll tell you what I believe," he says, taking a deep breath. "I believe that my son has never looked happier. I believe that my son is a changed man and that *he* now believes in the power of love. And I believe that it's all because of you, Dahlia."

"Really?" I ask, breathless. "But the wedding video..."

"Is exactly what I expected from my son," he says with a laugh. "You should have seen his college graduation video."

Tyler is grinning. "I was naked under my robe."

"Of course you were," I say with a chuckle.

"It's not important why or how the marriage happened," Mack says, standing up. "What is important is that you two are in it for real now, that you love and respect one another, and that you are in it for the long haul."

"I am," I say with a nod.

"I am too," Tyler says, smiling at me.

It's the closest we've come to saying our *I do's* sober, but it's good enough for me.

"Good," Mack says, walking around the desk to join us. Mack the billionaire is gone as he walks straight up to me and Mack my father-in-law takes his place as he gives me a warm hug. "I've always wanted a daughter," he says with a smile. "I'm so glad that I have you."

"Thank you, sir," I say, fighting back tears. "I mean, *Dad*."

He smiles at me. "Kirsten and I never gave you two a wedding present. I heard there's a company you're interested in."

"You're not giving us Hospitech, Dad," Tyler says, waving his hand. "It's an eight-million-dollar company. I'll buy it off of you."

"Save it to spoil your beautiful new wife," he says, giving me a little wink.

But Tyler doesn't back down. "It's too much."

I step back and watch as the two master negotiators dig their heels in and attack. It's clear that Tyler got his father's incredible negotiating abilities. That's going to come in handy when we're running Hospitech together.

When it's all said and done, Mack drafts up a contract for the insanely unreasonable price of two dollars. Tyler and I split it, a dollar each, and after signing our names, we are the new owners of Hospitech.

I collapse into the chair and stare at the contract with my head spinning as all of the pent-up worry, stress, and fear just washes away.

The town is saved, the company is ours, and I have Tyler.

Best dollar I've ever spent.

32

Dahlia

A MONTH LATER...

"CONGRATULATIONS," I say, grinning as I look up at my man. "You're officially a resident of the best town in the world."

Tyler is watching the empty moving trucks rumble away down my street. *Our* street. He takes a deep satisfied breath. "*And* I'm married to the best girl in the world. Lucky me."

"Lucky you is right," I say, grinning as I slip my hand into his. I smile when I feel the wedding band that I bought him wrapped proudly around his ring finger. He never takes it off, even in the shower.

It's been a month since Mack sold Hospitech to us for the price of a cheap coffee, and we've been living together in my place ever since. Tyler sold his condo in Vegas, traded his two cars in for a bike, and is now a permanent resident of house number four on Maple Ridge Road, Summerland.

We had talked about upgrading our house and even went to visit several properties, but after seeing a few, we decided to stay here. Every house we visited just felt wrong. They were too big, too impersonal, too flashy, too far from town. This house is just right. It's going to be the perfect house to raise a family in, and now that I have the start of one, I can't wait.

"Well," I say when the moving trucks turn around the corner, and out of view. "I guess I'm stuck with you now."

He takes my hand and pulls me toward the house with a smile on his face. "You guess right. Because I'm definitely stuck on you."

We head into the house and start unpacking his boxes, trying to fit everything into drawers and closets that are already stuffed to the limit with my junk.

"You brought these?" I ask, shaking my head as I pull out the whip and ball gag from a box.

"We still haven't officially had our honeymoon," Tyler says, walking over. "I thought they might come in handy."

"You thought wrong," I say, tossing them back into the box. "We tried that once, and it didn't work out so well." I laugh when I reach into the box and pull out a large framed photo. It's our wedding photo, the one that could double as a mug shot. "You got this framed?"

"I sure did," he says, taking it from my hands. He's all smiles as he walks over to the fireplace and puts it on display in the middle of the mantle. "Perfect," he says, taking a step back to admire it.

"Not perfect," I say, crossing my arms as I playfully glare at him. "I can't have that on display in my house."

"*Our* house," he corrects. "Dahlia, marriage is all about compromise."

"I'm willing to compromise," I say as I walk over and grab the photo. "I'll get my way and you can figure out a way to deal with it."

He laughs as he steps behind me and looks over my shoulder at the photo in my hands. We look like a hot mess. The strands of my hair are as tangled as a box of Christmas lights, and my makeup looks like it would be more suited on a clown caught in a hurricane. Tyler looks just as bad with his half-closed eyes, and the ball gag strapped to his mouth. A trail of drool is leaking from the side of his mouth down to his chin.

"You look worse," he says.

I burst out laughing. "Are you kidding me?" I answer. "Look at you! You look like you forgot what our safe word was."

He takes the frame from my hands and puts it back on the fireplace mantle. "I guess we'll have to let our guests decide who looks worse."

"Fine," I say, crossing my arms over my chest. "But don't expect them to come back for a second visit."

As if right on cue, the doorbell rings. "Are you expecting anyone?" Tyler asks.

"The moving trucks just drove through town," I say with a laugh. "I'm expecting *everyone*."

We walk to the front door and Tyler drops his jaw when he sees the whole town either on our front lawn or walking toward it with coolers, cases of beer, bottles of wine, home-made pies, and even portable barbecues that some of the guys are setting up on our driveway.

"Welcome to Summerland," I say with a giggle. "There's no place like it."

I look up at Tyler, hoping that he's not going to be overwhelmed and hide in the basement, but to my surprise, he opens the door, grabs my hand, and pulls me out onto the porch. "Hey, neighbors!" he shouts with a big smile on his face. "Welcome to our home!"

The huge crowd cheers as we walk down the steps to greet them properly. We get swarmed with hugs, warm welcomes, freshly baked apple pies, high fives, plants, bottles of wine, and even a handmade quilt with our names stitched on it from Mrs. Baker who lives down the street.

The alcohol starts flowing, the barbecues are lit, the music is pumping, and everyone is having a good time. I smile as I watch Tyler talking to a bunch of guys from the office. They're hanging on his every word as he tells them a story. I'm wondering what he's talking about when my old boss Mr. Wallace comes over holding a bottle of champagne with a bow on it.

"Congratulations, Boss," he says, handing me the bottle. "I'm really happy you two took over Hospitech."

"Thank you, Mr. Wallace," I say, taking it from him. With Tyler and I as the new bosses, we had to demote him to a lower position, but he was thrilled when we offered him a big raise to go along with his demotion. He's a good employee and we wanted to keep him happy. Even though I'm his boss now, I still can't bring myself to call him by his first name.

Emily comes over next, giving me a warm hug as she congratulates me on my sexy catch named Tyler. "I told you nothing good comes of drinking white wine spritzers," she says with a grin. "I'm glad you did Vegas properly."

"I'm glad you forced me too." We clink our beer bottles together and sit on the porch, watching the party. My eyes inevitably fall back on Tyler like they always seem to do.

He's taking over the grilling on the largest barbecue as the men of the town gather around with vigilant eyes. Tyler may be the new boss and the new cool guy in town, but none of that will save him if he burns the steaks.

"You better go save him from those barbecue Nazis," Emily says with a laugh. "He doesn't know what he's dealing with. They'll barbecue *him* if he flips over their steaks too early."

I laugh as I walk over and tap him on his broad shoulder. "Can you help me with something inside?" I ask.

He turns to me with a grin. "I'm doing my best Bobby Flay impersonation over here."

I step on my toes and lean into his ear. "Hey Bobby, these guys are going to *flay* your ass if you mess up their steaks."

"This one is burning," John from two streets over points out with a hint of panic in his voice.

"Alright," Tyler says, handing the spatula to Greg. "I'm better at ordering steaks than I am at cooking them."

The guys all turn back to the barbecue, arguing over who should get to hold the spatula.

"You can thank me later," I say as we head inside. "I just saved your life."

He grabs my wrist and pulls me into the hall closet, closing the door behind him. "How about I thank you right now?"

His lips come down on mine before I can answer. "Mmmm," I moan as his tongue slides over mine. "You're welcome."

"I'm just getting started," he says in a deep growl as his hands slide up to my waist. "It's time to show you who the master of the house is."

My breath quickens as his hands slide up and over my

breasts. His lips come back down on mine and he kisses me until I'm panting for more.

"I think I'm going to like living with you," I say between gulps of air.

"You better," he says as he pulls me in close. "Because this house already feels like home."

My heart swells in my chest.

I couldn't agree more.

EPILOGUE

Dahlia

5 YEARS LATER...

"WHAT MAKES your hospital equipment different from the competition?" Mr. Moreau asks, looking at us skeptically.

"Quality. Reliability. Service," Tyler says in an unflinching voice. I sit back and smile as I watch my husband do what he does best.

If we close this deal, Mr. Moreau will be Hospitech's biggest client yet. He is looking to purchase diagnostic and biomedical equipment for seventy-eight hospitals in France.

Tyler is a natural at making people want to buy from him. He speaks with so much passion and authority as he explains how Hospitech has an advantage over our competitors because our equipment is American made, and we don't skimp on the quality in exchange for larger profits.

It's not long before Mr. Moreau is eating out of his hand. The deal is as good as signed.

My pulse races as I watch Tyler, just like it has done for the past five years. We had our share of difficult times in the beginning when we first took over the company together, but once we found our groove, we became a formidable team. I took over the big picture planning and optimization of the factory, while he handled the employees and the day-to-day running of the company. After the first year, we moved Hospitech from the sixth largest hospital equipment manufacturer to the fourth. We're currently at number two, but if we close this deal, we'll be number one.

"It all sounds delightful," Mr. Moreau says, frowning as he looks at the contract. "But the price. It's ten percent higher than Medi-Ward."

"It is higher," Tyler says, leaning forward. "But think of the long-term savings. Broken machines, service repairmen, the inefficient running of the hospitals—those are all things you'll be facing if you go with a lower quality company like Medi-Ward. Not to mention the loss of lives that faulty equipment will inevitably create."

Mr. Moreau's face softens as he listens. We have the best running equipment in the world because we're all about quality.

After a few more minutes of convincing, Mr. Moreau shakes our hands and tells us we have a deal.

"You're amazing!" I say, staring at Tyler with pure admiration after our newest and biggest client leaves with a signed contract.

"*You're* amazing," Tyler answers with a smile. "I was only able to sell it because of our quality rating, and that's all thanks to you!"

"We're *both* amazing," I say as he walks over and gives me a kiss.

"Together we are," he says, holding me tight. "We're a good team."

"The best!"

It's the end of the work day on a Friday, and it's such a beautiful summer day that we decide to leave early to celebrate.

"I guess that makes Hospitech number one," Tyler says as I shut down my computer.

"It's about time," I say with a grin. It's been a lot of work over the past five years, but we've grown the company, added departments, and have developed three new pieces of equipment, including a new and improved electrosurgical unit that saves hundreds of lives every day. It's hard work, but it's rewarding, *and* it's fun because Tyler is by my side.

"Where is everybody?" I ask, looking around as Tyler walks into his office next door to shut down his computer for the weekend. It's eerily silent for four o'clock.

I walk to the large window that looks out onto the floor of the factory and frown when I see that everyone is gone and that all of the machines have been shut down.

"I told them they could leave early," Tyler says as he closes the door to his office. "Everyone has been working so hard lately and it's a nice summer day, so I let them enjoy it with their families."

I can't wait to enjoy the rest of the day with *my* family.

Our three-year-old daughter Mia is at home with her nanny, and I can't wait to see her.

We close up the factory and grab our bikes to ride home when I finally crack. It's our five-year wedding anniversary today, but Tyler has been so preoccupied with our meeting with Mr. Moreau that he's forgotten. He hasn't mentioned a thing all day. I knew he forgot, but I didn't want to distract him and make him feel guilty before the big meeting. But now that it's over...

"What's the date today?" I ask as we climb on our bikes.

"Friday," he says, pedaling away from me.

He's lucky he treats me like every day is our anniversary or I'd be really pissed.

I catch up to him, and we bike down the road side by side. The sun is out in full force, warming our faces, but the refreshing breeze is there to cool us off.

"I feel like today is significant for some reason," I say, hinting pretty hard.

He doesn't take the hint. "It is. Today Hospitech became the biggest manufacturer of life-saving hospital equipment in the United States."

I sigh as I look for a hidden present in his bike basket or a big lump that could be a jewelry box in his pants, but there's neither. It's not like him to forget.

He turns left on Willow Street when we're supposed to turn right to get back to our home. "Are you lost?" I ask with a raised eyebrow. "I know that Summerland is huge with its ten streets, but you have been living here for five years."

He doesn't respond as he bikes beside me, keeping his eyes ahead of him.

I smile as I pedal beside him. *Maybe he didn't forget.*

The huge park comes into view, and I gasp when I see it full of people. "What did you do?" I ask, forgetting to pedal. My bike slows to a stop and Tyler turns around with a knowing grin on his face.

He hops off his bike and walks up to me with his stunning eyes shining brighter than ever. My knees weaken when he drops to a knee in front of me.

"Dahlia," he says, reaching into his pocket. He pulls out

a huge diamond-encrusted wedding band and presents it to me. "Will you marry me?"

"You're five years too late," I say with a grin. "I already married the man of my dreams."

"Maybe you're right," he says, looking up at me with soft eyes. "But you didn't get the engagement or the wedding you deserve."

I glance up and see the entire town waiting and watching in the park. My heart starts beating faster.

"And you're missing a wedding ring to match the one on your finger," Tyler says, holding it up. "So, what do you say?"

I'm breathless as I stare down at the gorgeous ring that's shining in the sunlight and the beautiful man holding it.

"Yes," I say without a second of hesitation. I would marry Tyler every day if I could.

He looks thrilled as he jumps up and slides the ring on my finger. The crowd in the park cheers and claps as Tyler holds my hand up over my head. "We're getting married!" he shouts, and they all cheer even louder.

Kirsten comes walking over, holding Mia in her arms. "Mama. Papa," Mia shouts when she sees us. Kirsten puts her down and our daughter comes running over on wobbly feet. She's wearing a beautiful little white dress that makes my heart melt.

Tyler scoops her up off the ground and we both swallow her up in a group hug, breathing in that sweet toddler smell.

"Mama pineapple, pineapple," Mia says, pointing excitedly to the party.

"Oh, no," I laugh when I see the huge ice sculpture in the shape of a pineapple. "Where did you get that thing?"

Tyler laughs. "You should have seen the guy's face when I ordered a pineapple ice sculpture. He thought it was a prank call."

"I can't imagine why," I say, playfully rolling my eyes.

"Come," he says, taking my hand. "Let's go get married."

"Right now?" I ask, staring up at him in shock. I'm wearing a gray pantsuit, which is still an improvement on my last wedding outfit since it's not soaking wet and covered in dirt, but still.

Emily comes rushing over dressed up in a light blue bridesmaid's dress. She looks beautiful.

"Let's get you out of this thing," she says, grabbing my wrist as she looks down at my outfit. "This time you're going to look like a bride in a romance movie and not a horror movie like last time."

"You got me a dress?" I ask, staring at her in shock.

"Not me," she says, shaking her head.

"You picked out my wedding dress?" I ask Tyler. *Oh, my God, I love this man.*

He shrugs. "It wasn't hard to beat the last one. This one will cover both boobs."

Kirsten comes walking over, holding her arms out for her granddaughter. "Go get dressed," she says with her happy eyes locked on Mia. "I'll take care of her."

Mia runs into her grandmother's arms and gives her a big hug. Kirsten always looks so happy with Mia by her side. I'm really happy I could give her the grandchild she so desperately wanted. They look like best friends as they wander over to the park to play.

"I'll see you in a few minutes," Tyler says with a grin.

"Isn't it bad luck for the groom to see the bride before the wedding?" I ask, teasing him.

"I think those Lucky 7 drinks got rid of our bad luck forever. I haven't had any since you walked into my life."

He leans in to kiss me, but I put my index finger on his

lips, stopping him. "Seeing the bride, I can let slide," I say with a laugh. "But you're going to have to wait for a kiss."

"Let's go already," Emily says, rolling her eyes as she drags me away. "We're on a tight schedule. That dreadful pineapple ice sculpture is starting to melt."

I give Tyler one last look before I'm whisked away through the excited crowd. I'm surrounded by smiling faces and shouts of 'good luck' as Emily drags me to a high tent set up near the maple trees.

Wow. Tyler really went all out for this. There's an archway set up near the lake with folding chairs set up for everyone. There are flowers and wedding decorations everywhere, and the whole thing looks like it's out of a dream.

"You snagged yourself a good one," Emily says, nodding in approval. "You couldn't be luckier, and *he* couldn't be luckier too."

"Thanks, Emily," I say, giving my maid of honor a hug.

"Congrats on the engagement, cuz," Jason says, popping out of the crowd.

I wrap my arms around the boss of McMillan Worldwide Inc. and my favorite of Tyler's cousins. "Thanks, Jason," I say, giving him a hug and a kiss on the cheek. "I can't believe you flew out for this."

He's such a busy man with running Mack's old company, so it means a lot that he came. He's done an amazing job as the leader, and the company's profits have never been higher. The best part is that he's managed to do all that without closing down any departments, factories, or laying off any employees.

His brother Nick is out of jail after serving six months in a minimum-security prison for stealing just over three million dollars from the company. He found God while behind bars, returned the money to Mack, apologized to everyone, and has been living in Ghana ever since, volunteering his time to help set up hospitals.

"I would never miss this," Jason says. He glances at Emily and smiles. "I'm really glad I came."

Emily squeezes my arm as her cheeks turn red. "I have to get the bride into wardrobe," she says, smiling at the handsome millionaire in front of her. "I'll see you on the dance floor."

Jason never takes his eyes off her. "I can't wait."

She pulls me away and squeals when she's out of his earshot. "He's so cute!" she says, glancing back over her shoulder. "He's still looking at me!"

"It is a wedding," I say, grinning as I see hearts in her eyes. "You never know what's going to happen."

At that moment, I see a thick cloud of smoke drift out from behind the library in the distance and then Mack comes shuffling out with my parents behind him. *Yup. You never know what's going to happen. Especially when my parents are at a party.*

"Mom! Dad! Other Dad!" I shout, waving at them. They spot me and hurry over, trying to act like they're not stoned, which makes them look even more stoned.

"Dahlia!" Mack says, giving me a hug. I'm happy to say the man has loosened up in his retirement and is having a lot of fun. He comes and visits along with Kirsten every few weeks, and we've gotten really close. He's always good for a laugh or an interesting conversation, and his business advice can't be beat. "I hear you're marrying my son!"

"I always wanted to marry rich," I say with a playful shrug. "It will probably last one week before I divorce him and take all of his fortunes."

"One week with you, my dear, is worth all of the fortunes in the world," he says with a warm smile.

"Ahhh," I say, giving him a hug. He really is the best father-in-law.

"I'll let you get ready," he says, letting me go. "I want to get a front row seat."

I smile as he hurries away, and my parents step up to congratulate me next. I've been seeing them a lot more lately, and it's actually been nice. They helped me see that I couldn't keep pushing away love for a career, and I'm so glad they did. Having Tyler and Mia is better than any career in the world.

"Will you two walk me down the aisle?" I ask, getting choked up as I ask them.

I'm going to be the talk of the town if I get walked down the aisle with my father wearing that tie-dye shirt and with my mother in her burlap skirt, but I don't really care. I want them to be a part of this.

"Of course," my father says with a smile. "We're not missing Burning Man to sit in the crowd."

"We just have to go change first," my mother says, pulling my father away with a grin. "We'll see you at the start of the aisle."

Get changed? It must be a wedding miracle.

I head into the tent with Emily and shake my head in disbelief when I see my wedding dress hanging inside. It's stunning. A beautiful white sheath dress with a deep v-neck that is delicately detailed with lace and delicate beads.

"It's gorgeous," I say, taking it in my hands and running the long flowing skirt over my trembling fingers. "He knows me so well."

"He sure does," Emily says. "I tried to help him pick it, but he insisted that he knew exactly what you would want."

"Well, he was right," I say, swallowing hard. I try it on and it fits perfectly.

"Wow," Emily gasps when she sees me wearing it. "I think I'm a lesbian now."

"I think I'm going to marry this dress instead of Tyler," I say, staring at it with unblinking eyes. "It's perfect."

"I still like your first wedding outfit better," Emily says with a chuckle, "but this is a close second."

"Think Tyler will like it?" I ask, turning around with a gulp.

"I think he'll *love* it," she says with a wide smile. "Now let's do your hair and makeup."

"All of the guests are waiting outside," I say, feeling a flutter in my stomach. "We don't have time."

"This is me you're talking to," Emily says, pulling out a box full of hair and makeup products. "I sleep in until twenty minutes before I have to come to work. I'm a master at doing hair and makeup ridiculously fast."

Ten minutes later, I look like I should be on the cover of a wedding magazine. Emily heads out to let Tyler know we're ready, and I just stare at myself in the mirror, so thankful that I have a man who would do all of this work just to make me feel special.

Tyler makes me feel special every day of my life, and I don't want to know where I'd be without him.

"We're ready for you, Mrs. McMillan," Emily says, popping her head into the tent. "Ready to get married?"

"This time, yeah."

I should be nervous, but I'm not. Marrying Tyler is nothing to be nervous about.

Soft music starts playing through the park as my parents meet us at the tent.

"No way," I say with my mouth hanging open. My mother is in a beautiful red cocktail dress, and my father is wearing a slick tuxedo. "You guys look so... normal," I say with a laugh.

"I wanted to get dressed up for my daughter's wedding," my father says with a smile. He points to his bow tie, which is made from tie-dye material. "But I still have to keep a little bit groovy."

"I love it," I say with a nod. Really, I do.

"Beautiful dress, Mom," I say, admiring her dress. She looks stunning in it. I'm guessing she didn't make this one.

"It's so tight," she says, squirming around. "But I'm glad you like it."

"I love it," I say, offering them my arms. They hook their arms around mine as Emily brings us to the aisle.

The entire town is here, sitting on the chairs, standing on the grass, sitting in the trees, but I only have eyes for Tyler. He's looking ravishing, standing under the flower-covered archway dressed in a tuxedo. My chin trembles as we stare at each other with pure love in our eyes.

The music changes, and for the first time, I notice the string quartet playing by the huge weeping willow tree. *He thought of everything.*

"I'll see you up there," Emily says, giving me a wink as she starts walking down the aisle.

Jason is up there too, standing next to Tyler as his best man. I'm sure Emily notices him looking because she starts swaying her hips a little more as she approaches them.

All heads turn to me and everyone stands up as the quartet begins playing the Bridal March.

I take a deep breath, holding onto my parents as we start walking forward. I never take my eyes off of the man I love, so it comes as a surprise when I arrive under the archway and see Drunken Asian Elvis standing there ready to marry us for the second time.

He's wearing his rhinestone-covered onesie and looking odd without a bottle of alcohol in his hands.

"This is incredible," I whisper to Tyler when I arrive. "*You* are incredible."

"You deserve this every day," he whispers, staring into my eyes. "You'll never know how much you've changed my life for the better, and how much I love you."

I already know because I feel the same way.

"You even got Drunken Asian Elvis," I whisper, smiling up at the man who married us the first time. I didn't think this guy was allowed to leave Vegas.

"Just Asian Elvis now," he says with a nod. "I've been sober for a month and a half."

I nod back at him. "The King would be proud."

Just as Asian Elvis is about to start the hunk of burning love ceremony, Mia explodes out of Kirsten's arms and darts up to us.

"Hey, Baby," I say as Tyler scoops her up and holds her in his arms.

"Mama, you look pretty," she says, but she pronounces pretty as *preeetty*. She's so adorable.

She's a real Daddy's girl, and I can see why. She has Tyler's stunning smile and his bright green eyes. The two make a beautiful pair, and the three of us make a perfect trio.

Tyler holds her for the rest of the ceremony while Asian Elvis sings Can't Help Falling in Love in a thick Chinese accent and then marries us for the second time.

"Do you, Rainbow Solstice the First, take Tyler McMillan to be your lawfully wedded husband, to have and to hold, from this day forward, for better, for worse, for richer, for poorer, in sickness and in health, until death do you part?"

"You bet your rhinestoned ass I do," I say, making everyone laugh.

Asian Elvis turns to Tyler. "Do you, Tyler McMillan, take Rainbow Solstice the First, to be your—"

"Yes, yes. A million times yes," he says, looking ready for the kiss.

"I now pronounce you the first couple to get married at The Pineapple Chapel who stayed married for more than three months," Asian Elvis says. "And I also pronounce you husband and wife, again. You may now kiss the bride."

"Your Daddy has business to take care of," Tyler says to Mia before handing her over to Kirsten's waiting arms.

He comes back and takes me in his arms and gives me a deep kiss that has the crowd roaring. My legs go weak, but lucky for me, Tyler's strong arms are there to hold me up.

"Mmmmm," I moan as he kisses me like he's ready to suffocate before he comes up for air.

For some reason, Emily's words pop into my head: some people just can't handle Vegas.

I'm so glad that I'm one of those people.

AFTERWORD

Want more Tyler and Dahlia?
Sign up to my Exclusive Newsletter to receive a never seen before bonus chapter.

www.AuthorKimberlyFox.com/newsletter.html

Bonus Chapter: Dahlia and Tyler get into more trouble as they go tearing through a Casino on their drunken night!

I love to hear from my readers. You can email me at kimberly@authorkimberlyfox.com

***Keep turning the pages to read the first two chapters of The Best Medicine, a hilarious romantic comedy by Kimberly Fox!*

ALSO BY KIMBERLY FOX

The Best Medicine

Heavy Turbulence

Well Hung Over in Vegas

Bad Boys on the Beach Series:

Cancun

Belize

Aruba

Box Set of All Three

The Hitman's Baby

The Hitman's Second Chance

THE BEST MEDICINE

BY KIMBERLY FOX

I treat my female conquests like I treat my motocross stunts—I never stop trying until I nail them.

When Shane Winters rolled into my ER, I knew I had to save him.

I had an obligation to the human race to save the motocross star. He was too beautiful to have his DNA eliminated from the species. He had to reproduce.

For the sake of all humanity.

I fixed his back, but unfortunately there's no cure for a dirty mouth, and Shane Winters likes to use his. A lot.

But now that he's safe and healthy and constantly hitting on me, the only thing I want to do is put him back in a coma.

I've always had one strict rule as a doctor: *don't get close to my patients.*

But Shane is teaching me so much.

I'm learning that a hospital gown can look sexy, that a

medical exam can be erotic, and that a hospital cafeteria can be as romantic as a five-star restaurant.

So yeah, all kinds of rules are getting broken with Shane.

I just hope that my heart and my career don't end up in pieces.

From ~~Best Selling Author~~, okay let's be honest, Moderately Selling Author Kimberly Fox comes a sexy, new standalone romantic comedy.

CHAPTER ONE OF THE BEST MEDICINE

BY KIMBERLY FOX

Shane

"You absolutely have to nail this last course," my manager Christopher says as I climb onto my dirt bike.

I take a deep breath to calm my excited nerves as I grip the throttle and squeeze it. Christopher is right. I fucked up the last landing in the semi-finals when my bike slipped in the mud, and if I want to win the Freestyle Motocross gold medal, I have to do something big.

Something only a lunatic would try.

Good thing I'm the right kind of crazy.

We're at the EXXXtreme Motocross Championship, the biggest event in Freestyle Motocross, and this year I'm determined to go home with the medal. I finished second last year, and it's still a sore spot with me. I'm not going to fail again.

Christopher is biting at his lips as he looks up at the

clock. "They're about to announce you," he says, blinking rapidly.

I'm the one about to risk my life doing insane acrobatic stunts on a dirt bike in front of forty thousand people watching in the stadium and another million or so watching at home, and he's the one who's nervous.

"Relax, C," I say as I slip on my helmet. "I got this. I'm going for it."

"For what?" Christopher asks as his face goes pale. "Shane?"

I give him a playful grin as I lean back, completely relaxed. This is my moment. I've got this.

"The Kamikaze Twister. I'm going to do it."

Christopher rubs his sweaty forehead as he closes his eyes, trying to calm his nerves with deep breaths. I'm his only client, so if this goes bad for me, it's going to go bad for him too.

"Shane," he says, sounding breathless. "You've never landed it once in practice."

I grin as I look past him to the huge crowd of people in the motocross stadium. The flashes of cameras, the big screen, the energy of the crowd—it's all making me that much more sure of myself. If I can do it anywhere, it's going to be here in Seattle, the city I live in.

"This is not practice," I say, feeling more confident than ever. "This is where dreams come true."

"Shane," he says as I slap down the visor on my helmet. I rev the throttle, drowning out his negative words with the rumbling sounds of my motor.

I know I can do this. This is the moment I've been waiting for my whole life. The moment where I test myself to see what I'm really capable of. If I pull it off, I'm a hero. If I don't, I might be leaving here in a body bag.

"*Make a big Seattle welcome for Shane Winters,*" the announcer hollers through the stadium speakers. The crowd roars as I ride up to the starting line to complete the last tour of the night.

I'm competing in the Sexy Six. I have to perform six aerial tricks, and the rider with the best scores on style, level of trick difficulty, and crowd reactions wins.

I ride to the top of the ramp and grin as I look at my picture on the huge jumbo screen. I'm soaring through the air at last year's competition in the middle of a Fender Grab, my signature move. Until now.

Next year's competition will have a picture of me completing the Kamikaze Twister—the insane move that's going to win me the gold medal.

The crowd is going nuts as I take one last breath and drop down the dirt ramp with every cell in my body on full red alert.

Adrenaline is pumping through my veins like a broken fire hydrant, but I'm in perfect control as I hit the first jump and complete my signature move, the Fender Grab. The crowd goes nuts as I land it easily and turn toward the second ramp.

I whip around the course, nailing each landing after soaring through the air and twisting my body like a pretzel.

I can hear the crowd over the pounding in my ears as I line up for the last ramp.

"Let's do this," I mutter to myself as I take off at full speed, about to complete my destiny.

I hit the ramp at a breakneck speed, flying up the steep incline as I grit my teeth. It's the last jump. It's the time to lay it all on the line and win the gold.

My knuckles are burning as I crank the throttle to the max on my way up. The crowd explodes into camera flashes as my tires leave the ramp, and I soar through the air like a motherfucking fighter jet.

Time slows to a crawl.

I don't have to think. My body just reacts.

Turn hips. Release handlebars. Rotate. Faster. Faster. Good. Kick feet up. Dip head. Grab the handleb—

Fuck!

I stretch my arm so far that it feels like it's going to pop out of my shoulder, but only two of my fingertips graze the handlebars.

My bike dives to the ground as my body flies forward. A feeling of dread and panic fills me as the hard ground comes up insanely fast.

"Fuck!" I scream into my helmet through a clenched jaw.

The ground is racing at me. I close my eyes.

And then...

Nothing.

CHAPTER TWO OF THE BEST MEDICINE

BY KIMBERLY FOX

Madison

"Dr. Madison Mendes," a tight voice echoes from down the hospital hall.

"Shit," I curse under my breath as I force out a tight smile and turn around. "Hello, Dr. Clark. I was just about to check in with you after my rounds."

"Your rounds can wait," he says, staring at me through his thick glasses. The bright lights on the ceiling are reflecting on his head under his thin comb-over. "Follow me."

He turns his tense body and storms down the hallway to his office. I feel an empty pit in my stomach as I follow him.

Two nurses, Carol and Shondra, give me matching smiles of sympathy as I pass their station. They saw the whole thing and know I'm about to get chewed out by my boss, the medical chief of staff.

I swallow hard as I step into his office where he's already

sitting behind his desk, staring at me with a stern look on his face. He looks pissed.

He's been looking at me that way for the past five days.

"Everything okay, Dr. Clark?" I ask with a wariness in my voice as I slide into the chair in front of him. I keep my back straight as he crosses his hairy arms over his chest—staring me down like an elementary school principal on a power trip.

"No," he snaps. "In your case, Dr. Mendes, everything is certifiably *not* okay."

He pulls out a file from the drawer and slaps it onto the desk between us.

I lean forward and read the name. *Patient Louis Newport.* He was in here last week. Ruptured spleen. Bleeding internally. I diagnosed him and got him onto the surgeon's table just in time.

"What's the problem?" I ask when he just stares at me with a smug look on his face.

"What is the problem?" he repeats with a laugh. "Look at the paperwork. It's a mess."

"The paperwork?" I say, staring at him in disbelief. "I saved the man's life."

"Saving lives is your job," he says, dismissing it with a wave of his hand. He picks up the stapled papers and waves them around in front of me. "*This* is also your job. And it's unsatisfactory at best. Sloppy handwriting, writing outside the lines, and you missed your initials here."

He tosses the papers back onto the desk and stares at me with a triumphant look on his weaselly face.

"Is this about Anabelle?" I ask.

His hard look and authoritative demeanor crumbles like a house of cards. The threatening man who was sitting in front of me is gone—replaced with a wet-eyed, sniveling pathetic shell of a man.

"Did she mention me?" he asks, staring at me with wide hopeful eyes.

"Um," I say, trying to stall. He's wringing his hands as he starts breathing heavier, barely holding himself together.

He grabs his cellphone off the desk and looks at it with a hope in his eyes that quickly disappears once he sees that she didn't text him.

The text he's looking for is from my best friend Anabelle who dumped him after three dates. I'm so glad I set them up.

"I keep calling her," he says, looking frustrated as he runs his hand through his thin comb-over. "I always get her voicemail. Do you think she got the flowers I sent?"

I glance back at the door as my heart starts pounding. "I'm not sure," I say with a gulp. "Like I said, I haven't talked to her."

He frowns as he squeezes the cellphone in his hand, turning his knuckles white. "I better send her some more, just in case."

"No," I say when he hits a button that lights up his phone. "Maybe you should just give her some space."

Anabelle definitely received the flowers. All four dozen of them. She also received the oversized teddy bear that went straight into the dumpster, the chocolates that I helped her eat, and the singing Lady Gaga telegram who was no lady at all. Nothing says romance like a poorly dressed transvestite singing *Poker Face* in the hallway of your apartment building.

"I've given her space," he snaps. "What more does she want?"

A galaxy of space from what she's told me.

"Maybe," I stammer as I drop my eyes to the desk. "Maybe you two just aren't meant to be?"

His wet eyes narrow sharply on me, causing me to lean back involuntarily.

"That's the woman I want to marry," he says, taking heavy breaths like an angry bull. "We *will* get married. And *you* will help that become a reality."

I shift uncomfortably in my seat. "I will?"

"Yes," he says, picking up Mr. Newport's file off the desk. "Or we're going to have bigger problems than just sloppy handwriting."

"Sir," I say as my stomach hardens. "I think we should separate our work lives from our personal lives. I'm worried they're getting too muddled together."

He grins as he looks over the form. "And I think you should give Anabelle a call to put in a good word for me. Or you might not have a work life anymore to worry about."

My cheeks get hot as I stand up and shuffle to the door. I want to give him a piece of my mind for threatening my job over his dried-up sex life, but I just swallow it down instead. He's heartbroken and not acting rationally. Maybe in a few days he'll start thinking clearer.

I slip into a supply closet after leaving his office and sit on a stack of folded sheets as I dial Anabelle.

"Give me a second, sweetie," she says when she answers. *"I'm just ordering."*

I lean back against the wall and close my eyes as I listen to her ordering a late dinner at the drive-through.

"Yeah, I'll take the chicken burger with a salad... You know what? Fuck it. Give me the fries. Do you have turkey burgers instead of chicken?"

All I hear is a muffled sound from the drive-through speaker, but whatever they're saying, Anabelle doesn't like it.

"Well, maybe people would order it if you had it on the freaking menu. Ever think of that?"

More muffled sounds.

"A bottled water... No, wait. I'll take a Coke. No. A chocolate milkshake. Large."

I hear more muffled sounds, and then she's back. *"Sorry about that, sweetie. I was just ordering a salad for dinner. Work has been c-ra-zy. How do people have time to cook anymore?"*

I'm about to call her on her 'salad' when I decide that it's better not to get on her bad side right before asking for a favor.

"I just had an interesting talk with Mitchell," I say instead.

"Who?"

"Dr. Mitchell Clark," I say with a roll of my eyes. "My boss who you dated."

"Ew." I can hear the disgust in her voice through the phone. *"And we never dated."*

"You went on *three* dates."

"As a favor to you."

"I thought you'd like him."

She's laughing so hard that I have to pull the phone from my ear. *"That guy?!? Madison, he proposed to me on the third date! The third freaking date. I know I'm lovable, but come on!"*

"He's not *that* bad." He's definitely *that* bad.

"You know what he has tattooed on his arm? Alf."

"Alf? Like the alien guy?"

"Yes. Like the alien guy. He showed it to me proudly. God knows I could barely see it under all of his thick arm and shoulder hair."

"You wanted me to hook you up with a doctor and I did," I say, starting to panic.

"Yeah, but I was thinking George Clooney in ER, and the guy

you set me up with was more like Dr. Evil from Austin Powers. He had a comb-over! Why would you set me up with a guy who has a comb-over?"

Looking back on it, I can see that it was a mistake, but at the time I just wanted my boss to have a distraction so that he would get off my back. Talk about a backfire. He's even worse now than he was before.

"Can you just call him back?" I plead. "He's making my life a living hell."

"I did my part, sweetie," she says. *"I'm out. Plus, I'm already seeing someone."*

"You are?" How does she find these guys so fast? Anabelle seems to have a date every weekend. I'm lucky if I have one a year. "Where do you find these guys?"

"It's not hard," she says. *"Just put down whatever boring medical textbook you're reading, unbutton the top three buttons of your shirt, walk out onto the sidewalk, stick your tits in the air, and wait. It's like fishing, really. Throw the bait out there and wait for the fish to nibble."*

"That's so romantic," I say with a roll of my eyes.

"It's more romantic than watching Netflix every night by yourself. Gotta go. My salad is ready."

"Enjoy your fries, I mean *salad*," I say with a grin before hanging up. I walk out of the closet and find my resident waiting at the door of my office.

"Here's some medicine for the doctor," Ralph says as he hands me a foam cup of coffee.

It's cold, weak, and tastes like someone used it as an ashtray—Cherry Valley Hospital's finest brew. But I still drink it. I wouldn't be able to get through my grueling twelve-hour shifts without it. Especially when those grueling shifts start at ten P.M. like the one tonight.

"Thanks, Ralph," I say between sips. "Let's get started. What do we have first?"

My resident-in-training pulls the clipboard out from under his arm and frowns as he looks it over. His long shaggy brown hair falls over his furrowed brow whenever he concentrates. I'd like to prescribe this kid a haircut.

I'm already moving down the hall as he struggles to keep up while still looking over the notes.

"Walter is still here," he says as he narrowly avoids the garbage can. "The day shifters still haven't diagnosed him. I suggest we take more blood and—"

"Who?" I ask, skidding to a stop.

"Walter," he says, furrowing his brow as he looks at me in confusion. "The accountant. The big guy with the bushy mustache."

"Oh," I say with a quick shake of my head before I start walking again. "You mean Mr. Thatcher."

"Sorry," he mutters when he catches up to me. "I thought you knew his first name."

"I don't want to know anything but the patient's last name and medical condition," I say as we pass the elevators.

"How come?" Ralph asks. "Wouldn't it be better if—"

"Look," I say, interrupting him as I spin around. "Never get close with a patient. Never get personal. Never get attached. When you're in this building, it should only be about medicine."

He brushes the long hair out of his eyes, and I get a strong urge to grab the nearest scalpel and do some surgery on his bangs.

"But maybe you could help the patients more if you open up a little," he says with the wide innocent eyes of a resident-in-training. He hasn't been through what I've been through. He doesn't know what I know. He doesn't know how hard this place can be.

He doesn't know the kind of devastation that can result from bringing your personal feelings onto the job. I know. And I'm *never* going to put myself in that kind of position again.

"Maybe if we get to know them we can use that information to help them better," Ralph continues, sounding so childlike, so naive. He reminds me of me when I started. "Love and compassion can heal too. Isn't love the best medicine?"

I step in close, locking my battle-hardened eyes on him. "*Medicine* is the best *medicine*."

My pudgy sidekick takes a defeated breath and drops his eyes to the floor.

I rest a hand on his shoulder. He's still young and thinks he knows it all, but after he loses a few, he'll be singing a different tune.

"Just keep any emotions inside here," I say tapping his chest, "until after your shift. Keep all that love for Lacey and the new pups."

He looks up at me and nods.

"How's that going?" I ask as we continue walking. The stray Labrador that Ralph's roommate brought home had been pregnant, and she recently gave birth. On his living room carpet.

"How do you think it's going?" he asks with a shake of his head. "I have nine puppies pissing, shitting, chewing, and drooling in my little apartment. Do you want one? They're really cute."

"Yeah," I say with a laugh. "They sound adorable. But I'll pass."

I step into Mr. Thatcher's room with Ralph on my heels.

He's lying in the hospital bed, gazing down at the picture frame in his hands. I try to keep my eyes off it, but I see that it's a young pretty girl. Probably his daughter.

The room smells like fresh flowers from the arrangement beside him, mixed with the sterilizing smell of bleach.

"Hello, Mr. Thatcher," I say as his heart monitor beeps steadily in the background.

"Good evening, Dr. Mendes," he says, placing the picture frame on the nightstand beside him. I keep my eyes off it. I don't want to know anything but his symptoms. His face breaks out into a wide smile when he sees Ralph behind me.

"Did you finish it?" Mr. Thatcher asks as Ralph walks past me and sits on his bed. "I've been dying to find out." My resident grabs the patient's hand in his and smiles.

Ralph shakes his head as I watch with confusion. "One chapter to go."

"Promise me you'll let me read it when you're done," Mr. Thatcher says.

"You'll be the first one I give it to. I promise. Hopefully, you'll be out of here by then and you can read it in your favorite chair."

Walter smiles. "As long as I'm out before my daughter's wedding, I'll be happy."

I force out a cough, and they both look up at me.

"I'm writing a Sci-Fi book," Ralph says with a nervous grin. "Walter helped me with some ideas for the end."

I resist the urge to shake my head as I grab the clipboard at the foot of the patient's bed.

"Still having abdominal pains, Mr. Thatcher?" I ask.

"Yes."

"Has the severity of them increased? Pain-wise?"

"No. They're just as bad as before."

I tap my pen on the clipboard as I look it over. This guy's

case is a hard one to crack. Abdominal pains. Kidney damage. High blood pressure.

"Dr. Preston," I say, nodding to Ralph. "Take some blood from Mr. Thatcher. I want to run some more tests."

Ralph smiles at the patient as he gets up. "Maybe I'll rename the villain after you," he says with a laugh.

"Nah," Mr. Thatcher says with a shake of his head. "I like Doctor Mendestra better."

I follow Ralph out into the hall, grabbing his arm as he hurries away. "Doctor Mendestra?" I ask him with my eyebrows raised.

He smiles nervously. "She's an evil alien from planet Turkot."

"It sounds suspiciously close to my name," I say, pulling him closer as I narrow my eyes on him. "Doctor Mendes?"

He cringes. "Coincidence?"

"Sounds like a Freudian slip to me," I say, squeezing my grip on him.

I let him go and take a deep breath. "Ralph," I say, softening my voice. "This is what I was talking about. You get too close to the patients. What if he dies tonight? Or tomorrow?"

"Or what if knowing that his doctor cares keeps him alive for an extra night?" Ralph turns and hurries away to get the syringe before I can respond.

A small part of me envies his wide-eyed optimism, but a larger part of me wants to call him an idiot. He should keep his feelings to himself and let the medicine do its job.

My thigh buzzes and I pull out my phone. It's a text from Anabelle with a picture of Alf. *In a few years, guys who look like this are going to be your only prospects. Get 'em while you're still hot!*

I roll my eyes as I slide my phone into my pocket, grab

my now stone-cold coffee, and continue down the hall to finish my rounds. But Anabelle's words keep lingering in my head. I do have to do something. I have to be proactive. I can't stand here thinking that Mr. Right is just going to bump into me.

"Ow," I shout as a stretcher slams into my ass, making me spill my cold coffee all over my shirt.

"Sorry," one of the ambulance drivers says as he rushes past me. There's a man lying on the stretcher groaning. Tim, the ambulance driver, looks back over his shoulder as he rushes down the hallway. "Coming, Dr. Mendes?"

"Yeah," I say with a sigh as I squeeze the excess coffee out of my shirt. "I'm just redesigning my outfit first."

"Well, make it quick," he says when he stops at the elevators. "We have a hot one here."

My mouth drops when I hurry over and take a closer look at him.

"You got that right," I mumble under my breath. He's definitely a hot one.

Gorgeous, in fact. Even with the black eye and dried blood on his face, he's gorgeous. His dark hair is matted with blood and dirt, but strangely it suits him.

My eyes wander down his shirtless body, looking for injuries, but all I can see is a massive chest, shredded abs, sculpted tattooed arms, and colorful motocross pants.

He's perfect. I have to save him. I have an obligation to the human race to save this guy. He's too beautiful to have his DNA eliminated from the species. He has to reproduce.

For the sake of all humanity.

"What happened to him?" I ask Tim as the elevator bings open and we push him inside.

"Dirt bike injury," he says as I press my stethoscope to

his hard chest. "He was competing in the Motocross Championship and wasn't wearing his seatbelt."

I stare at the patient's face as I listen to his heart. The rate is fast. Just like mine.

"We'll get you fixed up, Mr. Right," I whisper to him only loud enough for him to hear.

He opens his green eyes a crack, and looks up at me through the glossiness. His mouth curls up into a weak smile.

The moment is over too soon. The elevator door bings open, and we rush him out to the ER.

It's time to get to work.

Available at www.AuthorKimberlyFox.com

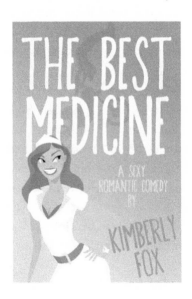

CPSIA information can be obtained
at www.ICGtesting.com
Printed in the USA
LVHW090456090519
617222LV00001B/1/P